Asked For

by

Colleen L. Donnelly

This is a work of fiction. Names, characters, places, and incidents are either the product of the author's imagination or are used fictitiously, and any resemblance to actual persons living or dead, business establishments, events, or locales, is entirely coincidental.

Asked For

COPYRIGHT © 2015 by Colleen L. Donnelly

Contact Information: info@thewildrosepress.com

Cover Art by *Diana Carlile*

The Wild Rose Press, Inc.
PO Box 708
Adams Basin, NY 14410-0708
Visit us at www.thewildrosepress.com

Publishing History
First Historical Women's Fiction Edition, 2015
Print ISBN 978-1-62830-609-5
Digital ISBN 978-1-62830-610-1

Published in the United States of America

She wore her auburn hair longer now because Cletus liked it that way, but it was pulled back out of Magdalena's and Betsy's reaches. And no makeup. She'd come plain, the way she always was, plain and tired.

"I probably am a sight." Lana felt her face flush, but tried to ignore it. She wasn't here to be told how good she looked. She was here to see Grandma, see herself and her new life against her old one and the person who'd told her how this new one was supposed to be lived.

"You look just fine, actually." A tall shadow filled the shed's doorway behind Grandma. "If anything, you're a sight for sore eyes."

"Jim..."

Jim Dillon stepped from the shed's dark interior. He'd changed. She was shocked at what he'd become. He'd grown in three years, muscles where scrawny arms used to be, tanned skin and chiseled features where softness used to be. There was still the boy in his eyes, though, the boy who'd helped her with chores before she left to get married. The boy Grandma had said really wasn't there to help Lana but was there because he needed the pay. A bucket half full of milk dangled from one of Jim's hands. Grandma was right again. He was here not because Lana was but because he needed the pay.

Jim didn't stare at her daughters, or the bulge of her stomach, or the worn dress that covered it. He just looked at her face, his eyes scanning every feature as if relearning, even admiring, who she'd become.

Praise for Colleen L. Donnelly

"After reading *ASKED FOR* I walked away with a renewed gratitude for the life I have. *ASKED FOR* is a work that will cause you to realize that no matter what you have been through, no matter what you are going through, there really is hope for us all."

~*Kacee Everhart, Ordained Pastor*

~*~

"I have truly watched [Colleen Donnelly] grow in her amazing talent of bringing the reader into the story and making them feel a real part of it. She has the rare gift of more than just entertaining us with a fictional story …making the reader feel uplifted and inspired along with the characters. You'll find you can't put the book down until you finish it and it will leave you wanting for more! It makes me see things in ways that I had never thought about before. A true work of Art."

~*Sherri Minick, Production Stage Manager*

~*~

Donnelly keeps the reader guessing until an unexpected but thoroughly satisfying ending. This is Colleen Donnelly's second novel and I think this one is even better than *Mine to Tell*."

~*Carolyn Paul Branch, Author and Librarian*

~*~

"Through the dark grittiness of this story, these characters shine. In a publishing world focused on slick commercialism, this was a pleasant change. I thoroughly enjoyed this novel and look forward to reading more from Donnelly."

~*Lori Robinett, Author*

Dedication

To my mom,
who inspired this story
and continues to inspire me as a writer.
And to my critique partners,
who have bettered me and my writing
with their diligent work.

Prologue

Magdalena 1960

Mama had six children after she had me, five of them one right after the other, mostly because Pop couldn't leave her alone. It wasn't that he was in love with her; he just loved hard the same way he worked hard. He worked her hard too, and us kids, keeping up with that patch of Missouri dirt he called a farm, and the welding shop he ran in town. Mama never complained, no matter what Pop did, and my brothers and sisters didn't either. They were too afraid.

My name is Magdalena. When I was growing up I was Magdalena Paine, but now I'm Magdalena something different. I've been several something differents since I was a girl, but none of them matter. What matters is the time I was Magdalena Paine, because that's when I first saw Mama for what she really was…beautiful. None of the rest of my family would have ever noticed if Glen Morgan hadn't said it to my littlest brother, James. "Your mother's the most beautiful woman I've ever known," Glen told him. That comment opened my little brother's eyes, and made me look at beauty in a different way, a deeper way. It just took me awhile to see it through my own eyes instead of Mr. Morgan's.

Chapter 1

James 1947

Is he coming? James gripped the thin wooden slats that lined the back of the dugout and peered between them. Maybe he wouldn't come. No, he had to! He stared at his mother in the seats behind the dugout, raising his eyebrows and widening his eyes to ask the question without speaking. She answered without a word, her smile saying something back to him, something thinly positive, even though the spot next to her was still empty.

"Jimmy, get ready! You're almost up to bat!"

James kept his back to the ball diamond, his knees planted on the wooden batters' bench where he knelt while he kept his eye on the space next to Mama.

"Jimmy! Come on!" Coach's orders boomed from near third base.

James tugged his lower lip between his teeth while he stared at the empty spot where his pop was supposed to be. *At least he isn't here to hear the coach call me Jimmy.* He scanned the park around the bleachers. Young kids were chasing each other across bare ground, clouds of dust bursting from behind their shoeless feet. Adults stood, arms crossed, engaged in conversations, like obstacles the kids were supposed to avoid as they wove in and out. It was the last inning, the last at bat. If Pop was coming, it would be any second.

"You hit a big one, *James,*" his mother called. The sunlight glinted off her auburn hair. She was tall and sat straight, even on the rough bleachers, the worn and faded housedress a little too loose as it fluttered where it wasn't tucked well around her slender body. She rarely had time to get out, what with seven kids, a house, chickens, and a garden to keep up with, but she always came to James' games, and she did her best to make sure the coach knew his name.

James smiled, but it felt feeble. It would have been better if the spot next to her wasn't vacant. Mama had told him before the game, "Your father will be there today." Then she'd added, "I'm pretty sure," as an afterthought. His eyes and heart had exploded when she'd said he'd be here. Pop never came to his games. He ran his own welding shop. He worked hard and came home hot, late, and dirty every night. He came home cranky, too. Mama said he was cranky because he was tired, not because James or his brothers and sisters had done anything wrong.

"James, you heard Coach. Get your bat." Andy shoved against James' side. "Stop gawking around!"

"I'm watching for Pop." James leaned to where Andy sat next to him and shoved his best friend back.

"Your pop never comes, so get your bat and get out there."

"Mama said he would. She said, 'Your father will be there today.' She said it right before the game." He omitted the "I'm pretty sure."

"She called him, 'Your father?' Since when do any of you call him Father?" Andy snorted.

"Jimmy!" Coach yelled again. The on-deck-circle

was empty.

James shoved Andy one last time, then stole a quick glance around the bleachers before he turned away from the crowd. Coach's eyes were on him, he could feel them, as he trudged to the row of bats leaning near the dugout's entrance. The lightest bat was his favorite. It was his, it was small, and it suited him. He rested his hand on the bat's handle. Pop said small meant sissy. James glanced at the other bats. He was six years old now, so maybe a bigger bat would be better, a bat for someone the coach would call James instead of Jimmy. He wrapped his fingers around the handle of a stout bat. It was fat, almost too fat for his hands. He stretched his fingers and wrapped them as far as he could around its base. Too much binding. Someone had wound layers of tape and cloth around the handle. He wiggled his fingertips until they touched his thumb.

This was the sort of bat Pop would want him to use. He glanced at the bleachers from the corner of his eye. If Pop was there, James would sling the bat up and take a couple of practice swings. His mother was there, and she was watching, just like she always did, no one at her side. He let go of the stout bat's handle and grabbed an even bigger one. He'd never touched this one before. He heaved it up to his shoulder, and it scraped his ear as it dropped into place.

"Batter up!"

James stole one last glance at the crowd. Mama had added, "I'm pretty sure." That meant she really wasn't. He stepped from the dugout onto the playing field, powdery dirt giving way beneath his shoes.

"Jimmy! Go back and get your little bat! That one's too big for you!" Coach clapped his hands like a seal. James ignored him and strode to home plate. Coach dropped his hands to his sides and shook his head as he paced off a circle near third base.

James bolstered his shoulder under the bat's weight as he stepped into the batter's box. It was heavy, and heavy meant more power. Pop would agree with more power. James would tell him about it later if he didn't make it to the game.

"You can do it, James," his mother's voice rang from the bleachers. James nodded and drew in a breath. He held it, and squeezed it in his chest until it was so tight it felt like a scream that needed to get out. He listened, his lungs burning, waiting for Pop's thundering echo. The voice that thundered every night, at Mama, at his six brothers and sisters, and especially at him. Surely Pop would shout something encouraging here and not pick on him for the things he did at home, like for being so small, for being so many years younger than Carla, the next oldest; for being a consequence instead of a blessing, something James never understood. If Pop saw him play, surely he'd thunder something better than the things he hollered at night.

The pitcher stared from the mound, waiting for James to get settled. It was too late for a practice swing, and the bat was too heavy anyway. James let the burning air seep out of his lungs like a slow leak. He bobbed his head at the pitcher like the other boys did, ready, still hoping to hear his pop shout, even if it was to go get the baby bat.

"Strike one!"

James wheeled to look at the umpire. The man was overweight and sweating. He raised a finger and a fist in the air at the same time.

"Okay, Jimmy, it's okay to take the first one. We got a man on every base and only one out, so pick your pitch and put one over the fence." Coach clapped his hands a couple of times and then leaned forward, propping himself with his hands on his knees like he expected to field the ball.

James looked around the diamond. Sure enough the bases were loaded. He'd spent so much time watching for Pop he'd lost track of the game. He gave the bat a tug, enough to lift it off his shoulder and get his mind back on what he was supposed to do. He leaned forward, his hands stretched as far around the bat's handle as he could get them. A pitch whizzed by.

"Ball one!"

James backed out of the batter's box. He could hear his coach, hear his teammates. He looked at the bleachers, even though he tried not to. His mother nodded and clapped. Andy's parents sat below her. They cheered for him, too. Pop must be busy. He had several guys working for him, all of them worthless, he said.

He stepped back to the plate and strained his fingers for a better grip on the bat. The pitcher bent forward, eyeing the zone he was going to send the ball. James read the pitcher's mind; he knew where the pitch was headed. The pitcher straightened, leaned back to cock his body for the pitch, and then launched forward, the ball rocketing toward home plate. James tugged at the bat, he knew just where to place it. It felt like lead, and he had to throw himself into the swing, dragging the bat through the air. It connected. It was late and the ball trickled along the first base line as the bat slipped from his fingers and skidded through the dirt.

"Fair ball!" the umpire shouted.

James jumped and raced toward first base. The pitcher came his direction, hurtling toward the ball. They reached the ball at the same time, and the pitcher's long arm whisked downward like a tentacle and snatched the ball up. He swung it at James' back, then fired it to home plate.

"Out! Out!" The umpire called.

James raced to first base and wheeled to the right. It had been an awful hit, but he'd made it. A grin gurgled deep inside as he circled back to first, glancing at the bleachers.

"Hey, you're out," the first baseman nudged him.

"I am not," James glared upward and looked the boy in the eye. He glanced at the first base umpire. The man nodded and jerked his thumb toward the dugout.

"But he didn't tag me! He missed!"

"He got both of you," the first baseman chided. "You and the kid who ran to home. Game's over, and we won."

"But he missed me…"

James' coach was waving everyone toward the dugout. The other team was cheering, jumping against each other, and slapping their hands high in the air.

James glanced at his mother. She was watching him, and now he was glad she was alone. She'd believe he wasn't out. He'd ask her not to say anything about the game to Pop. Pop would take the umpire's side and tell James to try harder next time. Or quit trying to play altogether.

His teammates gathered their equipment to go home while the coach said a few strained words. They filed out of the dugout, leaving James alone. He dropped to the bench and stared at the empty diamond as he spun the glove handed down from his brothers. He glanced at the baby bat, the one he should have used.

"Choke up when you use a big bat," a man said from behind him.

His heart jumped. Pop? James wheeled around. Tan fingers jutted through the fence's slats where his had been earlier. Mr. Morgan stared down at him, a black cowboy hat tipped back on his head. His hair was black, too. James couldn't tell where the hat started and where the hair stopped. "You grip a big bat a little higher than normal so you can control the weight better. You won't hit as far, but your control will be good."

James eyed the owner of Glen's Restaurant. What did Mr. Morgan know about baseball? He didn't even have a son. He'd opened his mouth to tell Mr. Morgan to leave him alone when his mother caught his eye. She was watching from the bleachers, her slender form in the background, just beyond Mr. Morgan's left shoulder. She was listening to what she was too far away to hear, and talking with her eyes the way mothers could.

James turned back to Mr. Morgan. What he had to say would have to be done carefully, without Mama knowing, but when he looked to Mr. Morgan, the man wasn't listening. He had turned away, his gaze on Mama. Mr. Morgan held there while Mama stared back at him, the two of them saying or thinking something, and James was afraid it was about him. Mama glanced away, finally, and Mr. Morgan turned back to James. Mr. Morgan's eyes were different then; they looked too much like James felt: like he'd just lost a game and the one person who mattered wasn't there.

James spun his glove in his hands. He would keep the nasty things he'd wanted to say to himself, but he still wished Mr. Morgan would go away. James wanted to be alone, he didn't want advice, and he didn't want to think about baseball now or maybe ever again. He glanced up at Mr. Morgan, into eyes as dark as his own. Dark and familiar. He thought he saw himself in there for a moment, but it wasn't him, it was Mama, and she was telling James to be patient, be kind, and fight above the hurt.

"Mr. Morgan, I appreciate your advice, but I'm okay. Thank you anyway."

"I imagine with a couple of older brothers and a father, you probably get lots of suggestions." Mr. Morgan kept his fingers around the slats.

A *ha* kicked up inside of James. He drew in a deep breath, one that felt like a scream again. Suggestions weren't real help, and they didn't make up for how small he was. That's why Pop never came to his games, why Pop was so angry at him all the time. He was small, he was sissy, and baseball was a waste of his time. If Mr. Morgan would go away, James would talk himself through Pop's list, tell himself just the way Pop would why he was no good at ball, and then he'd quit and be done with it. Just like Pop wanted.

"I realize your father used to play ball, and he was pretty good. I was younger than him and never played with him, or as good as he did, either, but I still know a thing or two about it."

Pop played baseball? James frowned. Why hadn't he ever said so? Why hadn't anyone said so? Maybe that was the real reason he never came to James' games. He'd been good when he was young, and James wasn't. Pop was old now. Too old to play or care about the game. Too old to be having little kids like James around, something he'd said more than once. He was lots older than Mama, and older than Mr. Morgan, too.

"He missed me," James said, looking at Mr. Morgan.

"Your father? He missed you?" Mr. Morgan's brows furrowed.

"No, I mean the pitcher. I wasn't out. He missed me." He saw it again in Mr. Morgan's eyes, the near reflection of himself and the reason Mama was there telling him to fight above the hurt. *Pop missed me, too. He missed my game, he missed my stupid hit, he missed seeing me lose the game for the whole team.*

Mr. Morgan's brows leveled out. "How about I show you how to choke up on a bat?"

James didn't feel like fighting or trying harder; it was easier to just hurt. There were things sissies could do; baseball just wasn't one of them.

"No, thank you." James turned away and stared at the empty diamond. Pop was probably a lot like that pitcher today. Long, lanky, a hero, arms as quick as snakes. Mr. Morgan didn't say anything, but he was still there behind the dugout. James could hear Mama in his presence. James sighed, dragged to his feet, grabbed his bat, and stepped out of the dugout.

Mr. Morgan stood back and waited until James came in front of him. "First off, that bat's too small for you," Mr. Morgan nodded at James' bat. "You were right to try a bigger one, but work your way up. Try one that's only somewhat larger next time."

James twisted the end of his bat in the dirt, waiting for Mr. Morgan to add "because you're so small."

"Now take a nice, slow, even swing with that bat. Feel the drag of the weight at its far end through the air."

James looked up. Mr. Morgan nodded at the bat. James dropped his glove and lifted the bat until it was level with his shoulders, then moved it in a semicircle.

"Now grip your hands a little higher on the handle, just above where they are now, and swing again."

James did as Mr. Morgan said. He felt the difference.

"I get it!" James wobbled the bat in the air with his hands near the end and then farther up. "I see what you mean."

"Come on, James!"

James glanced toward the bleachers. His oldest sister, Magdalena, stood next to their mother. She was seventeen, wearing too much makeup, and drawing on a cigarette.

"Pop will kill her if he sees her that way," James said, more to himself than Mr. Morgan, as he lowered the bat. Maybe it was good Pop hadn't shown up for the game, for Magdalena's sake. James shuddered as he thought what Pop would have said right there in front of everyone. Mr. Morgan moved alongside him. He wasn't big, but he felt steady, steady enough to absorb James' shudders. "Pop never lets Mama or my sisters wear makeup. He says makeup's for ugly hags, and cigarettes are for men and whores." He looked up at Mr. Morgan, wondering if he understood what Pop meant.

Mr. Morgan didn't say anything. Just like Mama never did. No one ever explained, nor did Mama ever complain at her oldest daughter or tattle to Pop how Magdalena looked or behaved in public. Mama protected her, just like she watched out for James. It was the way she loved them, her special way.

Mama said something to Magdalena. Magdalena looked straight at James. Whatever Mama said made Magdalena draw on her cigarette until the end flared bright orange.

James picked up his glove and slid its strap over the bat's end and rested the bat on his shoulder. "Thank you, Mr. Morgan. I need to go. Magdalena's here to walk home with us. We gotta get there before Pop does so Magdalena can wash that stuff off her face."

Mr. Morgan glanced at James' glove, touched it, and looked it over. "That yours?" he asked.

"My brothers, Harold and Alex, used it before me. It's mine now."

Mr. Morgan nodded, let go of the glove, and looked James in the eye. "Your pop was a good ballplayer, so when he gives you advice how to play better, take it. And you can tell your sister that what your pop really means about her is that beautiful women don't need makeup. Hags have nothing to do with her."

"You think Magdalena's beautiful?" James frowned at Mr. Morgan.

Mr. Morgan placed a hand on James' shoulder. "She's your sister, so you probably don't think so. But I can tell you one thing, she's your mama's daughter, and your mama sure doesn't need any makeup. I know."

James looked for his mama again in Mr. Morgan's dark eyes. Did Mr. Morgan see her the same way Pop did, and that's why makeup was forbidden? Mama would probably laugh at all this talk about beauty, she with her faded dresses and unpinned hair. James wanted to laugh like she would, but something in Mr. Morgan's eyes stopped him.

"Your mama's the most beautiful woman I've ever known," Mr. Morgan said. That was different from saying she wasn't an old hag. Just like saying choke up on the bat was different from saying James was small and sissy.

Cigarette smoke broke into their conversation. James turned and saw Magdalena near his side. He hadn't heard her approach, hadn't even noticed she'd moved. When he looked toward the bleachers, Mama was gone. Probably out near the road, waiting.

"Time to go, James." Magdalena seemed a little less brazen as she blew smoke into the air. She dropped the cigarette and rubbed it out in the dirt.

"Goodbye, Mr. Morgan," James said. "And thanks." There were chores waiting for him at home, and if they weren't done, he'd get a thrashing. Magdalena had to scrub her face, and Mama had to get a meal on the table. They'd all be hurrying, getting everything in place before Pop got there.

"Goodbye, Glen." Magdalena's familiarity shocked James. He looked up at Mr. Morgan, wondering if the man was as surprised as he was. Mr. Morgan nodded. There was a question in his eyes, something he chose not to ask. Mr. Morgan turned and walked away.

"Let's go," Magdalena said, and James ran ahead of her to the road, where Mama was waiting. Beautiful Mama. He glanced back over his shoulder. Mr. Morgan was far away, but he was watching them. There was something in his stance like there had been in his eyes.

James waved, then turned and walked with his sister and mother. They had to hurry. They had to get home.

Chapter 2

Lana 1929

"Lana, get back over here!" The way Grandma chopped her words, the way she barked rather than spoke, finally drew Lana away from the window. She left a smudge where she'd rubbed it all morning, watching, waiting for her parents to come. The window was clean enough, but she wanted to see her father when she looked out, see him coming up to the door and smiling, waving the way she'd imagined he would. He'd written…well, her mother had…promising they'd come…he'd come. Lana'd rubbed the window, over and over, trying to make him appear. "Get over here and stay put. We have to hurry," Grandma called again. She was impatient, her bark getting worse.

Lana moved near the cots she and Grandma slept on. Grandma lowered herself to the floor beside her, one bony knee at a time, grimacing as she knelt.

"He said he'd be here. Well, Mom said they would." Lana looked down at her grandma. She was too thin, not enough meat on her to be comfortable down there, too old to be crouching that way.

Grandma snorted, hanging onto the straight pins clenched between her lips. Lana watched her bunch the dress' extra fabric in her weathered fist and pin it at Lana's waist so she could baste it in place. It was

Grandma's best dress, the one she wore to church, and it was a little too loose for Lana, a little too straight, and a little too long. That's the way Grandma wore her dresses, especially her best dress, best but still old like the rest of them.

Lana strained to see herself in the cracked mirror that leaned against the wall near Grandma's cot. "You think your dress works good for a bride?" Lana eyed the dress her grandmother was giving her, faded gray fabric with only a hint of white where tiny daisies had once been. Lana's dresses were old and faded too, different colors than Grandma's, but so washed out they looked almost the same. If she squinted, Grandma's dress looked almost white all over. Lana knew nothing about being a bride other than what her best friend, Jeanie, had told her, and Jeanie had been firm that brides were supposed to wear white.

"You're going to be a wife, not a bride, and you're going to need your two dresses for everyday." Grandma muttered around her mouthful of pins, her needle and thread weaving in and out of the gathered waist. "Get silly notions about being a bride out of your head." Grandma knotted the thread and tugged the fabric tight, jerking Lana off balance.

Lana straightened and squared her feet on the floor. Every wife was a bride. Any woman…or girl…couldn't be one without being the other. Lana didn't know much about being either one beyond Jeanie's tales of princes and princesses, and the secret things that went on between them when they were alone at night. Grandma said Jeanie's tales were just that, stories designed to create flutters in little girls' hearts and make their eyes grow wide with silly expectations. Lana had never worried which one was right, Jeanie or Grandma, because there hadn't been a reason to. Not until now…now that a man had asked for her, told her grandmother he'd take her off Grandma's hands and provide for her.

Lana stared down at her grandma. She wanted to touch her shoulder, tell her it was okay, that both of them were upset. There was just too much rush, too much hurrying, and not enough time to turn Lana into a bride…a wife…and a woman…all on such short notice.

Lana glanced toward the window and strained to listen for the sound of a vehicle or wagon, whatever her father chose to get them here today. Lana's mother had written periodically over the years, always apologizing they were so far away, times being hard and work being so scarce and all. She described what the two of them were doing and how different each town looked that they went to, scratching out her and Lana's father's lives a few lines at a time on an occasional slip of paper.

Lana's mother was Grandma's only daughter. She'd been good about visiting on her own now and then, looking every bit as tired as she described in her letters. She looked older than she was supposed to be, too, something she tried to hide behind bright red lips and false highlights drawn around her eyes.

"Can you bring my father with you next time?" Lana begged her mother on each visit. There always a reason he wasn't there, always a hardship that kept him busy and away, until finally she brought him. Once. And unexpected. They appeared at Grandma's door, and Lana stared at him, her heart racing across the room and into his arms before she could get her feet to cooperate. He looked nervous, he fidgeted, he was a little uncomfortable, and he forgot how old Lana was and where she'd been born. But she forgave him because there was still something princely about him.

She'd eased across the room a little at a time instead of in full flight like she wanted. He smelled like smoke, like a thin layer of soap over hard times, when she reached his side. She laced her fingers through his and tried not to let him see how hard she was breathing. He had nice eyes, and she could see he was thinking as he looked at her. There seemed to be questions in his gaze instead of answers, but she didn't mind. This was the first time they'd officially met, since she'd been living her whole life with Grandma. She held onto his hand and refused to let go, looking for similarities between him and herself. She'd cried when he left. All she had of him after that was his best, sent to her in her mother's letters, a promise he loved her, and an apology he was so busy.

But now he was coming back, coming to see her for the second time, and this time to stand with her as she married. She felt his heart beating in hers, jumping off those letters her mother had sent all these years. He was making this one last trip to be by her side while she was still a girl to help her make the step from childhood into sudden adulthood. He'd be here. Her mother said he would. She couldn't wait.

"If Cletus had put this off a few more years, I might not have had to alter this dress so much," Grandma muttered from below, leaning back and eyeing the gathers. "You're still so gangly. Just a child. Not sure what he sees in you."

Lana hadn't met Cletus yet. He lived a few towns

away, and the deal had been made while she was at school. "Someone asked for you," was all her grandmother had said one afternoon when Lana came home. "His name's Cletus, Cletus Paine. He's got kin nearby, and he asked for you for his wife. He'll give me a little something too, to help out now and then." Grandma had refused to answer Lana's questions that afternoon, questions about where she and Cletus would live, how often Grandma would visit, and would she have to make new friends. Grandma was gruff, gruffer than usual, and kept her back to Lana most of the evening. Lana told Jeanie the next day at school about her arranged marriage, and Jeanie's eyes grew wide as she described men in greater detail for Lana, what they looked like all over, what they smelled like, and how they acted. Those details were frightening. They didn't sound princely at all, but Jeanie assured Lana they were.

"Will my husband want me to finish eighth grade?"

Grandma snorted and took a pin from between her lips. She tugged the bottom edge of the dress taut, the place where the hem had come loose, and she rolled the ragged edge up and pinned it. Grandma struggled to her feet. She was weathered from too many years of hard work, slightly stooped at the shoulders, but still stubbornly mulish in her frown. "I swear, I don't know where you get all these silly notions. From Jeanie, no doubt. When a man asks for you, he's just looking for a wife, and wives don't need to be educated for what they have to do. You don't need any smarts at all other than to cook, keep his house clean, and don't sass him. And whatever he wants to do, you let him do it." Grandma paused. She looked Lana in the eye, then stepped back to study the dress. The creases of her frown deepened.

Grandma had been a wife once, but Grandpa was long gone, and Grandma said he was dead. There were no reminders of him anywhere, just like there were no reminders of Lana's father other than the letters her mother had written that Lana kept. Grandma had been the only real family Lana had ever known, and Grandma took care of her with a grumbling determination to keep food in Lana's belly and a scrap of a dress on her long, gangly limbs.

Lana glanced around the house she'd grown up in, barely more than one room, barely enough furnishings to say she and Grandma did anything but survive. Grandma said things would be better for Lana this way. This man would make sure both of them had more— Grandma a little care sent her way once in awhile and Lana a home of her own.

Grandma stepped close. She lifted the hem where she could reach it and sewed around the pin, her hands working a little faster, a little rougher than before. Then she moved back again, still frowning. Lana watched her. She never knew for sure what color Grandma's eyes were. They were dark, but it wasn't their color that made them that way, it was depth, it was worry, it was frustration and hard work.

"Maybe it needs a belt," Lana suggested.

Grandma hobbled toward the front door, and Lana could hear her grunt and pant over their rag box. She came back with a long strand of yellow fabric. It was a remnant salvaged from some broken-down garment of long ago, longer ago than Lana could remember. "We'll try this," Grandma said. She bent around Lana and looped the yellow fabric like a belt about her waist. She drew it tight and tied it, letting the loose ends hang down. Grandma smelled like earth and sweat, the scent of her years of struggle to gather food enough for the two of them and keep their single-room home from caving in. Grandma straightened to survey the belt, a memory of some invisible happier time softening her face for a moment before it disappeared. "It'll have to do, I guess. He ain't gonna care much how you look anyway. He's too old for that. Probably why he doesn't mind you looking more like a scrawny boy than a girl."

Lana stared at her grandma. "Too old? How old? Won't he still care a little bit? Want me to be sort of pretty? Surely he wants his bride, I mean his wife, to at least look nice."

"You ask too many questions." Grandma let out a little grunt. She hated it when Lana was pesky, but more than that, she hated talk about beauty. She was worn and gray. Maybe she'd never been pretty at all. Whenever Lana stood too long in front of the mirror, trying different-colored rag scraps against her auburn hair, Grandma always snatched them away and told Lana to be content with what she had, which, Grandma always added, wasn't much. "And don't be setting any store by looks, young lady. Cletus didn't pick you for looks. He picked you to work hard and make babies."

Jeanie had said something about making babies. She had lots of brothers and sisters, some of them married, so Jeanie claimed to know a lot about husbands and families and being a wife. She said some people called it making love, not just making babies, and it was supposed to be deeply satisfying. According to Grandma it really wasn't; it only made babies and that was it. Lana couldn't imagine the act that Jeanie'd whispered as being something someone did for love, but it intrigued her. Grandma had snorted when Lana asked her about the act. "Ain't you ever seen what a bull does to a cow? Or one dog to another?" Lana hadn't. Or if she had, she hadn't thought anything of it.

Lana ran her hands down the soft, worn fabric of Grandma's dress. It was flat where she had no bosom and bunched where she had no hips. Jeanie'd said pretty mattered a lot when a man chose a bride…a wife. Jeanie'd seen things and heard things when men came courting her sisters, or when her brothers lived in her family's house for awhile with their new wives. She said having hips and bosoms helped turn making babies into making love.

Lana dropped her hands to her thighs and stared at her reflection in the mirror. She hoped Jeanie was wrong. Grandma said Lana didn't have what it took for love, and Cletus wasn't looking for it anyway. But she still wanted to look good, look pretty, look like a daughter her father would be proud of when he let Cletus take Lana as his own.

"Grandma?"

"What now?"

"Do you think my mom and dad will make it?"

Grandma held back whatever mean thought ran through her head, but Lana saw it, a flicker of fury that made her wince. Grandma shook her head and looked away. "No sense letting that spoil your day if they don't." She looked back at Lana and pursed her lips into a straight line. "I'm sure they'll try. That's what your mother said, anyway."

"I want you to go to the courthouse with me—I mean with me and Cletus—whether they come or not.

You raised me, so you can stand by me if my dad's not there."

"Child, you ain't gonna need me no more. You're going to be a wife now. You got to stand on your own." Grandma's voice was loud, louder than usual, but it didn't hide the guttural rasp. And her tone of dismissal didn't cover the wetness in her eyes or the worry on her face. "You'll be fine," she added, as she looked away. "Even if your dad don't make it."

Don't make it. Surely he would. Lana tugged at the yellow belt. No grandma, no mother there with her. And no father. She wanted them, she needed them—Grandma to tell her what to do, her mother to smile until the tired lines showed on her face, and her father… Lana needed him to be proud, to be there, to say she was special, a beautiful bride, even if she wasn't. Lana slipped a finger between the belt and her waist. It felt tight, too tight, and she wanted to yank it off. Throw it all off, the wedding dress, the slip she'd never worn before, and the belt. She wanted to stay here. She wasn't ready to be a bride…or a wife.

Suddenly she was swallowed in Grandma's arms, the earth scent overpowering as Grandma pressed Lana against her bosom. The dampness of Grandma's perspiration wetted Lana's face, and Lana inhaled, drawing in as much of her grandmother as she could.

"You'll be fine," Grandma said into Lana's ear. Lana could feel her tremble. It was slight, but it was there. "Don't worry yourself about little things like how you look. Just work hard, don't complain, and let Cletus be king of his castle. You got nothing here, nothing that's yours to keep or take with you, and nothing to offer him. Be glad a settled man like that has chosen you. Just do your duty. That's all you got, and that's what wives do."

Lana peeked above Grandma's shoulder, around their house, at the sparseness of it. It had always seemed enough before, but now that Grandma said it was nothing, it looked stark instead of sufficient. Would this little home be more stark when Lana was gone, when she took with her a nightgown, the two dresses she owned, the letters her mother had written, and the picture she'd drawn of her next to her father the day after his first and only visit? Surely Cletus would make sure Grandma had enough to fill this house, make sure Lana's absence wasn't bigger than the new things Grandma could buy. Lana nodded into Grandma's embrace. She'd do what it took. She put a hand on her grandma's back and squeezed.

"Do your duty," Grandma said, still close to Lana's ear. "That's all." There were tears in Grandma's admonition, deep tears Lana'd never heard before and she wondered who Grandma was crying for. Lana? Herself? Or maybe for Grandpa, the man Grandma'd been wife to when she'd really wanted to be a bride?

"Don't worry, Grandma. I'll be a good wife to Cletus. I promise I'll work hard and make babies, just like I'm supposed to. Just like you say."

A knock resounded throughout the house. Lana jumped, her heart kicked up like a young colt. Grandma's hug tightened.

"It's them," Lana said into Grandma's shoulder. "It's my mom and my dad. He came, he made it!"

The soft cocoon of Grandma's essence pulled back. It slowly peeled away, her warmth, her perspiration, and her scent, each leaving one at a time, until she let go.

Another knock, louder than the first, shook the lone picture Grandma owned, one of an angel looking down on a house. *Do I look all right?* Lana wanted to ask, but she didn't. She didn't want to upset Grandma.

"I'll get it. I'll let them in." Lana felt bubbles inside. They danced in her heart and widened her eyes. Grandma grabbed her hand and held on for a moment, almost holding her back. "They're waiting..." Lana laughed.

The knock came again. Lana's heart echoed the rapid banging. She straightened her dress. Grandma watched her, not paying attention to Lana's dress or the hair Lana quickly smoothed. Grandma's eyes were on Lana's, their dark color sinking into her own before Lana turned and hurried toward the door. She took a deep breath as she wrapped her fingers around the latch, kept her face in a welcome smile.

"Hello!" she sang as she swung the door open.

Hurry, an invisible little voice said as she looked up. It spoke from the pale blue eyes far above her own, telling her insides that *hurrying's what wives do.* Jeanie hadn't taught her that, and living with Grandma hadn't either. It was Cletus that told her, the way he stood, the way he towered above her as he surveyed his new bride.

"Oh. I thought..."

"I'm Cletus. You ready?" He didn't look impatient, but he looked ready.

Her heart continued to pound, thumping like a fist on a door. He was so tall, so lanky, already doing what, according to Grandma, a husband should do. She glanced behind him, listened, strained her ears down the drive and far away on the road. No one. No sound. Her father hadn't come. The thumping softened; it felt like sobs. She wanted to wait, give her parents a little more time.

"We need to hurry," he said. He twisted to the side, creating an empty avenue for her to pass.

Lana turned back to her grandmother, her face pinching tight. How could she go now? Couldn't they wait a few minutes more? Grandma nodded toward Cletus, her dark eyes hazy, her lips in a taut line.

Lana clutched the strings of the cloth bag that held her clothing, her mother's letters, and her drawing, all she had to take with her as she became Cletus' wife. Her heart ached; it was engorged with pain, making it almost impossible to walk.

Hurry. Lana followed the new man in her life to his truck, her heart throbbing with each step for the old one, the man she'd needed to come, to at least say goodbye as she left this place where she'd waited all her childhood for him. She glanced back.

"Wait," she said to Cletus. Her feet flew back to the house. She stuffed her hand into the cloth bag and pulled out her childish artwork from ages ago. "Give this to him." She handed it to Grandma. "When my father comes, make sure he gets this."

"Write," Grandma said as Lana backed away. She could hear the tears in Grandma's voice and see them on her face as Grandma clutched Lana's picture near her chest.

"I will." Lana nodded.

Write.

It's what families did. So far, it was all they did. Today was supposed to have been different.

Chapter 3

James 1947

Mama kept a small stool hidden behind the basket where they threw their dirty gloves and jackets when they came in from doing chores. James squeezed alongside the washstand and slipped behind the basket. He groped in the dark until his fingers found the rough wood. He latched on and dragged the stool to the front of the sink so he could stand on it to see in the mirror above the wash pan and pitcher.

Rain thrummed on the tin roof covering the back porch of the house as he set the stool in place. It sounded like thousands of pellets beating out a cadence, a drum roll that ticked away the minutes until Pop came home. James hopped on the stool and leaned over the wash pan, stretching toward the mottled mirror. He reached to the right and tugged the string on the small light Pop had hung there. Time was short. His brothers, Alex and Harold, would be in from doing their chores any minute, and Pop would be home from work soon, too. They would all want to wash, and he'd have to be out of their way.

He tipped his head and studied his face in the low light. His hair hung like black icicles over his forehead, drips of rainwater trickling from their tips as if they were melting.

If the rain had come earlier, his baseball game would have been canceled. Or at least the last at-bat. Then it wouldn't have been his fault his team lost.

He frowned and stretched farther over the wash pan. He stared at himself, swelling his chest and furrowing his brow even more, making his reflection look bigger, tougher, and better at baseball. He craned his head to the right, then the left, studying his reflection out of the corners of his eyes to see if he could look bigger than six, maybe two years younger than Carla instead of five. Carla was eleven, then Gail, Alex, Harold, and Betsy, all in stair-steps in their ages until they reached Magdalena, the oldest. Maybe he wasn't really so small. Maybe it just seemed that way because they were all so much older.

He strained farther upward and brought the top of his swollen chest into view at the bottom of the mirror. His toes stung as he perched on their very tips. He danced from one foot to the other, giving his toes a rest. He swelled his chest even more. He craned and studied it until something behind him caught his eye. It moved, it came his way, and he stopped. He dropped flat-footed to the stool, the breath still trapped in his lungs. He watched the shadow as it approached from behind.

"You about done?"

The trapped breath exploded in a choppy laugh, high-pitched and childish even for him. "Magdalena…" His sister stepped closer until her face came into the light, the scent of cigarette smoke still strong. Blue shone from her eyelids, red glistened on her lips, and a black line circled her eyes. "You need the mirror, don't you?"

"Just for a second." She smiled. Her smile was

nice, maybe not beautiful, like Mr. Morgan had said this afternoon, but nice.

James hopped off the stool and scooted it out of his sister's way with his foot. "Pop will be here any second. Go ahead, so you can get your makeup washed off."

Magdalena stepped in front of the washstand and leaned forward, pressing her face close to the mirror. The small light heightened the colors on her face, the pastes and powders Pop would scrub off if she didn't get it done herself.

"You need to hurry," James said.

Magdalena didn't reply. Her hand rose to her lips, her fingers blocking that part of her face in her reflection. James watched her hand make small circular motions around her mouth in the mirror. She tilted her head back and studied her hand's movements, peering from the bottom of her eyes. The smell of fresh lipstick filled the air. Her hand dropped, and so did her chin. Her lips were brighter instead of cleaned.

"Magdalena..." James moved closer. "Pop..."

"Pop what?" she asked through glistening lips. He watched her press them together, evening out the fresh coat.

"Pop'll be here any minute." He touched his sister's skirt. It wasn't worn like Mama's work dresses, or a hand-me-down, since Magdalena was the oldest.

Magdalena turned from the mirror and looked down at him. The color on her face was sharp, even with the light behind her. "I'll be gone before he gets home."

"But you'll miss supper! We're not supposed to..."

"You take my plate and silverware off the table before he gets here. And tell Mama I went out." She

29

turned back to the mirror, but her eyes in her reflection were on James' face instead of her own. "Tell Pop I got a job tryout, okay?"

James saw the way she set her face, the look his brothers said was desperate. Her gaze returned to her own reflection. She ran her littlest finger over her eyebrows, then reached up and fluffed her hair. She'd styled it like Mama's, but it wasn't the same color. Not as rich. Magdalena had Pop's fair hair and coloring.

"Magdalena," James whispered. "Pop's gonna be mad."

"Yeah?" She turned to James again. "No madder than if he finds out about this afternoon."

James thought of Magdalena at the ball park, smoking, and wearing all the colors Pop hated on her face.

"So don't tell him a thing, you understand?" Her face was set. "Don't tell him about the game, or Mama, or me, or nothing."

"I…I wasn't going to tell Pop about the game." James felt his face flush. "I never want Pop to know what I did…"

"Not just that, I mean *nothing*!" Magdalena's voice sharpened.

"I wasn't going to…"

"Listen." She leaned closer. "I know you don't want Pop to hear about the game. But he doesn't need to hear anything, you understand? Nothing."

Magdalena was like Mama, she helped him feel better when Pop was hard on him. But he didn't think she was doing that now. This wasn't about helping him. Maybe not even about keeping Pop from finding out she'd been looking like a hag and smoking like a whore in public.

Magdalena turned back to the mirror and focused on her hair, her hands whisking over it, making it look smoother than it really was. The rain was loud on the roof, and James worried they wouldn't hear Pop coming. They all did what they could to avoid Pop's criticism. Even Magdalena. But what she didn't do was care. She didn't care if Pop liked her or not. At least that's what she said. He didn't understand how she couldn't care. What Pop thought was important; he made that very clear.

"Magdalena, I heard Pop was a good ballplayer. Is that true?"

Her fingers stopped. He could hear her draw in a breath, slow and deep, as she stared into the mirror. "They say he was," she finally said, her reflection focused on James. "He doesn't like to talk about it, though. Where'd you hear that?"

"Mr. Morgan."

Kitchen noise rose above the pelting of the raindrops. Magdalena's reflection gazed at James long and hard, then she turned away from the mirror and bent close to him. He waited for her to talk, tell him what Pop had been saying all along: James wasn't a good ballplayer. But Pop had been, and that's why he didn't bother to come to the games. Magdalena lifted her hand, ran her fingers over his dripping hair. She picked up wet strands and moved them to the side.

"Wish I had your hair," she finally said.

"What?"

"Your hair's so dark. It's not nothing-hair like mine. You're special, James, You have good things about you I wish I had." She pressed her lips together in

31

a tight line, and he could see the fresh layer of lipstick squish between them. "Mr. Morgan say anything else?"

"He showed me how to bat better. He didn't say it, but he showed me how because I'm small. And he said you're not a hag. The reason you don't need makeup is because you're beautiful. Like Mama."

Magdalena's eyes grew wide; she looked surprised for a second. Then she snorted, unladylike, and dropped her hand from his head. She slumped back against the washstand. "He would know that much, I guess," she said, not even looking at James.

James frowned. "Know what much?"

Magdalena looked at him, her eyes bright and hard. Then they softened. "About baseball and being not so big. He's not all that tall himself. So maybe he had to figure out tricks to play better, if he played." She straightened. "But there's still something about makeup and beauty. Makeup makes women more beautiful. All women. And he knows it."

James didn't like the way his sister talked about Mr. Morgan. He'd been good to help James, and he'd said nice things about her and his family. "Mr. Morgan knows what he's talking about. What he showed me about batting worked. If I choke up on the bat, I'll hit better."

Magdalena started to snort again, but she stopped. "That's good, little brother," she said, twisting her mouth like she was thinking. "Mr. Morgan did right helping you. It took courage. He's a good man."

The way she said it didn't sound right to James, she wasn't talking about baseball as if it mattered, he could tell by her tone. "You don't think his tricks are really going to help me, do you?" James stared at her. "I really do need to be bigger to play baseball good, don't I? Well, I'll get taller. I'll be as tall as Pop someday, you'll see!"

Magdalena's face changed. Even behind the makeup he could see her tighten, a frown that didn't really show. She looked worried, but he knew whatever it was wouldn't last. Nothing bothered Magdalena for long, and she was never afraid. "You don't have to be tall to be good, you understand? Like I said, there are special things about you. If you need a trick, use it. But don't say nothing about any of this when Pop gets home. Remember that. Don't say nothing about this afternoon."

There was a roar in the distance. It sounded like thunder, but they both knew it was Pop's truck. King, their old black hound, barked. He knew it was Pop, too, and he was glad. Pop would pat King on the head and give him whatever scraps were left over from his lunch.

Alex and Harold could be heard running through puddles toward the back door, their voices playful, high and low octaves competing as they laughed, both of them on the threshold of turning into men.

"Tell Mama I left. Tell Pop it's a job I'm looking at." She stole one last glance in the mirror before she turned and stepped around James to the door.

Alex and Harold burst through as Magdalena opened it, flinging water everywhere in full body shakes.

"Try to leave some of that outside, will you?" Magdalena squeezed around her brothers.

"Well, look at you." Harold grinned. "You better clean up, and clean up fast. Pop's coming down the road."

"Not tonight." Magdalena slipped through the door and closed it behind her.

"Where's she going?" Harold asked.

"Job." James stared at the door.

"Uh-huh." Harold jabbed Alex. He grabbed the small towel that hung beside the dry sink while Alex poured water from the pitcher into the pan. "How'd the game go?" Harold sopped the rain from his hair, watching James from beneath the towel.

We lost and it was my fault.

Say nothing.

James shrugged. They would understand choking up on a bat better than Magdalena had, even though neither one of them probably ever had to do it. Both of them were good ball players. They were tall and strong like Pop, but they didn't care about the game like James did and had quit long ago. It was better if they didn't know about the game. The more people who knew, the more likely Pop was to find out.

"You do your best?" Alex asked. Alex was wilder than Harold, and got in trouble a lot more. He was a good big brother. He was like Pop, but without the meanness.

James wanted to ask them. Ask his brothers if choking up on the bat might have kept him from losing the game. But he couldn't. It was too big a risk. *Say nothing.* He shrugged again.

"Do your best," Alex said. "Every time. It's your best, and no one else's." Alex snatched the towel from Harold. "You need any help, just let me know," Alex added.

The roar increased. Pop's truck was on the road in front of the house. King's yelps sounded puppy-like, and James could envision their dog's happy leaps. Magdalena was probably gone. She had ways about her, but James still prayed she made it.

James snatched the stool off the floor and shoved it behind the washstand before Pop could see it. Pop hated small. That's why Mama kept it out of sight, far from Pop's eyes. He left his brothers and rushed to the kitchen, where Mama and his sisters were scurrying to have everything ready before Pop stepped through the door. Gail was aligning tarnished silverware beside each plate. Nothing matched, nothing was new, but it had to be orderly. Pop insisted, and Gail made sure things were perfect, that was her way. James put his hand on Magdalena's plate.

"Don't touch that!" Gail snapped. She rushed to his side and smacked his hand away. "What are you doing? Get out of the way!"

"Magdalena's not eating with us. I'm supposed to move her plate and tell Mama."

Gail's eyes grew wide and her mouth fell open. She closed it, scooped up Magdalena's place setting and ran it to the bureau.

"He's here!" Carla called from the front room. She wasn't one to shout, her voice could barely be heard above the reverberation of Pop's old truck as it rumbled into the lane.

Carla came into the dining room with a stack of cloth napkins and set each one on the table, dropping the plainest and most tattered one next to James' plate. He was the littlest. He was the last. That's the way things were, Pop said.

Mama darted from the kitchen, an apron tied over the same faded dress she'd worn to his ballgame. She started around the table to check the settings, make sure the plates, silverware, glasses—and one coffee cup for Pop—were all in the right place. James watched her, her movements, her quick and studious glances, all so familiar. Mama did this every night when Pop came home. She hurried. When James thought of Mama at home, he thought of *hurry!*

James came alongside her as she turned the last corner and approached Magdalena's empty spot.

Alex and Harold popped through the doorway. Mama stopped and glanced at the older boys, a smile of welcome on her tired face. They nodded, warm smiles returned, as they slipped to the backs of their chairs. They stood like sentinels. No one sat until Pop did.

James reached for his mother's apron, the soft fabric gripped between his fingers.

"Now, Mama?" Betsy poked her head through the door. Betsy always did what was right. It was her way of keeping things peaceful and in order.

The back door opened, and Pop's voice could be heard over the rain as he told King goodnight before stepping inside. Alex and Harold straightened. Betsy didn't wait for Mama's okay. She began toting steaming dishes to the table, a thin towel between her hands and the hot pottery. James heard Gail set a coffeepot on the stove. The coffee would be ready when Pop was, hot and thick, the way he liked it.

"Mama?" James whispered.

"James, get behind your chair." Her command came out in a sharp whisper.

"But, Mama—"

"James, I said get behind your chair. We're getting food on the table." She stepped toward the kitchen as the back door closed.

"But, Mama, Magdalena's gone."

Mama stopped and stared at him. Her *hurry* churned and stalled, but it didn't vanish.

"Gail put her dishes away. Magdalena said to tell you she's gone out, but to tell Pop she's trying out for a job."

Mama drew in a deep breath and dipped her head in a slow nod. He knew she was thinking about what he'd told her, and the things she would now have to say.

She started to push around James, but he held onto her apron. "Mama...the game... I don't want Pop to..."

This time the *hurry* vanished from her eyes. Her preoccupation was broken. A strange glimmer, a distant flicker appeared, then disappeared. She looked down at him. "No game," she said. "Nothing about the game. Nothing about the afternoon." She sounded like Magdalena. Warning him, more than just agreeing to keep Pop from knowing he'd messed up.

"What game?"

James saw what Pop looked like in his mother's face. He could smell the slightly burnt odor that was permanent in Pop's skin and clothing, tiny blackened holes testifying he was a welder. James turned and looked into his father's face. *The game you didn't come to. The one you don't even remember you were supposed to come to*. The game James was relieved he hadn't come to since it wasn't good, not good enough for Pop.

"Nothing. Supper's on the table," Mama said, as she slipped from James' fingers and rushed to the kitchen. James turned back and watched her, then took his place behind his chair.

Pop returned to the back porch. The sound of water being splashed came from the washstand where Pop washed away the grime but not the stench of welding. The towel always smelled slightly burnt after he dried his face and hands. Mama set a steaming dish of potatoes on the table and took her place behind her chair. James shot Mama a glance. The empty space where Magdalena should have been shouted her absence. Missing a meal would draw Pop's angry inquisition. Being late always guaranteed his strap. Mama looked taut beneath the flush of hurry. Pop's tall form could be felt in the doorway, then be seen as he made his way to the table.

James stared down at his plate. He knew by heart how Pop looked and what he would do. Pop's chair skidded backwards, its legs scraping across the floor. He dropped into it with a heave, and scooted it forward. The rest of them sat, their chairs silent as they settled into their places.

Dishes of food streamed Pop's way. He didn't even have to ask. Mama said he'd asked once, years ago, when they first married. She just passed them now, and she'd taught James, and his brothers and sisters, to do the same.

"Posts and wire in the shed?" Pop asked around a mouthful of pork.

"Yes, sir," Harold responded. "Fence is down and everything put away, just like you wanted."

Pop nodded. "Where's Magdalena?" Pop's attention was off Harold and Alex. His gaze went from Magdalena's empty space to Mama.

Mama didn't hesitate. She answered as suddenly as

he'd asked. "Trying out for a job."

Pop stopped chewing. "Restaurant?"

Mama shook her head, quick and sharp, as if the idea of Magdalena working in a restaurant was ludicrous. No one said a thing as Pop stared Mama down. "She wouldn't do that," Mama said, the muscles in her jaw tight.

Pop watched Mama a moment longer, then stabbed a chunk of meat on his fork and wagged it at her. "What else would a girl be doing this time of night?"

Mama took a bite and chewed. James watched her lower jaw grind, side to side, and up and down. She shook her head as if that was answer enough for Pop's question. *I don't know what our daughter is doing, but it's okay.* James wished Magdalena had stayed home and just done what Pop wanted.

Pop turned his gaze on James. James drew in a shallow breath and met his father's eyes. The fork pointed his way, and Pop's look sharpened. "What's in your sister's blood ain't fit to be discussed at this table." He shot a glance at Mama, then back at James. "I'll deal with her when she gets home." Pop's eyes carried the fiery spark of welding, pinpointed and hot, as he zeroed in on James. He didn't want to look in Pop's eyes, just like he wasn't supposed to look at the bright light of welding. "And you..." Pop's voice took on a darker tone. "You got some of your sister's blood in you, but that ain't your problem. It's what you ain't got that is. Forget about that game you were talking about earlier. Baseball's *not* in your blood."

Chapter 4

Lana 1929

The roar and rumble of Cletus' truck created a cocoon, a shell of noise around a wordless vacuum. Lana welcomed the silence the first hour they drove toward Cletus' home. She'd stared out the side window, the scenery a teary blur as she forced her heart to catch up to them. She was married now. It was senseless to linger over a childhood that was gone. Grandma'd told her what she had to do, and she'd do it, even without her father there helping her make the transition. She stole a glance to her left, across the seat, at her new husband. Cletus' large hands gripped the steering wheel, his gaze fixed on the road ahead.

Lana needed to see Cletus' face again, see more than the sallow blue eyes that had said hello and hurry at the same time. She'd been too surprised when she opened the door, too uncertain as Cletus' long legs turned and led her to his truck. Lana glanced again out her side window and rested her hands on the cloth bag on her lap. Grandma would give her father the picture Lana had left behind. He would surely know it meant come, come see me now.

Cletus had said very little since he'd taken her from Grandma's. He'd held the truck door for her while she climbed in. She thanked him, and he nodded before he took his place in the driver's seat and drove. When they reached the courthouse, and the justice of the peace asked him, Cletus had said, "I do." Then he asked the justice of the peace how much and paid him. Nothing more had been said. He'd eyed her when she climbed back into his truck, like he was studying something he'd just bought. He looked satisfied, and she'd smiled. He nodded again; then they drove on.

She ventured another glance his way. It would be nice to talk, hear more of his voice, learn what he thought, if he was happy now that she was his wife. She set one hand on the seat between them, she tapped a finger, but still Cletus stared straight ahead, tall in the seat, towering over her in height the same way he did in years. His legs were so long his knees bumped the dashboard, and the top of his head brushed the cab's ceiling. His hair was stiff and light, maybe whitish, maybe blondish. Maybe he really was too old to care if girls were pretty. She pulled her hand back to her lap. Grandma had said he was...at least girls like her. Maybe Grandma was right.

"Is it much farther?" she shouted above the truck's roar.

He looked at her then, his brows arching as if he'd forgotten she was there.

"I asked if it was much farther." She leaned his way, caught his pale blue eyes, and studied them. This was her husband, this was the man she would spend the rest of her life with. He wasn't handsome; he was rather ordinary looking. Her darker hair and complexion stood in stark contrast to his almost wan color. He probably wouldn't think she was pretty since she was so different from him, but that was okay because she didn't think he was particularly good-looking.

"Not much. Maybe another hour. I need to keep my eyes on the road." He didn't shout, but she heard him. He returned his attention to driving. She nodded and looked at the road too.

No boy had ever said she was pretty. Jeanie claimed that's how it started, that's what a prince did when he met the girl he wanted for his princess. A couple of boys in school had said they liked her. Jim Dillon, who used to come over and help her with chores now and then, acted like he maybe thought she was nice-looking. Grandma said he wasn't actually coming over because of Lana, he did what he did for pay, but with Lana watching he was too proud to take the canned goods or eggs she offered him. Sometimes Jeanie followed him over. Jeanie talked even more when Jim was around. He never really said much back to Jeanie. He just kept helping Lana with the chores, the two of them letting Jeanie talk.

Lana studied the passing grass and fields. Cletus was putting a lot of miles between Jim's kindness and her. Maybe she should have told Jim she was getting married. Grandma had said not to tell him, there wasn't time. She wished Grandma had let her. Jim probably would have come by today.

Cletus revved the engine, then let off the gas as he jammed the gearshift into another gear. The engine rumbled to a low hum as he turned into a driveway. He hit the gas again and accelerated over bumps and cuts in the lane. Lana bounced off the seat, the yellow sash on her dress flying up. Her head struck the ceiling, and her teeth bit hard when the truck hit the ground again. She grabbed for the dashboard as the truck lurched over the next rut, and the next. Cletus finally rounded an old house and yanked the truck to a stop. The engine cut to nothing, and the smell of hot fumes filled the cab.

"We're here?" Lana gazed at the two-story structure in front of her, thick gray boards laid one over the other in lines, each one beaten raw by the hot sun and icy winters. Upstairs, rags protruded from a couple of the windows, wads of faded cloth where glass should have been. She shivered and glanced at Cletus, wondering where her...their...bedroom would be. Rusty tin made up the roof of a low back porch, sloping their direction, protruding over a door in a windowless wall. "This is where you...I mean, we...live?" She pivoted in her seat when he nodded—an old barn, a smokehouse, an outhouse near a shed, and a fence that needed mending behind them, everything arching around the backside of the house and its parking area.

She straightened in the seat and glanced Cletus' way. He was watching her, one eyebrow hiked up as he did. Maybe he was hoping she liked her new home. "You can put in a garden over there." Cletus nodded toward a patch of tall, dry weeds.

She stared where he indicated. "Now?" Her voice sounded weak. "Now?" She tried again. She twisted the yellow fabric of her belt around her fingers.

"Tomorrow's fine."

She glanced at the house, then back at her new husband. "What's your middle name?" She could tell by the look on his face she'd startled him. She twisted the yellow belt tighter around two fingers. "I mean...well, I just want to know..."

"It's Anthony. We should go in." He slid out his side of the truck and slammed the door behind him. He walked to her side, opened the door, and waited for her. She slipped to the ground.

"Mine's Elaine. Now my name is Lana Elaine Paine. That sounds kind of nice, don't you think? It rhymes."

"Glad you like it." He turned toward the house, and she followed him.

A long narrow rut ran the length of the back part of the house where the slanted roof shed its rain, a gouge dug in the dirt along the wall. Cletus' long legs stepped over it as if it weren't there. He opened the door and paused, waiting for her to enter. She edged past him into a blinding dimness, a dank smell telling her more than her eyes could about this back room. He followed and closed the door behind him. She stood there, afraid to move until her eyes adjusted. She heard water to her left. He was pouring it, sloshing it in a pan. He splashed, then it splattered into a slop bucket.

"I eat at six on days I don't work," he said. He stood near her now, his expression hidden in the dim light. She nodded, hoping he could see how she agreed. She thought about touching him, curious what his arms felt like with all that hair she'd noticed earlier. He moved past her into the main house, and she followed. "When I work, sometimes it's later. But I like to eat as soon as I get home." He looked back at her. "That's how I've always done things."

She nodded, doing what Grandma'd said. She smiled, too, now that he could see her better. The room they were in was a dining area with a table and three chairs in the center. Two curtain-less windows on the right let in more light. To the left was his kitchen, through another doorway; a small window exposed the corner of a center chopping table there, and the edge of a wood-burning oven. She looked back into his face. He was watching her. She twirled the end of her belt.

"Your house is nice."

"Glad you like it." He nodded toward the doorway. "Kitchen's that way. It's almost six. You're probably hungry, too."

She looked at the kitchen through the doorway again.

"You can go on in there and get started."

Work, make him happy, let him be king of his castle. "I'm sorry. I didn't realize it was so late." She darted to the kitchen and glanced around in the window's light. Shadows began to take shape as she peered about the room. The stove, a cabinet, and, yes, a chopping table in the center of the room.

A chair scraped across the wood floor in the next room. She heard him sit, then scoot the chair forward. She peered around the edge of the doorway. *Hurry.* Cletus cleared his throat. Her husband was ready to eat. It was her job to feed him. She turned her focus back to the kitchen. She could do this, and she would.

The smoked pork she'd heated was just the right temperature, the gravy perfect and without any lumps. Lana hurried the last dish to the table, boiled potatoes, already soft with age even before she'd cooked them. The wood oven had warmed the house considerably, but Cletus didn't seem to mind. She chose one of the two remaining chairs and sat near him, realizing there were no plates or utensils on the table.

"I'm sorry, I forgot." She rose and peered through the increasing gloom of the room, wondering where Cletus kept his dishes.

"Over there." He nodded toward a bureau alongside the door they'd come through from the back porch.

She hurried and grabbed what they'd need. She glanced over the plates and silverware, making sure they were clean, then placed one set in front of him and the other where she was to sit. "I hope you like what I fixed." She smiled, took her seat, and dug a serving spoon into the boiled potatoes. His fingers, long fingers, appeared over her hand. She stopped, amazed at their size, and how rough his skin felt as it brushed against hers. "I'm sorry, you want to pray first? We always prayed at home, me and Grandma. I guess I forgot."

He shook his head. "I'm only religious about eating on time," he said. "But I do have a certain way I like things done when I eat." He aligned the plate and silver she'd slid in front of him, everything symmetrical, each item in its place. She watched, looked down at her own scattered utensils, and aligned them as he had his. "And you should always pass the dishes to me first." He nodded at the dish of boiled potatoes near her hands.

She slid the potatoes his direction. She reached for the platter of meat and the bowl of gravy, sliding both in front of him also. He said nothing as he filled his plate. She watched, the aroma of what she'd cooked filling the air. Everything looked good, it smelled good, and she could tell he was satisfied as he took his first bite. She settled into her chair and watched him eat.

"I'm not really very hungry," she said.

"You the nervous type?" he asked. "Been a big day," he said without waiting for her to answer.

He continued to eat, his head bent over his food, his big hands raking his spoon and fork across his plate.

She really wasn't the nervous type. Grandma always said Lana ate like a farmhand, often giving Lana her own small portions, claiming she was old and didn't need that much anyway. Maybe Cletus was right. It had been a big day. She'd married him and stopped being a child, was all on her own. She'd left Grandma and her friends behind, left the only place her parents knew where to find her. But her father would figure it out. He and her mother would come see the new her, the grown up her, the one who was going to make them proud by being a good wife.

****

Lana lay in the dark, colors drifting through her mind. Bright colors, like tinted clouds pierced by brilliant rainbows, the muted paleness of her wedding dress accented by the yellow of her belt. Fanciful parts of childhood—school, friends, the parents she'd dreamed of. She watched them drift, and she let them. Reality was a bit of a shock, but Grandma had warned her. She accepted the shock and the little bit of pain that came with it. She was a wife now, and both would eventually go away.

Cletus had set an old wooden box in the corner of the bedroom for her few clothes to go in. He'd said she could use it as a dresser. She and Grandma had shared an old two-drawer dresser, each of them folding their day clothes and draping them across the top for the night. Cletus saw no point in draping clothing across a dresser or a box. His clothes were in piles, some hanging out of an old chest of drawers he used for himself. She'd glanced at his clothing, snaking out of open drawers and clumped in wads around the room as she held her clothing, Grandma's dress, pressed against her body earlier. The top of his chest of drawers was different from everything else, almost bare; it was the neatest place in his house. A framed picture of an older woman stood in its center. She looked like Cletus, tall, slender, fair-haired and fair-skinned. To the side was another photo, a younger woman with a boy on her lap.

"Who are these people?" Lana had edged toward the chest of drawers, keeping her dress between herself and his eyes as he lay in bed watching her. She knew what she was supposed to do, she knew husbands and wives saw each other without their clothing, but she wasn't ready yet. She was still thinking about everything Jeanie'd described.

"My mother," he grunted. His eyes flickered across the photos and then back to Lana.

She peered at the picture of the younger woman. "So that's your mother when you were a boy?"

He didn't respond, so she turned. He was staring at the ceiling, a thin blanket molded over his long form. She looked back at the photos, and the other items he had arranged around them. Medals, war medals, were lined up precisely, the same way he wanted his plate and silverware aligned at the table.

"You fought in the war?"

"I did. Then I came back."

"But you must have been a hero."

"I survived. Sometimes living's heroic enough." He looked at her then. He looked tired, and older than she'd thought when she first saw him. "I built roads and bridges after I got back. Then I bought this farm, and I do welding in town." He paused, his face looking almost mummified. "And now I've taken a new wife."

"A *new* wife?" She glanced back at the young

woman in the photo, then at Cletus. "Are you sure? I mean, no one told me…"

"You ask a lot of questions. Guess I should expect that from someone your age." He ran a hand over his face. "Kind of wanted someone uncomplicated. That's why I picked someone so young, someone who'd just do what a wife's supposed to do, keep the house and give me sons."

Lana *was* young, still a child herself, and she felt like one compared to him and compared to the woman in the photo. She should apologize for acting like one, curious and full of questions, pesky, like Grandma always said she was. But no one had told her there'd been a wife before her. A real woman, not a child, like she was, standing here in Cletus' bedroom, hiding her shapeless body behind Grandma's dress. She pulled the dress tighter against her, ashamed she looked and acted so young, wishing she were fuller, the way Jeanie said she should be.

"Don't worry. You'll do, and you'll get used to things." He nodded toward the picture. "It was fever," he said. "I buried the two of them together."

"A boy," she whispered. "I'm sorry."

"Son." His brows pinched together. "Not just a boy. Sons matter. They'll work the land, help with the welding, and pass on what I build. What a father leaves a son is important. My father died and left us with nothing."

"Fathers want sons…I'm not your first wife…"

Cletus ignored her. He stared at the picture of his wife and his son. "I want a son again. For a long time I only wanted him back. Would've gone to him if I could. Got the medals to prove it." He leaned back against the headboard and looked at her. "You need to know that nothing scares me anymore. Nothing can hurt me worse than I've already hurt. And there's nothing I want except a son. I'll have one—I'll have dozens of them. And I'll do right by them."

Lana tried to shake away her shock as she stared at the determination on her husband's face. A chill ran over her nearly naked body as she grasped what he'd said. *Make babies. Mothers don't matter.* Daughters didn't either. Cletus only kept his first wife's picture because she was holding his son.

"My dad only had me, but my mom said he loved me."

Cletus frowned. "You have a dad?"

"Of course I do, he just never was around." It came out childish, her voice sounding high and screechy. She cleared her throat, drew in a long breath. "He was supposed to be there today. He was going to watch me get married."

Cletus frowned again, then shook his head like she was wrong.

Her heart pounded and she tightened her jaw. *Don't sass him.* She wanted to. She wanted to shout how wrong Cletus was, that her father was busy and tired and always far away, but she had one. Cletus still stared at her, the frown on his face making her feel like a child. She wasn't a child, not anymore. She drew herself up. She'd become a woman today. "You'll have sons." She looked her new husband straight in the eye. "Lots of them." She dropped the dress. The slip followed, and then her undergarments.

He looked her up and down. "You're awfully thin." He rolled onto his side and waited for her, facing the place she was to sleep.

"I can still carry babies. You'll have sons. Lots of them." She fought back the childish blush, the shock of womanhood, and the path it carved through her thoughts, the worry over having no noticeable hips or breasts. She'd seen his nakedness before he climbed into bed. He had no embarrassment or shame, not for himself or in front of her. He was her husband, her prince, and this is what princes were supposed to do. His eyes stayed on her as she climbed in beside him, the lamp at his side of the bed glowing, illuminating her lithe form.

He had been quick to pin her beneath his long body. She didn't cry out when he loved her, tried not to inhale the thick scent of his sweat, the aroma of something burnt emanating from his skin. She'd stayed quiet as labored breaths spouted from him. She'd gripped gritty handfuls of blanket and sheets and held on.

She lay in the dark and let go of the bright colors of childhood. Cletus was snoring, his back to her. She removed the blanket and let the night air cool his perspiration from her skin and dry the stickiness of her body. Had they made a baby just now? If what he'd done was making love, surely it wasn't supposed to have hurt so. She patted her belly. The hurt would pass, the shock would go with it. Surely they'd made a son.

Chapter 5

James 1948

"Where there's smoke, there's fire."

James glanced at Alex. His brother's voice was low, and the expression on his profile stern as he stared to the left, past Harold and out the driver's side window. Harold gripped the steering wheel with both hands and glanced to the left also, steering blindly, easing down the main street of town. James pivoted in the back seat, scanning the buildings and sidewalk, looking for the smoke his brother was talking about. No one was running, no one was screaming, everyone was quiet, minding his or her own business, just strolling along downtown.

"That Rick?" Harold asked while looking out the side window and then glancing ahead, checking where the car was going and straightening it a little.

"Uh-uh." Alex shook his head, craning to watch behind them as Harold drove on.

"Bases loaded. She'd better be careful. She's likely the one to be thrown out." Harold shook his head back and forth, his shoulders sagging. Alex said amen to his brother's sentiment, but his look was more fiery and his shoulders taut, his eyes riveted on whatever had their attention behind them.

James wheeled around once more. He looked for

"she," he looked for "smoke and fire," and he looked for someone not named "Rick."

"You better drive by Pop's work. That's one fire we don't want started," Alex muttered.

"Better." Harold blew out a breath as he veered to the left, heading one block off Main, then back the direction they'd come. The rear of Pop's welding shop butted against the back side of Main Street businesses, store owners often complaining about the noise and stench of a welding shop so near. Pop never cared. He ran his business the way he wanted and where he wanted, just like he did everything else. "Then we gotta get this car back to Ben, next door. Said he and his wife need it right after lunch, and I sure don't want him hesitating on loaning it to us again."

Alex nodded. "Hopefully this will be quick." Alex glanced ahead, then left and right as if looking for someone. "Pretty close to lunch time. He usually sticks pretty near the shop for lunch, but you never know." Harold hit the gas, hurrying toward Pop's shop.

James' stomach tightened. Lunch was supposed to be waiting for them at home. He had his ball shoes on, his ball shirt, and his glove. Pop would make some comment if he saw him this way. "Can you drop me off? I'll walk home." He put a hand on the back of the front seat.

Alex and Harold exchanged a glance. Alex looked back at James and the ball clothes he was wearing. "Yeah, sure," he said. Harold yanked the car to the right and pulled along the curb. "Meet you at home," Alex said as James opened the back door. "We won't be long. If you see Ben, tell him we'll be there in a jiffy. You can help mend the fence while I fix that gate Pop wants fixed, after we eat."

James nodded. He snatched his glove and closed the car's door behind him. He stood on the sidewalk and watched his brothers pull into the street and drive on. Pop's shop was a few buildings down on the left. Pop would be inside, probably having his lunch. If James headed back to Main Street the way they'd just come, he'd likely avoid being seen if Pop had gone out. The red brake lights of the car his brothers were in flared as Harold moved it into a parking spot across from the welding shop. James ducked his head, for once glad he was small, and headed the opposite way.

James rounded the corner and headed down Main Street, pausing in front of Andy's dad's hardware store. Andy had been at the baseball practice also, the one Harold and Alex held on Saturday mornings. When they finished their practice, Andy's mom had dragged him off to a haircut, Andy scowling and yelping he was about to be scalped. James grinned, thinking about Andy. He caught the grin in his reflection in the window. He looked different when he smiled. He looked good. Maybe that's why Andy always made him laugh.

"You been out practicing?"

James jumped. He thrust his glove behind his back and wheeled from the hardware store's window. Mr. Morgan was there, a sandwich sign on the sidewalk in front of him advertising his daily lunch special. James let the wind out of his lungs as Mr. Morgan toed the sign into place. He had an apron on, something Pop said was sissy. Mr. Morgan brushed his tan hands together and walked over to James.

"Yes, sir," James said. "I was." He brought the

glove around in front of him, relieved it wasn't Pop, and slipped one hand inside. He socked his other fist into it.

Mr. Morgan eyed the glove, watching James jab it with his fist. "With your brothers or with the coach?"

James stopped pounding the glove and looked up. "My brothers. How'd you know?"

Mr. Morgan grinned, and it made James grin back. He liked Mr. Morgan's eyes, especially when he smiled. He'd seen Mama in them the time Mr. Morgan showed him how to bat better. He thought he'd seen himself in there too, but his eyes didn't dance or talk the way Mr. Morgan's did. Mr. Morgan shook his head, a slow jovial wag, his dark hair glinting in the noonday brightness. "Small town. News travels fast when it doesn't have far to go. Good news, bad news, even fake news. It gets around."

James tapped his fist into the glove and squinted at Mr. Morgan, wondering if it was good news or bad that his brothers helped him and some of the boys. James ground his fist into the leather. "They always helped me a little. They used to use sticks and dirt clods when we were out doing chores. That was when I first started playing, though." That was when he was six. When Pop had said baseball wasn't in James' blood. He ground his fist deeper, remembering the thrashing Pop had given him one night, whipped him with his belt for not getting chores done on time when a game went into extra innings. Alex had stepped in and Pop thrashed him too. Alex didn't cry, but James did. "I quit once for awhile. But then Harold and Alex started helping some of my friends play, so I decided to join them."

"You've got good brothers." Mr. Morgan's eyes

were on him. James hit the glove hard. It felt right, he felt like he owned it. "You keep up the good work. You've really improved."

James stopped pounding the glove. Mr. Morgan came to a lot of the games... He must be watching him if he noticed how James played. "Thank you, sir." He cleared his throat. "I will."

"Well, I need to get back into the restaurant. Noon rush and all." Mr. Morgan stayed where he was instead of walking away. "I wondered...would you tell your..." He put a hand to his mouth, ran it over his lips, then dropped it. "Tell your brothers they're doing a fine job with you and the boys." He turned toward his café.

"Mr. Morgan?" James stopped him. "Was there smoke down here a little bit ago? A fire or something?"

Mr. Morgan stopped and looked back, his brow furrowed. "No. No smoke. No fire, either, that I know of. Thank God for that, right? Some would probably think it was coming from my kitchen."

Or from Pop's shop. Mr. Morgan could have said that, but he didn't. He raised his eyebrows in pretend alarm instead.

James smiled. "Just wondered. Good day, sir."

Mr. Morgan disappeared through the restaurant's door. James moved in front of the café's large front window and watched Mr. Morgan as he made his way to the back. Ida, Mr. Morgan's sister, was watching him, too. Mr. Morgan hesitated halfway and glanced to his left. His hand came to his chin. James watched him scratch it pensively before he resumed his trek toward the kitchen. He passed his sister, and Ida turned toward James, staring at him, a solemn gaze that didn't let up.

James had stepped back from the glass and started

to walk on, his fist hitting the glove, when he spotted the smoke. There in a booth along the left wall inside Mr. Morgan's restaurant. Magdalena. Her back was to him, her right elbow at the edge of the table, a long cigarette, balanced between her fingertips, sending smoke snaking toward the ceiling. A man sat across from her, a man James had never seen before. James pressed close to the glass and stared. The man was tall, he looked rugged, and his eyes were fixed on James' sister in a funny way. Rick never looked at Magdalena that way. That's who Magdalena was usually with.

James watched his sister, wondering if that was the fire Harold and Alex were trying to put out before it started. The man who wasn't Rick stood and moved to Magdalena's side of the booth. The smoke thinned and disappeared along with her arm when the man slid in next to her, scooting her out of James' view. Pop would be furious if he saw Magdalena this way. She shouldn't be in Mr. Morgan's restaurant, since Pop was at war with all the downtown merchants, and she shouldn't be smoking and sitting with a strange man. Pop would rage, and it would feel like a fire had struck when he was done. But not to Magdalena. She'd make sure she didn't care. It was Mama who'd suffer. Whatever heat Pop sent Magdalena's way would make Mama melt.

****

Magdalena was like cold water on a fire. She'd never burn; she did her best to make sure of it.

The heat rose during the night, late, so late it woke James, and probably the rest of the house.

"You know what you are, don't you?" Pop's voice boomed.

James sat up and rubbed his eyes. His brothers,

57

who slept in the same room with him, lay still. Maybe they didn't hear, but surely they did.

"I'm Magdalena Paine," his sister responded. There was no waver, no shame, no excuse for what she was. James admired Magdalena, but he feared for her, too. Pop was never one to strike them, other than to whip them with his belt. He didn't have to strike them—his temper was harsh enough. But James listened, still expecting to hear the sound of Pop's large hand across his sister's face.

"Say it, Pop," Magdalena's voice went on. "Say, 'No Paine would ever be a whore or a hag.' "

The silence that followed felt heavy, so heavy James could hardly breathe. He fought to listen through it, praying Pop would drop it, let Magdalena go, and not call her the names James was finally beginning to understand.

A door slammed. Someone had gone out into the night. James threw back the covers to run downstairs and find Magdalena.

"Don't." Alex lifted his head from the pillow. "Stay where you are."

"But…"

Then James heard it. Female voices, soft and quiet. He wanted to go to the door and listen, but Alex's gaze held him. He stayed on his bed. The voices were low. Mama's was there and it rose; he recognized it.

"If Pop hurts Mama," James muttered.

"Just stay put," Alex said.

Harold lifted his head. "Pop's outside."

"But that was Magdalena that left…" James listened harder. The voices contrasted, Mama's soft one and Magdalena's coarse one. His brothers were right. "I thought… Why'd Pop go out?"

"Got a lot to think about," Alex said. Both brothers dropped their heads to their pillows. "I imagine he'll get another jab at Magdalena, but she'll do what she always does and get him back."

"Get to sleep, little brother," Harold said. "Someday Pop and Magdalena will figure out this battle's already done and realize who the winner is."

Chapter 6

Lana 1930

No one had ever told Lana how beautiful a baby could be, or how wonderful she'd feel as she looked at a child of her own. She'd been just a child herself when she'd come to be Cletus' wife, and now she was a mother. Cletus had done his part making this baby, and now she had done hers. Almost. This new daughter, their first child... Lana saw her as a good beginning, proof of what she was capable of, a promise she would bear more for him, especially sons.

Ella Canfield stood at the side of Lana's bed, stains from the birth discoloring her hands and apron. Ella tipped her head and brushed a wisp of gray hair aside with her shoulder as she gazed down at the new baby. "She's beautiful. Just like you."

Lana shook her head. *I'm a wife, but I've made a beautiful baby.* Jeanie's notions about love and marriage had been wrong. Marriage wasn't like those childish fairy tales. Cletus wanted uncomplicated, he wanted his meals on time and his silverware in a line. He had been good to her, considerate of her condition while she carried what was supposed to be his son, but he didn't care about beautiful. And she knew he didn't care about daughters. But this baby was perfect. "She is beautiful, just look at her." The fact his first one wasn't a son wouldn't matter when Cletus saw his new baby girl. He would feel like Lana felt, he would say this daughter was wonderful and their next one would be a son.

The still air in the bedroom felt almost cool, she and the baby both still damp. Soft grunts came from the bundle, making the infant quiver in her arms. Lana stared at their new daughter, admiring the fair-haired, red-skinned baby in her arms. Ella tucked the small blanket under the baby's chin, her hands like Grandma's, worn, leathery, and kind. Wife hands. What Lana's would become with time.

"Thank you," Lana said. *Thank you for helping me with the birth, and for all of the invisible lessons you've given me since I married Cletus.*

Ella lived more than a mile down the road, and little in these months of learning to be a wife had made Lana's heart beat with more excitement than the stout form of Ella coming over the rise, plodding through the dust and rocks to see her, to show her how to do things good enough to satisfy Cletus. "You think I can handle a baby all right?" The baby squirmed, emitted a soft cry that made Lana feel as helpless as it sounded.

"Of course you can, even though you're barely older than she is." Ella laughed. "Brides get younger and younger every year, I swear."

Lana tried to smile. *Grandma was right about that, too. Lana hadn't been a bride, only a wife. But wives sure made beautiful babies.* She thought of the nearby picture on Cletus' chest of drawers, the wife who was bright, happy, pretty, and holding onto his son. Lana didn't look up at the woman. She hurt, she was bleeding, but she was alive, and so was Cletus' daughter. Their family was started. This was a new beginning.

Cletus had touched her belly while she carried this child, his eyes prying to look inside at his son. He had tamed his passion at night, made sure she was comfortable and her belly out of his way, all the while explaining sons' value, how they kept a man alive. She'd slowly begun to understand the liberty sons had. It didn't matter if they were beautiful, it didn't matter if they were there or gone. Making love wasn't an issue for them, either, only making babies, and having a wife who gave them sons.

Lana drew her daughter against her breast and held her there. If this baby had been a boy instead of a girl… Lana pressed the baby tighter, leaned close, and whispered against her head. *You'll always be beautiful. Someday you will be a bride. You're a girl, and that's still special.*

"What are you going to name her?" Ella asked. Lana looked up. Ella was gathering wet and bloody towels and rags from around the bed, taking away the stains that said this had been a painful experience. It had been painful. Lana relaxed her hold on the baby and drew in a long breath. It was still painful. This tiny bundle had stretched and torn Lana's body to make its way to her arms, but it was worth it. The pain was welcome. None of what she'd gone through would frighten her away from the marvel of having more children, lots of sons, maybe even another girl.

"We never talked about what to name her. Cletus planned on a boy, so he probably never thought much about a girl's name." Her head felt heavy, and she let it sink deep into the pillow. She was so tired and yet so exuberant.

"What about you? You thought of any names?"

Lana looked down at her daughter. Her misshapen face, her matted light hair, her puffy eyes. Ella'd told her all infants looked like this right after birth, as if the shock of leaving a womb was something to be apologized for. It didn't matter to Lana how her baby looked now or a year from now. She was precious, and she always would be. It was the rest of the world that would think differently, the men who needed sons, Cletus who was outside waiting to greet his new boy. "She has to have a special name," Lana said in a whisper. "One that will shout how beautiful she is."

Ella tucked the dirty towels into a bag and leaned over the bed, peering down at Lana's daughter. "You could call her Rose," she suggested. "Roses are beautiful."

"They are." Lana nodded. "But I want a name even more special than Rose. I want a name that will remind her and everyone else she's exceptional."

Ella straightened and frowned.

"You know. A name people will notice." Lana traced a finger around the dried crust on her baby's skin, thinking of the few women she'd known, books about heroines she'd read, and stories Jeanie had shared about fabled princesses. "Like Magdalena," she said. Magdalena Trenton was a girl from Jeanie's tales, a girl who'd suffered years of desolation and hardship, only to find out later she was actually royalty, mistakenly thrown into the wrong environment as an infant, but related to a king.

The back door opened and closed. Ella puckered her lips as she looked from mother to daughter. They both listened to the sound of Cletus coming through the house. "Your husband's here." Ella shifted her gaze to the door.

Knuckles rounded on the door in sharp, distinct raps.

The knock that had said *hurry* the first time Lana heard it said *hurry* again. *Hurry* and marry me. *Hurry* and fix my supper. *Hurry* and let me see my son.

"Magdalena and I are ready." Lana nodded to Ella. She winced as she straightened in the bed and snuggled Magdalena even closer to her breast. "He'll love the daughter I've given him. You can let him in."

Chapter 7

Lana 1932

Three years. Three years of being Cletus' wife. Three years of being mother to his children, first to Magdalena, now to Betsy, and soon to another which was well on its way. Two girls in three years. Two reasons Cletus was disappointed in her, two reasons that proved Lana wasn't being the wife she was supposed to be. Lana squeezed her daughters onto her lap as Ella's husband, Carl, closed his truck's door for her.

"Want me to take one?" Ella twisted Lana's way from the center of the truck's seat, extending her forearms to take one of the girls.

"Here, take Betsy." Lana wrapped an arm around Magdalena and let Betsy be drawn from her small lap onto Ella's much fuller one. Carl climbed into the driver's side, slamming the door behind him. The farm truck roared and smelled of fumes as he pushed the starter and revved the engine. Both girls jumped, Betsy fading into Ella's soft skin and Magdalena giggling with delight. Lana smiled. Magdalena always managed a laugh, even though she had little to laugh about in her small world. Betsy was the opposite. She mirrored the quietness of their home, the disappointment there were no boys, doing her best to stay invisible even at her tiny age, mostly vanishing into the woodwork.

Magdalena squirmed while Betsy burrowed into Ella's arms, her eyelids already half closed as Carl pulled onto the dirt road.

"You want to trade girls?" Ella whispered, even though she could have shouted since the truck's engine would have muffled her yell.

Lana tried to manage Magdalena's wiggles around her protruding belly, rolling the truck's window up against the dust that was swirling in. A trade would be wonderful, but Ella would be better off with Betsy. "Magdalena might take over the driving if she gets close to Carl." Lana laughed.

The scenery hadn't changed much since three years ago when she'd traveled this road the opposite way, going from Grandma's to Cletus'. She had come his way shattered, a child with a heart that was broken from missing her father. She was going to Grandma's a woman, a wife with her heart in her throat, terrified this unborn baby was going to be a girl, another girl. Cletus probably worried about the same. She saw it in the way he looked at her, the way he looked at his daughters every day.

Lana needed answers, going this way from Cletus' to Grandma's. Grandma'd sent her his way with the orders to work hard and let him do whatever he wanted. Cletus had sent her Grandma's way with the reminder he'd be home at 6:30 and expected his supper then. She promised she'd be back in time. She'd touched his arm, felt the bristly hair she'd longed to feel three years ago. He'd pulled away, nodded goodbye, then glanced at the girls. Grandma would surely have the answers. Grandma would know what to do.

Lana showed Carl where to turn after an hour and a half of dusty roads, jarring ruts, two- and three-word conversations, and soft snores from Ella between them. The truck rumbled down the narrow dirt road, and Lana's heart beat harder as the terrain changed from familiar to home, grasses that were common everywhere suddenly waving at her as if they recognized her and welcomed her back. These were her grasses, grasses that didn't, yet did, belong to Grandma. A road and fields that weren't Grandma's either, but they *were* hers, because they were landmarks of home. Lana pinned her gaze on the horizon, waiting for the low-pitched roof that was theirs—Grandma's—and the cottonwood tree next to it she'd never thought much about until now. Why hadn't she cared about it when she was a girl? Now that tree was like a beacon, a comfort, a memory of the way things used to be.

"Right there!" She didn't mean to shout, but she did, and she pointed, acting like Magdalena instead of herself. Ella stirred, Betsy opened her eyes, and Carl gunned the engine, eating up the last of the road between her and her old home. The truck bounded into the lane the same way Cletus' had bounded out. Lana squeezed Magdalena tighter as she scanned Grandma's weedy yard, unpainted chicken coop, and sagging shed where they always kept a milk cow. She and Grandma'd written letters to each other, Grandma with little to say and Lana with little she wanted to say on paper. She'd told Grandma she'd be here one day this week, depending on Carl's schedule and Cletus not changing his mind. It didn't matter if Grandma didn't know what day they would come. Grandma would be here. Like Lana, she rarely went anywhere.

Before Carl stopped, Grandma's thin form appeared in the doorway of the shed. Her hair was neat, neater than usual, as if she'd taken more care this morning. Her dress was tucked evenly within a makeshift belt, another scrap of material promoted to something more glorious than being just a rag. Lana pressed her hand against the truck's window as Carl slowed to stop, watching Grandma's form disappear on the other side of Lana's fingers. She wanted to grasp her grandmother and hold on as she passed, remake the connection she never realized they had until it was gone, soak in some of Grandma's wisdom that had always been there teaching her, though she just hadn't realized it until now.

"Grandma," Lana said to Magdalena. Her daughter stared out the window, lifted her tiny hand, and plastered it next to Lana's on the glass.

Lana dropped out of the truck's cab the instant Carl stopped. With Magdalena on one hip, she reached for Betsy and settled her sleepy daughter on the other, her stomach, where the next child lay, protruding between her two girls. She balanced herself like a tightrope performer, pivoted toward Grandma, and waddled her way. "Grandma…" Her voice sounded like a child's, the knot in her throat choking the confidence she'd meant to portray. Grandma's face looked just like Lana felt, and Lana knew she understood.

Betsy nuzzled her head against Lana's shoulder as they drew up in front of Grandma. Magdalena squirmed and made gleeful nonsense noises. Lana gripped her tighter.

"My, aren't you a sight!" Grandma tried to sound brash and bossy, but her eyes betrayed how happy she really was. Lana hadn't thought to come here not looking like a sight. Her dresses were all baggy—until she was pregnant, like now. Then they bulged forward, hiking the skirt up in front, making her dress look like a bell in the middle of a toll. She wore her auburn hair longer now because Cletus liked it that way, but it was pulled back out of Magdalena's and Betsy's reaches. And no makeup. She'd come plain, the way she always was, plain and tired.

"I probably am a sight." Lana felt her face flush, but tried to ignore it. She wasn't here to be told how good she looked. She was here to see Grandma, see herself and her new life against her old one and the person who'd told her how this new one was supposed to be lived.

"You look just fine, actually." A tall shadow filled the shed's doorway behind Grandma. "If anything, you're a sight for sore eyes."

"Jim…"

Jim Dillon stepped from the shed's dark interior. He'd changed. She was shocked at what he'd become. He'd grown in three years, muscles where scrawny arms used to be, tanned skin and chiseled features where softness used to be. There was still the boy in his eyes, though, the boy who'd helped her with chores before she left to get married. The boy Grandma had said really wasn't there to help Lana but was there because he needed the pay. A bucket half full of milk dangled from one of Jim's hands. Grandma was right again. He was here not because Lana was but because he needed the pay.

Jim didn't stare at her daughters, or the bulge of her stomach, or the worn dress that covered it. He just looked at her face, his eyes scanning every feature as if relearning, even admiring, who she'd become. Lana's hand twitched. She wanted to run it over her hair, smooth it, or pull it out of its knot and let it hang loose so she'd look like the girl she used to be, not the worn-out housewife she'd become. Her face warmed. She was being silly. Jim didn't care, he was just a childhood friend.

"Let me take one of those girls." Ella appeared at Lana's side and took Magdalena from one hip. Before Lana could reposition Betsy, the tiny girl was lifted away also, up into the air, Jim's big hands around her ribs. Lana watched her shy daughter go, bracing herself for the wail the frightened Betsy would let go. Jim talked to Betsy, let her have a good long look at him, then settled her gently at his side.

"She looks kind of like you." He turned to Lana.

Betsy was actually pretty. She had Lana's complexion and some of her fine features. Lana looked at her daughter, a semblance of what Lana used to be when she grew up here near Jim. She glanced at him. *Please don't say it, don't say what's too late to say.* Too much had happened, too much had changed. A strand of hair came loose and blew across Lana's face. She didn't straighten it. She let it blow.

"And this one's like her daddy," Ella chimed in, bouncing Magdalena on her hip. "Got his fair hair and skin."

Every eye went to her oldest daughter, the lanky girl who really was like her father, except she knew how to laugh and smile. Lana hurried to say everyone's names and explain who everyone was. Everyone except Cletus, the daddy Magdalena favored. He wasn't here, and Ella's comparison was enough of a tribute, so she finished the introductions and left it at that.

Ella and Carl had family nearby, or at least they'd said they did when Ella offered to bring Lana to see her grandma. Lana wondered if they'd go down the road and just sit in the hot sun all day, waiting, letting her have a much-needed moment with Grandma. Ella and Carl climbed into their truck. They knew to be back in time to have Lana home to fix Cletus' supper before 6:30. She waved as they drove away. So did Magdalena, from Lana's hip now that Ella was gone. Jim waved Betsy's little hand for her. Lana watched, surprised. She'd never seen that done before. She'd never seen Betsy held by a man before.

"Well, I'll finish taking care of the milk," Jim said to Grandma. He brought Betsy to Lana and set her easily on Lana's hip.

"You're good with little girls," Lana said. He smelled like milk, like their—Grandma's—shed, like home used to be.

"It's the big girls that baffle me." His mouth took on a grin, but his eyes were serious. He picked up the bucket and turned away.

"I'll pay you tomorrow," Grandma said to his back. "You can head on home and take some eggs tomorrow."

"No need to give me anything," he said. He stopped and turned around. "Glad to help out." Then he looked at Lana, his dark hair glistening in the sun. She felt herself redden as he studied her. A smile appeared, an inward one that didn't really show, yet it was there in his gaze. She recognized it—she knew it well. It revived the one that used to be in her, even after three long, difficult years. "Glad to help you too, if you ever need it," he said to her. "Just let me know."

"She's fine. You go on, and I'll pay you tomorrow." Grandma was at Lana's side. She took Betsy, dragging her from Lana's hip as Lana watched Jim walk away. He disappeared back into the shed as Grandma created a commotion with Betsy.

"Here, let me keep her," Lana offered.

Grandma held onto Betsy like a sack of potatoes. "Let's just get inside. Come on." Grandma hurried toward the house.

Lana turned from the shed and followed her. "Jim's just being neighborly to me for old time's sake."

"That's right. Now come on." Grandma moved even faster, folds of her dress gripped in Betsy's small fists.

Grandma's house hadn't changed, not as much as Lana would have expected with Cletus' promised care. It was even smaller than she remembered, now that she lived in Cletus' much larger home, and still empty except for a cabinet she didn't recognize.

"Grandma…" Lana began, making a sweep around the room—the small dresser, the cots, the stove, the lone picture of an angel watching over a small house. "I thought there'd be more…"

Grandma dropped into her rocker, Betsy bouncing and flopping on Grandma's lap. Magdalena slid from Lana's hip to the floor and began to explore.

"Has Cletus been sending you something, like he said he would?" Lana came and stood near Grandma's rocker.

Grandma thrust forward, then back, rocking hard, squeezing a frightened Betsy tight. "Notice the cabinet over there? Got that right after your wedding."

Lana glanced at the cabinet. It was old, probably used, but new to Grandma. "It's nice," Lana said. "But it's been three years. I thought there'd be more..." Lana looked at Betsy, terror in her eyes as Grandma flailed back and forth in the rocker. Then Lana looked at Magdalena, roving around the room, running her finger over what little Grandma had. Cletus thought there'd be more too, more than two daughters.

"Don't need more." Grandma snorted. Betsy let out a whimper, and Lana saved her from Grandma's grasp, then knelt beside the rocker. She wanted to set Betsy on the floor and crawl onto Grandma's lap herself, have both of them rock hard to fling the hurtful things away.

"Grandma..."

"Those girls look plenty healthy," Grandma interrupted her. Lana watched Magdalena toddle around the room. "Can't be easy supporting a wife, two girls, and a third on the way. Especially at his age."

"He doesn't want girls, Grandma, he wants sons." Lana looked at Grandma, the determined fix of her face, but she thought of Cletus and how much he smelled like burnt metal when he came in at night. Their bed smelled like welding and hot skin. He did work hard, so hard she couldn't clean it out of their blankets, no matter how much she tried.

"Looks like your husband's doing what he's supposed to, no matter what." Grandma slowed in the rocker. "You just gotta keep doing what's right, so he will too."

Keep doing what's right. Two girls in three years. What if this third child was another daughter? What if Cletus left, left these two girls alone? Lana had cooked and cleaned, done all the outdoor work Cletus asked her to. She never complained and she always let him have his way. She'd done the best she could. She'd tried to be a good wife. Betsy nestled into Lana's lap, and Magdalena rounded the room for the third time. Lana rested her chin on Betsy's head. "He's not happy with me. He's sorry he asked for me, and now he's taking that out on you. What if he…"

"Oh, posh." Grandma rocked hard again. "I'm fine. He knows that."

"I thought things would be different." Lana watched Grandma go back and forth. "When I married him, I thought it would be like living here with you. I thought it would be easy." Lana hesitated. "And someday, we'd be all settled, and my dad would come and…"

Grandma stopped and turned in her seat and looked at Lana. "It wasn't as easy as it seemed. Your mother just made it seem that way. That wasn't right, and I told her so, but it was her way of taking care of you. You're grown up now, and you've got a chance to do things really right. Work hard and be satisfied with what you got. You know how, just like you and I always did."

"But…" Lana saw it then. She'd missed it before. Her little drawing, the one of her holding hands with her father. Grandma had pinned it to the wall above Lana's old cot. "He never came, did he?"

Grandma set her jaw; her lips formed an even line. "Do you want me to say never?"

It sounded like a scream inside, one that was trapped and wanted to get out. It had started on her wedding night, but she knew when she heard it that it had always been there. She tried to ignore it, keep a deaf ear to its cries. In the evenings, when Cletus came home and gave her that look, the one that said how disappointed he was, the scream reared up and grew louder, almost as loud as now. When he rolled off her at night, for some reason it wanted to wail. She never let it. She didn't want to hear what it said, or hear what it was shrieking now. *He'd never come because he'd never been.*

"Oh, Grandma." Instead of the scream of a wife, Lana's voice came out like a child's.

"Lana, you listen to me. You know how to get by on little. You did it for years, here with me, and finding out now what you thought you had wasn't really there doesn't change the fact that you were strong and we made it. Whatever you didn't have, or don't have now, remember it could always be a lot less."

Lana gazed around the room at a lot less, a nearly empty house made even emptier without Lana here, without a father here. Ever. Tears blurred the lone cabinet Cletus must have decided was enough when he didn't get his part of the bargain. Grandma's house felt like Lana felt—bare, empty, only the fear that there could be a lot less to get by on keeping them going. Cletus could leave, just like her real father must have.

She slid a hand between Betsy and the child that lay in her womb. She wouldn't scream, she wouldn't cry.

"The best thing you can do is to love those little girls," Grandma said.

Lana raised her head. It felt heavy. She felt tired. But Grandma had never talked about love before. The word seemed foreign, coming from her lips with her voice.

"I know you'll do right by them yourself, but if you want to really love them, you'll do right by their father, too."

Do right...let him be king, no matter what. She'd never felt so hollow. Lana didn't know if she could. "Like Mom pretended she was doing?"

Grandma frowned and rocked a little harder. The pain Lana felt at her mother's deception looked like anger on her grandmother's face. Magdalena grabbed Lana's arm while Betsy stayed plastered against her chest.

"I know growing up here, just you and me, we did okay, but if there'd really been a man around, a good man, not just an imaginary one..."

The door opened and Jim stepped in with the milk, freshly strained and in a crock, the same crock Lana had used when she lived here. She looked from the crock to Jim, a man now, but once upon a time the boy who'd come and helped her...not helped *her*, but come and helped for pay.

"Thank you, Jim." Grandma's voice sharpened. Jim seemed not to hear her, his attention on Lana. "Put it on the table, and that'll be good. Then go." Grandma spoke louder, like a hammer shattering crystalline memories.

Jim set it on the table, but then he paused and looked at Lana again. Something in his eyes made her hurt even more than she already did. She clenched her teeth so nothing would get out, and she looked down and aside at her girls. He walked away, she heard him, and then he was gone.

"Jeanie's sweet on him," Grandma said.

"She always was." Lana choked, she batted away

tears. "Jeanie had a way around him, teasing and talking in ways I never knew how." She swooped Magdalena onto her lap and squeezed her and Betsy into a powerful embrace. "Thank you, Grandma," she said into their hair. "If I can make sure Cletus stays, I'll be fine, so will these little girls, and so will you. I'll do my very best."

Grandma rocked herself forward and shoved to her feet. "Don't worry about me. It's those girls that matter most. Not many get a good father," Grandma said, glancing down. "As you know. Just do your best. That way Cletus will stick around and be there as theirs."

Grandma's frail form went across the room to her "new" cabinet. Lana watched her do what she'd always done for Lana, without ever having to say it out loud. Take care of the little girl...in this case the little girls. That was loving. Lana buried her face in her daughters' hair. She could do this. She would love her daughters by being a very good wife to their father. She could. She would.

Chapter 8

Lana 1933

Cletus stared. His blue eyes had grown hazy around the edges from looking too often near the hot flames of welding. "What's that?" His voice rattled, as indistinct as his irises, raspy from a throat abraded by the same heat that burned his eyes.

"A flower."

"A flower? Why?"

The single flower stood in the center of the table, not big enough to bring inside the color or life she'd meant it to. It looked too thin, too incapable of doing what it was supposed to. It looked too much like her.

"I thought it would be nice. For you. And the girls, and Harold." Harold wasn't old enough to care about flowers, or food that needed to be chewed, or anything else she put on the table, but he was Cletus' first son and therefore important, especially in matters where Cletus' opinions outweighed hers.

Cletus looked at the flower, its stem leaning against and over the rim of the jar she'd put it in. Magdalena loved the flower and hopped up on a chair to stretch over the table and touch it. Cletus' gaze shot to their daughter. Lana wrapped her arms around Magdalena and swooped her off the chair, holding her in a hug she couldn't squirm out of. *Get down,* rang in Lana's ears.

Cletus hadn't said it. She'd been quicker than his impatience. But he'd said it often enough, even said worse. *You're a bother. You're just in the way.* Lana had learned to be quick, quicker than his tongue, keeping him from eroding little Magdalena's laugh, keeping him here where he was supposed to be.

Cletus frowned at Magdalena until she stopped squirming. She caught her father's glare and returned it with a stare of her own. Lana knew who would come out the winner of this battle of wills. She pivoted to the side, breaking the father-and-daughter deadlock. Magdalena wasn't afraid to challenge her father. She instinctively knew what should be hers, and she was determined to get it, her way, every loss still a victory in her young eyes.

You did okay without a man here, but it would have been better if... She set Magdalena down in the next room, then carried Betsy over to join her. *Love those little girls by doing right by their father.* Betsy cowered next to Magdalena. She knew, too, what was supposed to be hers, but she didn't fight for it, she beat it down inside and melded into the woodwork. Lana glanced over at her son. Harold would be fine right where he was, in a small crib near the table. He was a boy. His battles were already won.

Cletus watched Lana as she returned and stood near the table. "Magdalena loves the flower. She helped me…"

Cletus raised a hand. He was no longer watching her, he was looking elsewhere, staring at the curtains she'd made from Grandma's dress that morning, the dress that had been Lana's wedding gown, both panels tied back with the yellow material she'd used for a belt on their wedding day. She said nothing as he looked farther along the walls, to the place she'd hung his medals. She'd lined them up on a board and tacked them where he could see them while he ate.

She'd added little things to their home ever since her trip to see Grandma. It hadn't been easy to find items to add to their house. She never went anywhere and had no money to buy something even if she did. But she found little ways to improve it, change it, clean and organize it so it was slowly becoming a home. But today she'd done more, put him on display, added color to their dining area. Cletus finished, and his gaze returned to her.

She smiled. "Do you like it?"

He tipped his head as if considering what she'd done. "It's different." He drew back his chair from the table and dropped into its seat.

Lana hurried to set the meal in front of him, keeping all the dishes near his plate and away from the flower. She brought both girls from the other room and settled them in their chairs. Cletus waited until she sat before he began serving himself. She watched, glad Harold was quiet in his crib. When the ladles were back in their serving dishes and the only sound was Cletus eating, Lana served her daughters and then herself.

"So where'd the flower come from?" Cletus asked around a mouthful of food.

"The pasture." She was surprised he wouldn't know that. She always tended to the cow, but he would know about the wildflowers spread throughout the grasses. She looked up. He was staring at her, but his thoughts were far away, maybe sorting through memories of the pasture while churning his food.

"There are lots of them out there," she added. "All kinds. I should have picked more, but I had my hands full with the kids. I got that one today when I called in the cow. I thought it was pretty. I thought it was…"

"Whereabouts?" Cletus watched her over the top of the flower.

"What do you mean, whereabouts?"

"Where in the pasture?"

There was something about his question, or maybe the way he looked at her when he asked. His eyes were different, the watery blue irises sharper and more distinct. Her heart beat hard in her chest. Where had she picked the flower? She set her fork on her plate, trying to think.

"Rock."

Lana turned to Magdalena. She was facing her father. She was right. Lana had picked the flower where Magdalena had fallen over a rock.

"To the right of the gate," Lana said. It came out in a rush. "Maybe two yards to the right."

Magdalena looked back at her plate and resumed eating. She wasn't proud of her first real conversation at the table. She'd come to Lana's rescue, and Lana wondered if her daughter somehow understood that. Magdalena continued to eat, just like her father always did after a brief conversation.

"I guess it's all right." Cletus dragged his spoon across his plate and scooped up another mouthful. "Women need those sorts of things. Just wondered where you got it."

"We do, you're right. Well Magdalena does, but I don't. I never expected you to bring me flowers. I wasn't trying to say…"

"I prefer uncomplicated." He gave her a small smile.

Lana retrieved her fork and scraped and rearranged what was left on her plate until Cletus was finished. She gathered their dishes and hurried them to the kitchen. She set them down near the stove and looked around the room. She drew in a deep breath. Thank God the smell of lemon was gone. She returned to the table and set his cup of coffee and a plate of leftover oatmeal cookies in front of him.

"I'm sorry. I didn't have time to make a new dessert."

He took a cookie off the plate.

She returned to her seat, leaving one cookie each in front of her daughters. Later, when he was asleep in his chair in the next room and the children were in their beds, she would take his favorite lemon cake she'd made for him out to the pasture and dump it there. Something would eat it, it just wouldn't be him. She had to do things his way, she had to keep them uncomplicated. The way he wanted.

Chapter 9

James 1950

There were more gifts under their tree this year than any other Christmas James could remember. He sat cross-legged on the floor next to Carla, the rest of their family behind and around them, waiting to open their presents. He was too old this year to have poked and prodded the wrapped pencils and oranges they always received, pretending they were fancy pens and baseballs, things Mama always said they couldn't afford. He'd skirted the corner where the tree stood, pretending he didn't care. Like Pop, the way Pop said men should be. But now, sitting next to Carla, he stared at the gifts and wondered. He was anxious to see which presents were for him.

Magdalena yawned behind him. She sat farther back at the edge of the family, old enough to be married by now, as Pop often remarked, her hair in matted tufts, smudges of black mascara still under her eyes in defiance of what he said. James prayed Pop wouldn't notice, even if Magdalena didn't care. She should have taken more time to scrub her face. It was Christmas, and he wanted things to be happy for a change.

Pop thumped his pipe on the arm of his chair, the wooden armrest blackened where he knocked ashes from the pipe's bowl. This was Pop's ritual. It gave him a distinction as head of the house. They all waited, letting Pop go through the steps they had all memorized—thump, dig, thump, fill, tamp, light, puff quick and hard, then blow out a cloud of smoke. The ritual made home seem like home, and it made Pop content.

When the scent of tobacco filled the air, Mama stood. "Merry Christmas," she said. She looked tired and happy at the same time.

"Merry Christmas," James answered along with his brothers and sisters. His siblings were all older, the voices responding like adults instead of children. But still he felt it, maybe they all felt it, the excitement the season was supposed to bring. "Merry Christmas, Pop," he said without thinking.

Pop stopped mid-draw on his pipe. He glanced down at James from his chair, his blue-eyed reserve shattered. He lifted one eyebrow, nodded, and looked away. Sometimes at night James heard Mama and Pop talking about him. Neither said his name, but when Pop said, "That boy," James knew it was about him.

Magdalena rose from her chair. One hand tussled James' hair as she passed toward the tree. "Merry Christmas, little brother," she said while her fingers were still on his head. "Love that dark hair."

Pop took a longer draw on his pipe as she stepped toward the tree. He blew hard into the air, a cloud of smoke hiding him as it swirled in front of his face. James smoothed his hair where Magdalena had mussed it. He wished she'd sit down before Pop said something about her face and the traces of last night that looked even more obvious against the morning pallor her fair skin had.

She bent and picked up a package. She read the name and handed it to Harold. Then she sat, and Harold shrugged, then stood. Everyone knew Harold was anxious to get to Sandra's house, his steady girlfriend for over a year now. James was glad Harold had stayed home this morning, that they all were here. Harold chose a package, read the name, and handed it to Carla. This was new. James had never seen this done before, but his brothers and sisters understood the rules as the gifts were distributed, each one receiving and then giving. Alex handed a gift to James. James stood, found a package, the one he'd wrapped for Mama, and he handed it to her. She looked uneasy as she smiled and took the present from his hand.

"You'll like it, Mama." He'd found a picture of her hidden away, and he'd framed it with wood he'd whittled and smoothed with a knife. He wanted her to put it on Pop's dresser, next to the other two photos Pop kept there. She thanked him, her eyes on Pop. James glanced at his father. He was staring straight ahead, a shroud of smoke hanging around him. Mama stood, took a gift from under the tree, and passed it on.

James returned to his spot on the floor and watched in fascination as his brothers and sisters and Mama received and gave. This had to be something they used to do, that they stopped doing for some reason after he came along. He wanted to do it again next year, and the next, and forever. It felt good. He wanted to always feel this way.

There were two gifts left under the tree. Magdalena picked up the one he recognized, the gift they'd all shared in for Pop. She carried it to Pop's chair and stood in front of him. The gift hung in her hands, the dark smudges under her eyes making her look like a fighter instead of a daughter, or a hag or a whore. James saw then how much alike they were, his sister and his father. Not just their hair, and their fair skin, and their height, but something else, too. She was like Pop on the inside, the place that gave her the courage to stand there with last night's makeup still on her face. Mama said Magdalena had been her happiest baby, but James couldn't imagine his sister that way. Her happiness was like a thin covering over a deep sore, one that never seemed to get better. It was the sore he thought she relished, that was her strength, and it made her do the things she did.

Pop nodded at his lap, one hand holding the pipe he was nursing, the other gripping the arm of his chair. James prayed Magdalena would set the package on his lap, not drop it, not throw it, not insist he reach up and take it.

She smiled. If her eyes hadn't glistened, James would have thought it was respectful. "You need to get up and hand that last gift to whoever it belongs to. Do that first, and I'll put this on your lap so you can open it."

"I'll get it." Mama jumped to her feet. She started toward the tree, but Betsy latched onto Mama's skirt. Mama was yanked to a stop and glanced down at her daughter. Betsy's fingers twisted around Mama's hem. Mama bit her lower lip and backed toward her chair. Slowly she sank into it.

"Last package, Pop." Magdalena nodded toward the tree.

Pop's pipe clattered into the ashtray on the floor near his chair, and he gripped both armrests and hauled himself to his feet. In one stride, he reached the tree, bent down and swept up the gift. James' jaw dropped. Pop still had the ballplayer in him. He'd never seen Pop move that way. Pop straightened and glanced at the name. He turned to James, waved the package like an underhand pitcher, and lobbed it into James' lap.

"Thank you." James could barely speak. He watched his Pop; he memorized that move.

Pop stepped backward and sank into his chair. Magdalena laid his package in his lap. "Merry Christmas, Pop." He reached for his pipe, relit it, and puffed silently, his gift balanced on his knees. "Okay, everyone, open your gifts!" Magdalena's eyes were like fire, venomous fire, instead of yuletide flames. She waved her arms to encourage them as she waded back to her chair.

James prayed Magdalena would open his gift first. It wasn't much, but she needed it. He'd found an old mirror, a small piece of a bigger one, and he'd made it a frame just like he'd done for Mama's picture. He wanted Magdalena to get a closer look at what she needed to see to keep out of Pop's way. He wanted to protect her even if she didn't care. He turned and watched as she dropped into her chair. She looked like she wanted a cigarette.

James turned back to his gifts, amazed again there were so many. Surprise and small gasps rose up around him amidst the rustling of paper being torn aside. He unwrapped pencils, and looked at Mama and Pop and thanked them. Mama smiled. A book about baseball was next. It was old and used, but it made his heart leap. Harold grinned. New napkins for his spot at the table sewn by Betsy and Gail, a shirt, blocks cut from wood from Alex, an orange, and cookies from Carla. He thanked them all before he opened another orange which lay still wrapped near his knee, alongside the last package Pop had handed him. He lifted the orange first. It wasn't easy to find oranges this time of year, and he could tell it wasn't ready to eat yet, by the feel. It was hard, probably slightly green like the others. He peeled the paper aside, and saw white instead of orange. White leather with neat lacing. He tore the rest of the paper away and gripped a baseball in both hands. He looked up at Mama, then at his brothers. They smiled, they grinned, but they nodded toward Magdalena.

"Like it, little brother?" Magdalena was holding the mirror he'd made her. She winked.

"How did you…" He clasped the ball in both hands, feeling its smoothness, gripping its hardness.

"I'll expect great things out of you," she said. "Now you got one more there. Open it."

James had forgotten about the gift Pop had handed him. He had his own baseball, and nothing else mattered. He held the ball in one hand and grabbed the soft package with the other. He stabbed a finger through the paper. Brown appeared beneath, soft, dark brown. The ball slipped from his fingers as he tore the paper away, the smell of cowhide overpowering Pop's sweet tobacco smoke. A baseball glove. His hands quivered. He could barely breathe.

"Who's that from?" Pop snapped to attention, his voice sharp. James looked at Magdalena. She'd pay dearly if she'd given this to him. The ball was enough. Pop would be on her for sure, now.

Magdalena grinned at James then looked up at Pop. "Not me." She shook her head, a slow shake she enjoyed. James heard Pop come to his feet, the box he hadn't opened hitting the floor. It was a new pipe, and an ashtray they'd carved from wood. Neither would break, but the thud was awful, like the pounding in James' chest. He heard Pop leave the room. The back door opened and closed, the dog letting out a yelp of welcome, and Pop was gone. Mama's face was white as she looked at Magdalena, her eyes huge question marks. Magdalena nodded, and her grin deepened.

James didn't understand his mother's look. It was an expression that had never been there before. He pressed the glove to his face and inhaled the leather. He grabbed the baseball and tucked it into the webbed pocket. Mama watched, the look still there. Suddenly he saw what Mr. Morgan had said ages ago. She was beautiful. A beauty James had never seen lit her face with the flush of being alive. Her eyes seemed darker as she combed her fingers through her hair. She took a long, deep breath, her eyes intense, her focus far away. He wanted her to stay this way so Mr. Morgan could see he was right. The clock on the bureau chimed, and Mama jumped to her feet. The light in her eyes vanished. It was time to begin lunch. She had to hurry.

She scooped paper from around her chair. As they scurried to help her, she came close to James. He had paper in one hand, his new glove and ball in the other. She looked into his eyes, farther than she ever had before. But it wasn't him she was seeing, it was someone else, maybe someone like him. "That's a really nice glove, James."

The back door opened.

"Hurry," Mama said. Then she glanced one last time at James. Whoever she saw, or wherever Mama'd been, it was just her now. She was back and the other person was gone.

Chapter 10

Lana 1933

"Grandma?"

The shadow Lana thought was Grandma moved away from the bed. Maybe it wasn't her, or maybe she hadn't heard Lana call. The room was dark, and the squat form blended in, making it hard to discern the dusky figure whose edges blurred within the fog of gray. Lana opened her mouth to call again—she didn't want to be alone—but nothing happened. Nothing came out, not even air. She winced. Why did it hurt so much? Having her other babies hadn't hurt like this, hurt enough she felt like crying instead of crying out.

She lay smothered under a heavy blanket of warm air. The room was stuffy like her kitchen, but she shivered, a cold inner chill creeping through her. Maybe Grandma had gone across the room to open and close the window to even the temperature. She listened for the creak of the wood, the window being forced up, and the thud of the weights in their channels. Everything was quiet. There was no sound.

The pain struck again. She tried to ignore it, think about Grandma instead...wherever she was. The darkness thickened, blocked all sight and sound, leaving her isolated with a pain she couldn't ignore. She groaned. The air was heavy and grew even hotter. She couldn't breathe; the pressure and pain were too great.

A scream came from somewhere. It startled her, a piercing cry that ripped through the blackness. Lana trembled. The gloom split in two. The shriek was shrill and sharp, like a vocal knife. It cut through the dark, slicing down from above and dropping onto her. It severed her, separating her top half from her bottom. Lana screamed. It was the same horrible sound she'd heard just a moment before: anguish, and a plea for relief. She screamed again. And again. Louder and louder. Lightning shot through her abdomen and burned down her legs.

"Grandma!"

Someone moved, came through the darkness to her side. She lifted a hand, but as she did, agony gripped her, coiled her into a ball. Hands tore at the wet bedding around her. She cried, and slapped at the hands. They wouldn't stop, but everything else did. Everything else began slipping away. Shuddering and hot, she was unable to scream again. The darkness consumed her.

****

There were voices. Voices so soft she couldn't tell what they were saying. A man. A woman. A man with two heads and two different sounds; Grandma, when she was younger, a little younger, but not much. It was too dark to see them. Maybe she'd died, maybe these were mourners. She wanted to tell them she really wasn't dead, they just needed a light so they could see she was still breathing. At least she thought she was. It was too dark to tell.

****

The scream came again. It shot from her depths, seared through her abdomen, knotted her chest, and raked her vocal cords as it escaped. It hurt, everything hurt, she was too hot, there were too many hands. They pushed, they pulled, they pressed. She wanted to bat them away, but she couldn't. Her arms lay dead at her sides.

****

The scream went away. A soft whimper took its place, a sweet muffle. It jarred her, its gentle cry far more powerful than the scream. Her arms flailed when she heard it, dragged her upwards through layers and layers of murky water, the darkest being left below, a glow of soft gray above. Voices were in the thin grayness overhead. Men, a woman, maybe two of them. The whimper increased. Her heart pounded and she swam harder. Something touched her, something cool on her forehead, something warm beneath her legs.

"She can't do this again." It was a man. Someone she didn't recognize. The gray was gone, a foggy glow in its place. She frowned, tried to see who he was, her eyes squinting through the haze.

"She's waking up!"

Grandma? Ella? The whimper became a wail. Her eyes opened. She was sure they did. Tall shadows stood like trees around her. One moved close and touched her.

"Lana...Lana, can you hear me?" It was Ella. Her voice gurgled, like she was talking through the water, or maybe it was tears. The wail came nearer. A soft, warm bundle pressed against her. Her arms were too heavy to move, too exhausted from swimming to the light. She dropped her chin down near the cry at her side, rolling her head close to the squirming warmth. What if she really was dead? Or dying? What if she

93

couldn't find the tiny voice? Her limbs lay lifeless, joined together by dull pain and exhaustion.

"You understand?" It was the same man as before. He sounded firm. "She can't go through this again."

A grunt answered him, another man. The tallest form moved away. A door opened and closed. The two remaining shadows moved close together and stayed at her side. The bundle began to cry, and her heart came alive.

Chapter 11

Lana 1933

Carl's truck rumbled slowly up the lane. Lana listened from her chair near the table, the motor much smoother than the one in Cletus' truck. Carl was here to pick up Ella, just like he did at the end of almost every day. Lana sighed. She was ashamed things had to be this way, but she was too weak to change them. The aroma of roast wafted from the kitchen, where Ella worked to complete another meal. On occasion Lana was strong enough to cook on her own, but most of the time she couldn't. Growing new blood was a slow process, and that's what the doctor said she needed to do. Alex had torn away at her insides too much, his birth almost violent. So violent that Ella's face turned white when Lana asked her about the two days she couldn't remember.

"Carl's here," Lana called into the kitchen. Magdalena romped by, riding an invisible horse. "Go tell Ella Carl's here," Lana said to her daughter. Magdalena galloped away, bounding over her little brother, Harold, who was crawling across the floor. Harold didn't flinch. He was peaceful, like Betsy, just not withdrawn. He was a combination of Lana and Cletus, the best of both. Harold would make a fine man someday.

"Call's here," Magdalena's small voice piped from the other room. Then the beat of her little feet could be heard as she spun her horse around and galloped away, making another circuit through the house. Alex was propped with his back against Lana's stomach, the two of them slouched in the chair. His eyes were pinned on his sister. He had spunk, just like she did. His legs stiffened and kicked. If he could figure out how to use them, he'd gallop after her, a mini Magdalena, racing from room to room.

Ella stepped from the kitchen, wiping her hands on a towel. "Supper's done," she said.

"You make enough for you and Carl too?" Lana asked. It was their arrangement. If Ella cooked here to help Lana, she took enough food home for herself and Carl. It was a battle every evening, who would give and who would receive. Lana knew it was her weakness that was her strength. She won these tussles because Ella watched her as they bickered, Lana's skin turning cooler, and no doubt paler, whenever they locked horns.

Ella studied her as she gauged the battle, drying her hands far more than they needed. She nodded then, her jaw set and her lips in a thin line as she retreated to the kitchen. Lana smiled, victorious. She must look especially bad this evening.

Another truck rumbled in the distance, rougher and growing stronger as it approached. Harold stopped crawling and rolled onto his bottom. He sat up and listened to the sound he recognized as Pop's. Magdalena rode harder. Lana lifted a hand, ran it over her own head to straighten her hair as she listened to her daughter slap her hip, urging the horse to go farther and faster.

Cletus' truck pulled into the lane. Carl would stay outside, now. Sometimes he came in and played with the kids while Ella finished up. But he wouldn't when Cletus was here. They would stay out, Carl helping Cletus with the chores. Ella stepped once again from the kitchen and glanced the direction the men would be.

"Guess I got a few more minutes," she said, looking back at Lana. "What else you want me to do?"

"Sit," Lana said. "Pull up a chair and sit with me for awhile."

Ella hesitated, then waddled over, lifted Alex off Lana's lap, and took the chair next to her. "Cow's milk isn't hurting him any, is it?"

Alex looked far healthier than Lana felt. He was rounding out and rambunctious. She envied him, wished she had his strength so she could get back to being wife and mother the way she was supposed to. Nursing Alex what little she could helped him get a good start, but it slowed her down. She straightened in the chair and smoothed her skirt where he'd been sitting. The skin of her hands looked old instead of young, thin and dry instead of well. She flexed them. They would improve with time. She'd eat more, drink more water, get back on her feet so some of her vibrancy returned.

"Cletus helping you plenty in the evenings still?" Ella asked.

Lana nodded, clutching her hands on her lap. He held the boys and corrected the girls, well, corrected Magdalena. Betsy stayed quietly out of the way while Magdalena took advantage of her father being held down by two babies.

Ella jostled Alex as his head swiveled from side to

side, keeping an eye on his brother and sisters, especially the sister racing from room to room shouting at her horse to go faster and faster. Ella watched the back of Alex's head, her mouth working before she finally spoke. "Cletus behaving himself?"

Lana kept her face toward her children. Ella's question embarrassed her, but it also exasperated her. Such things were no one's business, just hers and Cletus'. Ella had told Lana the doctor warned Cletus she shouldn't go through another childbirth. The first time Ella said it, vague memories of a tall shadow leaving her bedside, the sound of a door opening and closing after a man had said, "Do you understand?" ran through Lana's mind. She'd hoped it was part of a dream, not Cletus leaving her side after his second—maybe his last—son had finally been born.

"He's fine," Lana answered, hoping Ella would be satisfied. Behaving himself was too much for Cletus, and Lana knew it. She saw it in the way he watched her when he was home. The doctor's edict and the fact she'd been slow healing and too torn up inside to be the wife he needed had toppled her king from his throne. The hunger in Cletus' eyes, the wolfish appetite which lay behind them, made his celibacy, even though temporary, look intolerable. His eyes stalked her, followed her around the house, viewing her as if she was a meal withheld instead of a wife. He was hungry, he was frustrated, he was a pot of simmering fury, waiting to see if it was true she'd never give him another son. *Let him do whatever he wants.*

"Good." Ella gave a sharp nod of approval. "He doesn't need to bury another wife. I know that sounds harsh, but you're a treasure, whether he realizes that or not."

A treasure. Lana felt cold inside. She thought of Cletus' first wife's photo on his chest of drawers. Had that woman been a treasure before she died? Or even afterwards? Sons were his true treasure, not her, not his other wife. If she stopped giving him sons, he'd blame her, say it was her fault, and he'd be right. She'd given him two. She glanced from Alex to Harold. Two wouldn't be enough. If she was no longer able to give him babies, especially sons, Lana may as well not even be here, not even to satisfy his nightly yearnings. She might just as well be a photo on Cletus' dresser.

The back door opened and men's voices flowed into the house. Lana straightened as much as she could. Her skin felt cool and clammy. She brushed her hair back with her hands.

Magdalena shot into the room and back out again. Harold watched the doorway he knew his father would walk through, a bounce in his excitement. Ella became quiet, the men's voices and Magdalena's foot-beats the only sounds.

Cletus' voice overpowered Carl's. It rose, gruff around the edges—he sounded upset. Lana watched the door. Cletus had been more and more upset lately. Tension had grown along with the hungry look in his eyes. Lana clasped her hands and buried them in her lap.

"Morgan." Cletus spit the name. Mr. Morgan. He owned a restaurant in town. Lana'd never eaten there, but Cletus had. He used to eat lunch there often, especially since his welding shop was across an alleyway from it, directly behind the business next door to it. Cletus had an ongoing battle with the owners of the businesses downtown, men who preferred a welding shop be relocated farther away. Mr. Morgan was on the city council. As far as Lana knew, Mr. Morgan had stated no preference one way or the other, but he had authority, he had influence, he was like God, and he had power over the thing Cletus loved second most.

Cletus said Morgan's name again. Lana had only seen the man once or twice, but Mr. Morgan had the reputation of being good and honest; his gentle smile, his friendly dark eyes, all making what she'd heard of him seem true.

"My shop… Odors… Fire…" Cletus went on, Mr. Morgan's name again, and then another, a Mr. Kline.

Lana knew nothing about Mr. Kline. But Mr. Morgan… She and Mr. Morgan were the same. They shared the responsibility for the suffering her husband felt, or at least Cletus thought they shared it. She was taking away the main thing Cletus loved, his sons, and Mr. Morgan was a threat to the other, his work. She and Mr. Morgan were inadvertently intertwined. They were Cletus' enemy. In his mind, she and Mr. Morgan were one.

Harold struggled to his feet, then toppled over. He rolled onto all fours and struck out toward the door that led to the back porch. Carl stepped through the doorway, Cletus' tall form close behind. Carl stopped and scooped Harold off the floor and settled him on his hip. Harold watched his father as Cletus moved past, giving his son a pat on the back as his eyes sought out and found Lana.

He was angry, starved and angry. Roast wasn't going to satisfy the sort of hunger he had. He needed something more. She needed to satisfy him, answer that look in his eyes, assure him he would have more sons from her, lots of them. She touched her hair, smoothing it back again while she held his gaze.

The red hot flames in his eyes smoldered. Lana grabbed the back of her chair with one hand and forced herself to her feet. Her lower half felt as if it had remained on the seat.

"I'll help you gather your things and your supper," Lana said to Ella. The room swam, and her skin felt wet and cold. She gripped the chair until the wooziness passed.

"Here, you take Alex." Ella was on her feet.

"Cletus will take him," Lana said. She didn't look his way. She was waiting for her legs to steady and the ache in her pelvis to subside.

"No, you sit…" Ella held Alex her way.

"Cletus will take him," Lana said again. She looked at him this time, sent him a reminder this was his family, that was his son, and she was his wife that had given him to Cletus. Her fingers slowly released the back of the chair. She stood all the way and faced him. "Please take our son while I help Ella."

Cletus stepped forward and took Alex. Magdalena galloped into the room and back out again. Normally he would have yelled for her to settle down, but he didn't. He didn't even look Magdalena's way. He was watching Lana, the smoldering embers licked by tiny flames.

She looked into his fiery countenance. She was and would be his wife. Tonight, and always. And she would give him more sons.

Chapter 12

James 1952

James heard it again. He'd heard it most of his life, but he'd never really listened until now, now that he was older. *That boy. That boy. That boy.*

If Pop talked about Harold, he said Harold. If he talked about Alex, he said Alex. But late at night when Pop talked about James, it was *that boy.* James lay stretched on his bed and stared at the dark ceiling. That's what Pop called him behind his and Mama's bedroom door, his voice carrying through the walls and up the stairs where James could hear.

"Hey, you asleep?" The door to the room James shared with Harold and Alex cracked open. His brothers were both out, double dating, they called it, two fun times for the price of one, even though Harold wasn't looking for fun. He was unofficially engaged to Sandra. A silhouette of mussed hair came into view. Magdalena was slender enough to fit through without opening the door very wide. Her outline and form were black, but James knew, even in the dark, she would be bright, her face highlighted with vivid color, her clothing the same, her whole style vibrant and alive.

"I'm awake." He sat, drawing his knees up to rest his arms on. He propped his chin on his folded arms and watched her slide into the room. Pop's voice grew louder while the door was open. She shut it quickly, *"that boy"* and a faint glow of downstairs light still able to slip through.

The bed sagged as she sat near the center. She smelled of smoke, cigarette smoke, and something else. Harold and Alex said she drank, but James didn't believe it. She never acted like drinkers acted. She was always alert and in control.

"How was the game?" she asked.

"We won." Mama had been there. So had Harold. Alex stayed at work at Pop's shop, but Harold had slipped out to watch James play. Pop was mad at Harold for leaving early, but he'd blamed James. Pop's voice rose again from downstairs, his irritation filtering through the ceiling and floor.

"Sorry I missed it. Had to work, or I would have been there." Magdalena cleaned houses for people too old to take care of their own. She worked irregular hours, claiming the pay was good and the old folks didn't mind if she wore makeup and smoked. She seemed content with these jobs, happy to have a schedule Pop couldn't control or predict. She dug a dollar out of the front pocket of her blouse and handed it to him. "Here, this is for winning. Did you pitch?"

James shook his head at the money. "Yeah. The full game."

She slapped the dollar on his arm near his chin. "Buy yourself a couple of sodas or whatever you want. You deserve it." Her hand went to his head and tousled his hair. Magdalena did that a lot. She always said she liked the color.

"Magdalena?" Her hand dropped, but she was still looking at him.

"Why do they fight like that?"

Her silhouette turned to the side, as if she was listening to Mama and Pop. Mama never hollered like Pop did, but she always responded. She just never won.

Magdalena rotated his way again, the fuzzy curls making a loose halo around her head in the faint backlight.

"Mama doesn't fight," she said. "Just Pop."

"Why does he yell? What did I do?"

"Nothing." Magdalena stood. Her voice had an edge. Her anger was never far beneath the surface, and now it was palpable, even though the dark hid it on her face. "Nobody did nothing except Pop. His problems are his own fault. It's what he did and what he didn't do. He's no one to blame but himself." She strode back and forth in the dark, fury exploding with every step. James was afraid she'd make too wide of a turn and trip over his ball shoes he'd left at the foot of the bed.

He lifted the dollar bill and rubbed it between two fingers. He couldn't imagine what Pop had or hadn't done that was so wrong. He went to work, he worked hard, he came home, and he slept. He was sour most evenings, but he did everything he was supposed to.

"You're different from him." Magdalena stopped pacing and came back to his bed. She sat on the edge, nearer this time. "There's something about you that's better than him. He knows it and he hates it."

Magdalena sounded a little vindictive, but more than that, James knew she was sincere. She was wrong, though, no matter how certain she sounded. She was only trying to make him feel better, the way Mama did. Actually, the way they all did, except for Pop. He always made James feel worse, just like now, when he wasn't even really trying to.

"What about you? If I'm different and better, so are you."

"I'm the same as Pop is. And I hate it, but believe me, I'm trying to get out."

James scratched his head. Magdalena didn't make sense. They were all different from Pop. No one was the same as him, because none of them were good enough. Pop made that more than clear.

The door opened a crack, and they both turned. It was Carla, the gentle way she carried herself giving her away.

"What are you doing?" she asked as she slipped into the room. The downstairs was quiet now. Pop was done for the night, but it would take awhile before James would be tired enough to sleep. *"That boy"* had to quiet down in his head just like it did in the downstairs.

Carla eased to the side of his bed. She resembled Mama. Even her silhouette spoke of Mama's lithe grace.

Magdalena put a hand on James' leg in the dark and squeezed. "Talking about family stuff," she said.

"About Mama and Pop?" Carla asked, glancing back toward the door.

"Kind of, but more about James."

They were quiet. The uneasiness that was always there was even worse when they talked about it. No matter how apparent the bad things were, they stayed invisible if no one said them out loud. James wanted to change the subject, talk about anything except what they'd all heard Pop shouting, but he couldn't think of anything to say beyond the two words that were stuck in his head.

"I saw part of your game today," Carla whispered.

James groaned. Baseball was not the way to keep the bad things invisible. *That boy* made them obvious enough, but baseball made them inimitable.

"You're a good player."

The bad he'd hoped to avoid exploded in his gut. He'd improved enough to be kind of good. He'd worked hard, but still, kind of good hadn't been good enough. Not good enough for Pop to come to a game, or help him practice, or ever say James played fairly well. For years he'd waited for Pop to come to a game, give him some advice. But he never did. James stole a glance at Magdalena. He envied that hard place in her, the one that didn't care. The bad stuff hurt because he'd always cared. He wasn't full of stone like Magdalena was.

"Is he like Pop?" Magdalena asked.

James gaped at the question. He didn't want Carla to answer. Everyone knew he didn't play as good as Pop. It wasn't like Magdalena to be so careless. Maybe she did drink. Maybe Harold and Alex were right. He rolled and wadded her dollar in his fist until it felt hard and tiny, like a miniature baseball.

His sisters stared at one another in the dark. He could see their faces pointed, each at the other, saying something without speaking. Carla's head began to shake slowly from side to side. Then she turned his way.

"You are different from Pop, James." Carla's voice was quiet.

James wanted to fire the wadded dollar bill into the dark across the room. "Of course I'm different, but it's not a good kind of different." He shouldn't yell, but he couldn't help it. "I'm smaller, I don't play ball like he did, and I never do anything right!"

Carla's hand touched his shoulder. It was like Mama, the way she touched him. It quieted him, at least his voice. He was still yelling on the inside, screaming that things would never be right, not the way he wanted them to be.

"You are a good player," she said. "Even if Pop never says so." She brought two coins up and held them where he could see them. Then she set them on his blanket and pressed them down with one finger before she let go. "There."

"What are those?"

"Two tokens for ice cream at Mr. Morgan's restaurant. He handed them to me downtown this evening. He said he gave the boys on your team one apiece, but you deserved two because you pitched a winning game." Carla smoothed the blanket around the tokens. She straightened, studied them a moment, then looked at James.

James had seen Mr. Morgan watching the game. He came to lots of them, but James avoided him now. Pop hated him. He had for years, a squabble about his shop, or something the two of them could never resolve. James stared at the tokens, rolling the dollar in his hand.

"It's not baseball," Carla said. James glanced up and saw her watching Magdalena as she spoke. "It's not even how you look. It's deeper."

Magdalena stood. "You're different from Pop. You're better than him. That's all."

James opened his mouth but closed it again.

Better? Never. He'd be happy just to be like Pop in baseball, but it wasn't working.

"Gotta go." Magdalena laid a hand on his shoulder.

"Where? It's late."

"More work."

"Now? Really?" He could feel her grin in the dark. She liked her world and her schedule. It gave her power.

"Old people keep odd hours. I make myself available to suit them. See you tomorrow." Magdalena left the room. Carla and James watched her go. They looked at each other after they could no longer hear her creaking down the stairs.

"I wish Magdalena'd be more careful," Carla said.

"It's just old people."

Carla stared at him, the worry lingering on her face. "Yeah," she said, "just old people."

He didn't understand his sisters, not about this, not about him being different, and certainly not about him being better than Pop. "I don't understand," he finally said.

"Oh, it's nothing," Carla bolstered herself. "She'll be okay. Magdalena has a way of getting by."

"I mean I don't understand about me and Pop."

Carla looked at the door. She twisted her hands the way she did when she was thinking. "That's how it looks, James, in ways I know you can't see." She turned his direction, her face only half lit by the glow from the doorway. "You're different. You can be better than Pop if you want."

He stared at his sister, waiting for her to see how ludicrous that sounded. "You're crazy. You and Magdalena both."

"Magdalena told me once Pop picks on the things that defy him or scare him. He picks on her for the first reason. He's not afraid of her like he is of you." She dropped her hands to her sides. "See you tomorrow." Carla slipped away from the bed and through the door, closing it softly behind her.

James stared at the tokens, then swiped them off the blanket into his hand. He stuffed them and the dollar beneath his pillow and slid between the sheets. He stared at the door. The glow around its edges began to waver, distort, and move like a luminous snake in the blackness. Wet trickled down the side of his face, leaving a streak of cool in its path. He squeezed his eyes. The snake disappeared, and his lashes felt cool with moisture. He rolled to his stomach and buried his face in his pillow. He would stay this way, forever if he had to, until everything disappeared.

Chapter 13

James 1952

The tokens bumped together in James' pocket, their sound a dull ping, a reminder that Mr. Morgan thought he was good, good enough for two tokens instead of just one. The tinny noise jangled out its compliment, one he decided he didn't need, and one he'd decided to return.

James turned down the sidewalk toward Mr. Morgan's restaurant. He'd slammed the ball harder than ever at practice today. It was his first homerun, an electrifying jolt of wood against ball that still vibrated clear to his teeth. *Hustle it up a little*, the coach had yelled at the outfielders when James' hit dropped behind them. They saved their best for the games, making it look like James' homerun didn't count. But it did count. He'd torn around the bases because it meant everything to him—meant he didn't need compliments or tokens to spur him on. Not from Pop, and not from Mr. Morgan.

James' reflection appeared alongside him in Andy's father's hardware store window. He paused and glanced at himself, at the James that had hit his first homerun. He straightened and wished he had the long, lanky limbs Pop had. He jabbed his arms to the right and the left. They didn't react like snakes. If long legs and quick arms were what he needed to be really good, then Pop was right, baseball wasn't in his blood. He dropped his arms back down to his sides. Something was in James' blood, though, and that something had sent him around the bases for a score today. He studied his dark hair, his tan skin, his stout build. Magdalena said he was handsome, handsome like Mama was pretty, just neither one of them knew it. He thought that was a funny thing to say. Handsome wasn't what helped him hit a homerun today.

Andy appeared within James' reflection. Funny expressions, contorted mouth and eye gyrations, and silly faces blurred James' image enough it looked like there were two of him, one handsome and fairly sensible, the other not quite as handsome and rarely sensible. James grinned. Andy ran along the inside of the store's front to the door and popped out onto the sidewalk.

"You looking for me?" He still had his ball clothes on from practice, just like James did, but Andy's were dirtier because he fell a lot. James thought it was to make everyone laugh, maybe to hide the fact Andy wasn't a very good player. Or maybe Andy didn't really care.

"Naw, I was heading home." He glanced at Mr. Morgan's restaurant next door and jangled the two tokens in his pocket.

"Whatcha got there?" Andy tipped his head to the side and stared at James' pocket. "You got money? You never have money."

James tried not to blush. No one in his family had money except Pop. Harold and Alex made enough to go out on their double dates now and then, but Pop didn't give them any more than that for wages. He said they were old enough to earn their keep, and they were expected to help at the shop to pay their way. James had given them the dollar Magdalena had given him. He knew they deserved it, and they'd been excited. Magdalena always acted like she didn't have much for all the work she did, but James knew better. She bought little things for Mama and his sisters, just none of them ever let on.

"It's just a couple of tokens. I was taking them back to Mr. Morgan to…"

"To get two ice creams?" Andy's eyes lit up and his tongue ran over his lips. Andy bounced up and down on his toes. Andy was right, except for Magdalena's dollar he'd given away, James never had money. He pinched the tokens together. He'd never had a thing he could share with his friend.

"You want ice cream?"

"You betcha!" Andy raced to the restaurant's door and yanked it open. "Come on!"

James hesitated. This wasn't what he'd intended to do. If he hadn't jangled the tokens he could have returned them privately, thanked Mr. Morgan, and been on his way. He would have been in and out and no one would ever have known. James had never gone into Mr. Morgan's restaurant before. They all knew how Pop felt about Mr. Morgan, and only Magdalena dared to go in. Andy opened the door wider, sweeping his arm to usher James in.

James stepped to Andy and dug the tokens out of his pocket. He held them out. "Take these and go have a double. On me. Well, on Mr. Morgan."

"You aren't coming in? Don't you want ice

cream?" Andy let the door close.

"I need to get home. You go on." James jiggled his hand, the coins clinking like dull little bells. "Take them. It's fine."

"No, thanks. I'll wait until you can go with me. It's more fun that way. And besides, they're yours. I already used mine."

James dropped his hand and stuffed the tokens back into his pocket. He looked at his friend and then at the doorway. "Oh, all right. Come on, I've got a little time."

Andy's long thin arm shot out and yanked the door open again. He stood back and waited for James to walk through first.

"You go ahead," James said.

Andy darted through the door and held it from the other side for James. James drew in a deep breath and followed him.

Mr. Morgan looked up as the door closed behind James. The light from the front windows highlighted Mr. Morgan's face. His look of casual welcome changed to surprise when his eyes lit on James. His features became animated with a boyish excitement as he set the glass and the white towel he was drying it with aside. James had never seen him move so quickly. Mr. Morgan nearly ran around the counter as he hurried to meet the boys.

"James, Andy, come in. Come over to the fountain, and I'll make you both something." He waved them in the direction he'd come from.

Andy beat Mr. Morgan to the counter. He hopped onto a red stool and was swiveling in circles before either Mr. Morgan or James reached him. James watched his friend spin. It looked like fun and he wanted to do the same, but it wouldn't be right. He didn't intend to come in here for fun, and Pop would have something to say if he spotted him.

"Have a seat." Mr. Morgan nodded toward the stool next to Andy, who was nothing but a blur now. "What can I get for you boys?" he asked from the far side of the counter, wiping his hands on the towel again.

Andy screeched to a halt. "Anything?"

James frowned. Andy surely was in here often enough to have plenty of ice cream. He didn't know how Andy's parents could keep him out, with their store being right next door. James laid his glove on the counter and dug the two tokens back out of his pocket. "We want two ice creams."

Mr. Morgan didn't answer. He was eyeing James' glove. He touched the soft leather and looked up. "You like this glove?" he asked.

James watched Mr. Morgan's fingers trace the smooth leather that had broken in so well. "It's the best," he said. "Much better than the old one my brothers handed down to me." James cupped the tokens in his hand and extended them across the counter. "I have these for our ice cream."

Mr. Morgan looked at James' hand. He nodded and took the tokens and stacked them near the register. "It's the best there is. Your glove, I mean."

Andy resumed spinning, and Mr. Morgan turned his back to the boys, his hands and arms reaching and dipping and spooning up ice cream like a master. James glanced at the front windows, the tinkle of silverware and glass in the background as Mr. Morgan worked.

James would only do this once, only because of Andy.

Mr. Morgan finally turned and presented them with two dishes of ice cream. Three candied mountains were aligned in each bowl, white mounds dripping with a sugary sheen of chocolate lava, forests of fruits and candies sprinkled down their sides. James tried not to let his eyes pop or his mouth drop open like Andy's had.

"That's…that's a token's worth of ice cream?" James finally asked.

"Yep." Mr. Morgan scooted the dishes in front of him and Andy. Andy's finger made a road through the running chocolate as Mr. Morgan handed them spoons. James looked up. Mr. Morgan's gaze caught him, it was so familiar. It was the same one he'd seen a long time ago, the time Mr. Morgan showed him how to choke up on a bat, the time he said Mama was beautiful.

"Thank you, Mr. Morgan." James touched his spoon. Andy tried to say the same, his mouth full, chocolate smeared over his lips. Mr. Morgan smiled, his eyes a mix of white and dark brown. James thought his eyes were exactly like his sundaes—white, chocolate, and something very sweet. How could Pop hate him so much?

"Dig in." Mr. Morgan nodded at James' dish. James picked up the spoon he'd been toying with. He'd never had a sundae before. Never had ice cream much to speak of, at all. Once at a birthday party Andy had. James had never forgotten it. Mr. Morgan resumed washing and drying glasses. "I see you're both in uniform, and you've got your glove." Mr. Morgan nodded toward James' glove on the counter. "So let's talk about baseball. What do you say?"

James set the spoon back down. If Mr. Morgan had mentioned fishing, building fences, pulling weeds, any of those things, he would have been fine. But baseball? He stared at the ice cream. It would have been better if he'd kept Magdalena's dollar and given it to Andy to buy ice cream instead of using those two tokens. He wasn't supposed to be here. This wasn't the way he wanted to play baseball.

"You boys have improved. I've been watching you." He'd turned. His eyes were on James, and he was talking to him. Andy wasn't paying attention. His eyes were full of love over what little sundae he had left. "Your brothers still helping you and your teammates practice?"

James shook his head. "Well, once in awhile. They work for Pop now, so there isn't much time."

"They like girls now, too," Andy finally spoke. His spoon clattered to the counter, and he rubbed his stomach. "Not as much as I like ice cream sundaes, though."

Mr. Morgan laughed. "That will change in time. Someday you'll discover how sweet young ladies are. Even the ones you never thought it of." His smile deepened and his gaze drifted away, possibly to some faraway sweetness, one maybe even sweeter than the chocolate covering Andy's face.

"Glen?"

Mr. Morgan's smile disappeared. He looked to the door that led to the kitchen where Ida, his sister, stood.

"Yes? What is it?"

Ida resembled Mr. Morgan. She even wore an apron like his. She started to speak but paused and wiped her hands on the skirt of her apron as she stared at the two boys.

"Hi, Miss Morgan," Andy chirped. "Mr. Morgan gave us ice cream. It was delicious!"

She nodded. "I see that. I'm glad you liked it."

James wanted to thank her, too, and tell her how good it tasted. But he hadn't taken a bite yet. His shiny, clean spoon twinkled, catching a glint of light from the front windows. His ice cream had changed from three mountains to a swirling sea of white and brown, islands of fruit and candy floating on top.

"Me too," he offered lamely, hoping no one would look at his dish. "Thank you."

Ida glanced his way, then looked back at Mr. Morgan, her brows drawing together.

"I asked what you want," Mr. Morgan reminded her.

"When you're finished, I need your help in the back. I hope it's soon." She glanced one more time at James, then retreated through the doorway she'd been standing in. When she was gone, Mr. Morgan rubbed his hands on the towel again, cleaning them, scrubbing them harder than he needed to.

James dug into his ice cream pond, ladled a thick scoop of chocolate and vanilla into his mouth. He would eat it and go, head home, let Mr. Morgan do whatever needed to be done in the back. The syrupy, cool sweetness jarred him. He slowed, let it trickle down his throat, then ladled another spoonful and slid it into his mouth. He could feel Andy's eyes on him. He could hear him toying with his spoon. James looked at his friend and shook his head. Flavor and sugar flooded his senses as Andy's eyes begged for a bite. He'd never tasted anything like this; he didn't think he could share it. "Mmmm, mmmm," James muttered as another cool sweet bite filled his mouth. It was better than Andy's birthday. It was like he imagined heaven.

Mr. Morgan watched James. His face was all business now, the glow in his eyes gone. James scooped another spoonful from his dish. The sundae was divine. Bite after bite sweetened James' world, erasing everything else, making him forget that not all of life was wonderful.

"You gonna eat it all?" Andy looked distressed. James grinned, he could feel the cold chocolate on his lips. Maybe pitching a winning game warranted a treat after all. If Mr. Morgan thought his pitching deserved something like this, maybe small rewards now and then were justified. He scraped every glistening spot of sweetness from the dish with his spoon. He wanted to lick it clean, but he didn't. Andy's shoulders sagged and his spoon clattered back to the counter.

"No need to talk about baseball, sir," James said, running his tongue over his lips. "You just said it all."

Light filtered back into Mr. Morgan's eyes. "Sundaes open doorways to the soul," Mr. Morgan said.

James looked at Andy. Both of them frowned.

"They're the key that unlocks doors. Serve them to the right person at the right time, and they're medicine for the heart." He paused and looked at the boys hard. "You deserved these. Now I expect great things from both of you on the diamond."

Andy slid off his stool, grinning, and headed to the door. James could hear it open and knew Andy was waiting for him. James paused. He thought Mr. Morgan might be right. The sundae wouldn't make him a better player, but it had certainly brightened his outlook. Mr.

Morgan must have served other sundaes to people like him, people who needed it but didn't know it until the sundae unlocked their door. "Thank you, Mr. Morgan. We'll play extra hard."

Mr. Morgan nodded. He wadded the towel in one fist and propped himself on the counter, leaning on both straight arms. He looked at James, then at Andy, then back to James. "It's almost a handicap to be born with natural ability at something. You never have to work hard, you just do what's easy and stay satisfied because you're a little better than everyone else. But other people are born with heart instead of talent. That's actually better. Heart is God's greatest gift to pass from a parent to a child. People with heart never stop getting better. They press onward, they love in exceptional ways—maybe sometimes in unconventional and unexpected ways—but still exceptional."

James looked at Mr. Morgan. His heart rate kicked up and he could feel it beat a little harder. Mama. His chest swelled. Mama. It was her heart in him. Her heart, her soul. Not Pop's. Not Pop's natural ability. He saw it now. That's why he was different from Pop, and that's why he could be better. He didn't need baseball in his blood, because it was her he had, her heart. He was like her. That's why he worked hard. He saw it. He saw it all as if the door had just opened.

"Mr. Morgan? Would you serve my mama a sundae someday? I know she hardly ever comes to town, and never comes in here, but if you get the chance, would you do it for her? I think she needs it."

Mr. Morgan glanced at the counter and scoured a spot with his towel. His face took on a hue even darker than his usual deep tone. "There is always that right time, remember that." Mr. Morgan looked up. "And it's wrong to pass it up. I always watch for it in everyone, and that includes your mama. When the time's right, I'll make sure she knows there's a sundae waiting for her here. Now you get on, and in the meantime you be all the sundae she needs, okay?"

"Yes, sir." James smiled. "I will." He chased after Andy, and they bolted through the door. Mr. Morgan wasn't so bad. Too bad Pop wasn't more like him.

Chapter 14

Lana 1934

"Magdalena has turned into a good helper," Lana said from a chair near the table. She'd been standing but had to sit, her newest infant, Gail, heavy against her shoulder.

"Here, let me take her." Ella was quick to Lana's side, lifting the sleeping infant away.

Gail was healthy, her birth not as difficult as the doctor had feared, but Lana had seen the scolding in his eyes every time he looked at Cletus during his visits to their home. She'd never had a doctor attend a pregnancy before, but when he'd heard she was expecting, he stopped by, checked her, taking great pains to assure she and this infant were safe.

Lana had told the doctor that it wasn't Cletus' fault she was pregnant. She'd consented, knowing full well, when she resumed being Cletus' wife, this might happen. The doctor tried to weigh his expression before he let it show on his face, but it was there in his look, the thing he must see too often, and the thing that was true. She was a woman who was a wife, doing what she had to do, whatever the cost. And Lana had survived the cost. Physically. Cletus had warmed to her while Gail was invisible in the womb. Now that Gail was out, Cletus was cold again, unforgiving in his disappointment. Lana didn't know if she could survive the emotional cost, she didn't know if her daughters could, either. She didn't know if he'd let them.

"You really don't need to be here." Lana looked up at Ella. "It's not like last time. I'm stronger than I was after Alex."

Magdalena marched from the bureau, four plates stacked in her little hands. She set them on the table, then arranged them perfectly, just as Lana had taught her, just as Cletus had taught Lana years ago.

"You need one more plate," Lana reminded her. Magdalena looked at her, then at the table where her father's spot was missing a plate. *She's pretending.* Lana gauged her oldest's face. *She rides a horse that doesn't exist, and she's pretending her father doesn't, either.* Lana waited. Magdalena stood for a moment, then returned to the bureau where the plates were kept. She brought one more to the table and set it near Pop's spot, far from the edge and off center. Magdalena turned to the bureau for silverware, tall, straight, and stubborn. Just like her father.

Lana looked at Ella, the older woman biting back a grin. Ella pulled a chair near Lana's and dropped into it, Gail still sound asleep. "Your babies are all such sweet things," Ella said, patting Gail. "Even that one." She nodded toward Magdalena.

Magdalena marched back toward the table, four spoons splayed erect in her fists, like the winning hand in a round of poker.

"She's very special." Lana watched her daughter stop at each of the four meticulously arranged plates. With great precision Magdalena aligned a spoon near each. When she finished, she marched back to the bureau for forks, not risking a glance at Lana.

"Lord help that child's husband someday," Ella mused, the grin surfacing.

"Husband?" Lana asked. "I hate to say it, but it might take a whole army of husbands to rein that girl in."

Ella turned Lana's way. "Dear, if that husband of yours can't rein her in, no army of men can, either."

They laughed. It felt good. They watched Magdalena return, four forks proudly fanned out like the tail of a peacock. She set each one in line with its spoon partner, then slapped her hip and galloped away. She was done. She'd made her statement, one Lana would make sure Cletus never heard. She would fix his setting before he came home, just like she always did, something Magdalena always noticed but never commented on. She'd had her say and it placated her, even if her father never knew.

"Your grandma still coming for a visit?"

Lana's heart skipped a beat, and she nodded. Grandma's first visit after all these years. She had a guess what prompted it. Worry, something Lana had detected more and more in Grandma's letters. Grandma chewed on worries the same way she fought a bite of tough meat. It was the only emotion that could undo Grandma's sense of what was supposed to be and fire her with the fury of what should be. Love was in those letters, too, laced between lines of admonishment and the dull details of Grandma's daily life. Lana feared Grandma was coming because of Gail. And therefore, because of Cletus. Grandma might come to do the very thing she'd taught Lana never to do—interfere with a man's castle, make sure the prince was behaving himself and not doing anything that might endanger the girl he'd taken as his princess.

"When will she be here?"

"I think tomorrow. She said the neighbor was coming this way, and she insisted he bring her along. That's not like her, but I'm glad she did it. I think."

"What day depends on the neighbor, then. I hope it's tomorrow and the two of you have a wonderful time."

Lana nodded. Grandma here. Protecting her young, trying to be Lana's hero. Someone was going to be hurt. Grandma? Cletus? Herself and her girls? Magdalena galloped into the room, bolted past her and Ella, then charged out again. That was when she knew. It would be Magdalena. Her pretend pony could never take her away fast enough or far enough. Just like the one Lana's mother had constructed for her. Fake ponies don't last. The truth eventually comes.

Chapter 15

Lana 1934

The sound of a truck coming up the road had been there all day. Lana had heard it hundreds of times, but each time she ran to the window and looked, it hadn't been there. But this time it was. A strange truck, without a roar. Different from Cletus', much milder, much less obtrusive as it turned into the lane.

Lana glanced around the house. All of the rooms were perfect. Scrubbed clean, everything picked up, her children all in freshly laundered clothing. She was exhausted, but the extra effort was worth it. It was Grandma's first welcome. It had to be just right.

The truck eased along the lane and around the house. The outdoors wasn't as tidy as it was in here, and she knew it was mostly her fault. She hadn't been able to do as much since Gail was born, and Cletus wasn't inclined to help, since Gail was another girl. Lana tried to pretend it didn't matter, that she could handle the load, but she had five little ones to tend to, and still wasn't back to normal since the birth. Not as much as she should be, but close. Close enough she could rally and hopefully fool Grandma.

Lana scooped Alex off the floor, muffling a groan. Gail was asleep. Magdalena and Harold had stuck close all day, Magdalena understanding someone special was coming, Harold mimicking her excitement. They followed Lana now, Betsy quiet in the front room just as she'd been all morning, off to the far side, away from her father's chair. That was Betsy's place. No one disturbed it. Lana wished Betsy would ride a pretend horse with her sister, but she never suggested it, afraid such an idea would shatter her daughter's delicate world, a place they all pretended not to notice.

Lana opened the back door and hurried outside. A thin cloud of dust settled around the truck as it came to a stop. Both doors of the truck opened, but only Grandma stepped out, slowed by her age but still surprisingly quick. Magdalena ran as if she remembered her, calling her Grandma, just as Lana had taught her.

"Aren't you a sight," Lana called. She laughed. Grandma grinned and let Magdalena tow her by the hand in Lana's direction.

"Sight for sore eyes," a man's voice answered.

Lana stopped watching Grandma, and looked back to the truck. Legs dropped beneath the opened driver's door, long fingers wrapped around its edge and drew it closed. Jim stood there grinning, taller, darker, and so much more the man that boy was always meant to be.

"I thought…I thought…" Lana stuttered.

"He's a neighbor, ain't he?" Grandma sounded defensive.

"Yes, he is. Of course. Welcome, Jim." Lana's cheeks burned, and her heart beat too loud as Jim stepped their way. He looked so content; he looked so kind. She squirmed in his gaze, ashamed she was a sight herself, but certainly not one for sore eyes. Jim's smile danced over her, as if he saw only the gangly girl of years ago instead of the worn-out woman she was beginning to be.

"Got some new ones, I see." He patted Harold's head and looked at Alex in her arms. "Boys now."

"Too many of them," Grandma blustered. "Enough's enough, I say."

"It's all right, Grandma," Lana replied, her cheeks growing even warmer. She shouldn't have shared what the doctor had said about Alex's birth in her letters. But in those two days of pain and delirium Grandma had been there with her, even if she really wasn't. That's who Lana had communed with in that darkness, that's who she'd called to when the agony sucked her away.

Grandma gave a gruff grunt and looked around the barnyard. She'd taught Lana to be a good wife. Keep her place in relation to her husband, perform her duties without complaint. But Lana was certain now that Grandma wasn't here to make sure those rules were being kept. She was here because of love, a force that superseded the laws of subservience. Grandma had been Lana's true father, the one who had always been there for her when there was no other. She hurried to Grandma in a rush of gratitude and bound her in a one-arm hug, little Alex squashed between them. He yelped, and kicked and squirmed his way to the ground. Lana wrapped both arms around Grandma and held on. She'd had no idea while growing up that Grandma had this in her, this much love, this much willingness to defy what she believed, in order to protect her granddaughter. Grandma was the perfect parent, the perfect father.

"Well, invite us in," Grandma growled from Lana's arms. Lana let go and smiled. Jim winked at her from behind Grandma's back. He took Harold's hand and they walked to the house, keeping Alex in front of them, Alex's determined but awkward toddle slowing them down. One by one they streamed through the back door Cletus had taken her through years ago, past the dim washroom where she'd waited while he washed his hands, and into the room they ate in after she'd survived cooking their first meal. This room was much brighter now, much more homey, Grandma's gift of Lana's wedding dress still making fine curtains for the windows, the yellow makeshift belt tying them back to let the sunlight in.

Lana watched Grandma take a slow toll of the house, item by item, a glimmer of pride on her face. Lana relaxed. She glanced at Jim. He was looking at her, not at the house.

"You're all grown up," he said. He sounded surprised, like it had just dawned on him they no longer milked together or pulled weeds.

"I'd say you are, too," she canted back. He had changed for the better, whereas she hadn't. Anyone could see that. He was handsome, and she wondered if Jeanie had snagged him yet. She couldn't tell by his smile. It was warm and comfortable, free and generous. Would he smile that way if he was in love with someone? Engaged? She smiled back, just the way she had when she was a girl. She looked at Grandma, at her children, then back to Jim. "Well, I should probably get us some lunch."

"I'll help," he said. And he followed her, boy and girl, friend to friend, just as he'd always done.

****

Cletus kept his eyes on Jim throughout the evening meal. It didn't matter who was speaking, it didn't matter that Magdalena was showing off, it didn't matter that Grandma's comments to him were brash and stinging with hints she was here to protect her granddaughter. All he saw was Jim, and Lana wished Jim would cage his childhood warmth toward her, temper his smile.

"Who is he?" Cletus asked when they were alone in their room. Grandma was in Magdalena's bed, Lana's oldest daughter squeezed in beside Betsy. Jim was in the living room, a little too long for their sofa but not complaining when she handed him a blanket and pillow and asked if he minded sleeping there. Everyone was quiet, and Lana cringed, hoping Cletus' voice didn't carry through the walls or up the stairs.

"Grandma's neighbor," she answered.

Cletus watched as she cleared his trail of dropped clothing. She was exhausted, every muscle tired, her insides still weak from childbirth and feeling like they were about to fall out and drag the floor. She folded his pants and draped them over a trunk he'd brought home when she'd asked for more storage space in the bedroom. She neatened his dirty clothing. She'd sort it tomorrow. She just couldn't do it tonight.

"He's more than a neighbor," Cletus said. He was in bed, sitting up, tired but not sleepy, she could tell by the glint flickering in his eye.

Lana's heart beat a little harder, she felt the flush rise to her cheeks. Jim was kind, he spoke the language of goodness in all that he said or did, something Grandma had pointed out more than once that evening, hoping Lana's husband would understand. But that language was foreign to Cletus. It made him wary, and he would never allow his ignorance to leave him feeling insulted. "He's just a neighbor. He has helped Grandma for years. She pays him however she can."

"How many years?"

Lana stopped what she was doing and looked at him. He was waiting, his face as rigid as the metal he forced to bend, his eyes like the heat of the fire it took to transform it.

"Always," she said. "Ever since he could. He's always been this way." She said it soft, wishing Cletus wouldn't hear, and praying Jim couldn't. She wouldn't be able to face Jim in the morning, she'd never be able to face him again, if he heard this conversation. She straightened, drew in a deep breath, and steeled herself to look at her husband.

The wolfish hunger Cletus had been trying to hold back since Gail had been born emerged. Something else came along with it, something that made him look desperate, afraid, a little bit threatened. She'd never seen him this way. He was afraid of nothing. Lana dropped his clothing she'd picked up, and began to undress. He breathed a little shallower, his worry waning as her clothes fell to the floor.

Cletus watched her walk to their bed. He was listening to what she'd said only through his eyes, a language he understood. He wanted her; she saw it. He looked up.

"I don't like him. He watches you too much. And your grandma, she doesn't like me."

She saw it even more clearly then—all the things he wasn't afraid of. They worried him, teetering his throne, and he was looking for someone to blame. It would eventually be her. She paused and stared at him. "I've missed you."

"Come to bed." He lifted the blanket.

Lana hurried, hurried to crawl into bed, relieved, afraid, and praying Cletus would be quiet. She knew what was coming would probably hurt, since it would be the first time since Gail's birth. But she would bite back any sound.

She wanted her husband to be satisfied, wanted him to know everything was safe, but she didn't want Jim to hear, hear Cletus grunt and breathe hard, expel that one last gush of air when he was done. And Grandma. Lana prayed she wouldn't know, either. She didn't want either of them to see the look of a wife on her face in the morning, judge the very private thing Grandma had come to monitor and gauge.

Cletus rolled against her the moment she slid in beside him, and dropped the blanket over both of them. He smelled of burnt metal, hot fire, and soap where he'd tried to scrub some of it off. His arm stretched across her chest as one leg edged over her thighs. She lifted a hand and touched him, waited for him to top her so she could wrap both arms around his back.

She could hear his thoughts. She felt them stop as he paused.

"Cletus?"

He retracted his arm. His leg dragged back over her and away. He turned and rolled to the far side of the bed.

"Cletus," she whispered. She scooted his way, laid a hand on the back of his shoulder. "It's okay, really. What's wrong?"

"Maybe another time."

She stayed there beside him, near his back, listening to what he was thinking as he pretended to sleep.

She silently tried to erase his thoughts, undo what everyone else was doing to him, against him, to them.

Chapter 16

James 1953

James stood behind his chair along with the rest of them, all of them at the table for once, no one out with a girlfriend or beau. Steam rose from the dishes and platters on the table, an enticing aroma circling upward that almost drowned out the brash sounds of splashing water and Pop grunting into a towel as he dried his face and hands in the back washroom. James drew in a deep lungful of the warm roast and potatoes while he waited. Waiting was as much a part of their meal as eating was. Everyone stood, stiff and still, everyone except Magdalena. She fidgeted with the back of her chair, tapping out impatient clicks with her fingernails. She rarely joined them for a meal, and tonight she looked tired, distracted, and impatient, too preoccupied to care whether she waited the respectful way Pop wanted or not. Pop strode from the wash room, easy heavy strides that brought him to the back of his chair. The smell of burnt metal overtook the pleasant odors of their supper, more powerful than ever now that it came from three of them—Pop, Harold, and Alex. Alex followed Pop with his gaze. He worked hard at the welding shop all day and came home famished, famished enough to barely tolerate Pop's rules until they could sit down to eat.

James' stomach growled, and he glanced at Alex.

All of the outside chores were his ever since his brothers began working in Pop's shop. He also had school, he had baseball, he had everything else anyone added to his list, and he did it all. He worked hard, and like Alex, he came to the table starving.

Pop stayed behind his chair, eyeing the food. Everyone waited for him to sit and begin to help himself to whatever Mama and the girls had prepared, but he remained standing, his head down. The solemnity of his stance made it seem like he was praying, but Pop never prayed. A thin sheen of perspiration broke out over James' palms, and his hands turned clammy. He knew why Pop just stood there, so James prayed, even if his father never did, and his hunger disappeared.

"How did our cow get into Colson's field?"

James closed his eyes, and kept his head down. He clamped his fingers on the back of his chair.

"No harm was done," Mama said. "His wife shooed it out when she saw it, and Ben drove it back home this afternoon. Gail's boyfriend, Jackson, was here, and the two of them helped him."

James prayed Pop would listen to reason, that no harm was done.

"I didn't ask about harm. I asked how the cow got into his field."

"The gate broke, Pop." It was Harold. It was a lie. James opened one eye and glanced at his brother.

"You were at work. You rode home with me. How would you know?"

"I told him." Alex cut in. Alex's voice was like Pop's. It was decisive and sharp. James knew Alex liked talking that way, especially to their father. James opened both eyes and looked at his brother. Alex's knuckles were white, his fingers biting down on the back of his chair just like James' were on his. "I checked the gate when Mama told me tonight the cow'd gotten loose."

"How could it break?" Pop changed his tone, contrasting his voice with Alex's, sounding smooth and steady instead of abrasive. Pop was mocking Alex. Pop knew Alex and Harold were both lying. He wanted to catch them at it so he could blame James.

"The wood was too old," Alex answered. "Ben just wired it shut to hold it till we got home. I'll prove it." Alex thrust away from his chair. It rocked forward, its back smacking against the table's edge and its legs thumping against the wood floor as he disappeared from the room. The back door opened and closed with a bang.

James' skin turned cool, the clamminess of his hands spread up his arms and around his neck. The gate wasn't broken; he'd left it unlatched. Or loosely latched, when he'd finished feeding this morning. He was running late for school. His sisters had gone on without him.

Let's sit down while we wait." Mama's interjection surprised him. Her voice was soft, but her suggestion was bold. She'd never countered Pop's rules this way. James glanced his mother's direction. Every eye at her end of the table was on Pop, instead of her, waiting to see what he would do. James was afraid to see his father's face, see who he was looking at, but he turned his head and peered Pop's direction. Pop was staring the length of the table, his eyes on Mama, a silent fiery command directed her way that they would remain standing until he sat. James clenched his teeth as he breathed a little deeper and a little harder. Pop shouldn't look at her that way. James would take a thrashing before he'd let Pop treat Mama bad or yell at her for something that was his own fault.

"Pop. I…" James straightened as he spoke, forcing his voice to hold steady.

A chair scooted back, wooden legs skidding across the dry floor. Someone sat, and the chair creaked, then dragged forward. "Good idea, Mama. I'm ready to eat," Magdalena said.

James closed his mouth. Pop disappeared from his eyes. He only saw the gate in his mind, even when he turned toward the far end of the table to look at his sister who'd just defied their father. *I'll never leave it loose again. I'll always make sure it's fastened like it's supposed to be. I'll always double check it…*

The table creaked, and James looked Pop's direction. His fists were balled and his arms stiff as he leaned over his chair, propping himself against the table's top. His gaze had shifted from Mama to Magdalena.

Another chair slid backwards before Pop could speak, its movement silent and almost without a sound. James looked, and Betsy sank silently into her seat. She didn't scoot forward, she just sat, sitting out her support of Mama and James, sitting still enough to not upset the household she was apparently content to stay in all of her days.

All of them knew the gate was James' responsibility. And, like Pop, they knew Harold and Alex had no idea what had happened but were just coming to James' defense. James looked at Mama.

She'd tried to soothe Pop for James' sake. She loved him, all of them, in ways he'd never realized. Mr. Morgan was right. Mama had heart. What she was doing was unconventional, and it would surely bring Pop's wrath down on her as quickly as it did on James.

Alex burst through the back door, and it slammed behind him. He marched to Pop and dropped the top end of a broken post on the table, the end James should have secured with a wire loop over it to hold the gate in place. "There. You happy?" Alex returned to his chair and stood behind it, his eyes glued to his father.

"Looks like the cow rubbed against the gate and broke it," Magdalena said, slumping down in her chair, one elbow propped on the table. "Probably scratching her side."

Pop stared at the broken post, too thick for an easy break. James wanted to look at Alex, look at the muscles that loved him enough to snap that chunk of wood with his bare hands and slap it on the table in front of their father. He didn't look. He didn't want Pop to yell at Alex. To Pop it was bad enough to make a mistake like James had made, but it was worse to do what they were doing—lie, defy his rules, band together against him.

Pop shifted his gaze from the broken post to Harold. He stared at his oldest son. Harold was softer than Alex. He was like Mama. He was good and thoughtful. Harold didn't flinch under his father's glare. He held still without looking away.

Pop switched to Mama, then Gail, then Betsy and Carla. He skipped Magdalena and stopped at James. "Pick this post up and take it outside. You and I will talk about it later."

James' legs nearly gave out as he stumbled away from his chair. He started his father's direction, but stopped when thick fingers wrapped around his arm and held him where he was. He glanced at the hand, then up into his brother's face. Alex nodded, then released James' arm and marched to Pop. Alex swiped the wood from the table and walked it to the woodstove and threw it in.

"The cow broke the gate. That's it," Alex said above the ring of the iron door slamming. He strode back to his chair.

Carla slid her chair backwards, softly like Betsy. She sat, then gently scooted forward. Gail did the same. Tears welled in James' eyes, tears he couldn't stop. His brother Harold tugged his chair out and sat also.

"I say we're ready to eat." Mama sounded less steady than she had before. James wanted to look at her, but he couldn't. If he turned his head, his tears would spill over and run down his cheeks. "Please sit down, James," Mama added. She was helping Pop, not contradicting him. It was in her tone, it was the special way she loved that she was so good at. James fumbled with the back of his chair. He dragged it out from the table and sat. Its legs thumped in the silent room like gunshots in a cavern as he scooted forward. "You'll feel better if you eat," she said. James knew she was talking to Pop now. She left her end of the table and walked to Pop's. "There's lemon cake for dessert. We can talk after that."

Only Alex remained standing, of all James' brothers and sisters. Stubbornness resonated from him, from the way he stared at Pop, in the way he stood fixed behind his chair, how his hands flexed open and closed on its back. Alex stood in defiance, while Magdalena sat in defiance.

Pop yanked his arm from where Mama touched him. He shrugged her off and glared at James. "I said we'd talk later, and we will, with or without that hunk of wood."

"You'll talk to me," Alex shouted. "I'm the one that made it, and I'm the one responsible for it. If it's broken, it's my fault for choosing bad wood, not James'!"

"I'll talk to that boy, not you."

That boy. James jerked to his feet, Magdalena along with him. She was behind him, her hands on his shoulders. Her fingers dug into the skin around his collarbones, gripping, squeezing the pent-up scream that needed pried out.

"I'm not *that boy!* I'm James Paine, and I'm your son! I'm not a nobody, and I'll take full responsibility for my actions!" It came out in a flood of words, it came out violent and full of anger.

Cletus moved in a jerk, so quickly Mama tumbled aside. He rounded the table, tall and fierce. James clutched his fists and looked up at the giant advancing on him. He was ready. He would lose, but he didn't care. Alex shot between them, Magdalena with him. Pop tried to round James' brother and sister, but Alex was quick.

"You'll deal with me, not James. Pick on someone your own size for a change."

Pop swung. James wasn't sure Pop wanted to hit his second eldest son. Maybe he didn't, but Alex ducked and Pop's fist missed.

Alex was upright before Pop regained his balance.

Alex leaned into him. "*That boy*, as you call him, is James. He's your new welder, because I quit!"

"Alex!" Mama wailed.

"I'm joining the army." Alex glanced his mother's way. Her hands rose and covered the lower half of her face. "They're always looking for men."

Then Alex turned again to Pop. "Be good to James." Alex looked back at James. "Don't stop playing ball just because you work at the shop. You're too good."

No one moved except Alex. He looked at each one before he turned and disappeared through the door to the back room. They listened as the outside door opened and then closed, softer than before, yet it still said he was gone. Mama stifled a sob. She fumbled for her apron, drew it up, and buried her face.

"Get his chair away from the table. We won't need it anymore." Pop's voice was husky.

"Get rid of mine, too." Magdalena stiffened to her full height. "I'm getting married." She returned to her seat, took her own chair by the back, and carried it to the far wall. She set it there, then looked back at Pop. "It's Earl. He asked the other night. He's a good enough guy, so I'm going to do it."

"Earl?" Pop tried to say it with a snort, but it came out wrong. He almost choked. "Earl Long? You waited all this time for someone like him?"

Magdalena stared at Pop, then headed for the stairs.

"If it is, you'll be begging to come home again in a week," Pop called to her back. "No Long is worth marrying."

Magdalena turned. "He's better than this." Magdalena threw a glance around the room. Then she looked at James, and went on up the stairs.

Mama moved. She stepped back from where she'd stood at Pop's end of the table. She followed her oldest daughter. So did Betsy, Gail, and then Carla.

"I gotta tell Alex goodbye." Harold stared at Pop. "Come with me," he said to James. James' legs trembled as he stumbled behind his brother. He urged them forward. He didn't want to say goodbye, but he needed to say thank you.

"Tell him… You can tell him…" Pop didn't finish. James wanted to turn, but he didn't. He followed Harold out of the house.

Chapter 17

Lana 1934

Lana stared into the small mirror over the washstand on the back porch. A mature woman gazed back at her—not a girl anymore, but a woman who was tired, tired and afraid.

She yanked the cloth tie from behind her head. Auburn hair fell, loose waves tumbled down and drifted beyond her shoulders. Her hair was thick and heavy. It shone, almost sparkled, even in the meager light.

She shook it out, tilted her head to one side and then the other, studying her face and craning to see her profile. She turned quickly, her tresses yanking like whips with every twist of her head. Photographic glimpses of her image looked almost pretty as she whisked back and forth, but when she paused and stared at herself straight on, the pretty woman vanished and the tired woman returned—the worried eyes, the frightened stare. She pressed her fingers against her skin. It had a good healthy texture in spite of all she'd been through, and her eyes still bore their rich hazel color. What if Grandma was wrong? What if in this one thing she had erred? What if Cletus really would respond to pretty? What if pretty gave her that "something more" that she needed?

She gathered her hair in both hands, twisted it into

a rope, and lifted it on top her head. She moved it from one side to the other, holding it back and high. *He won't care how you look. He's too old for that.* Grandma may have been wrong…

Lana dropped her hair and stared. Stared at the wife with too many daughters and not enough sons. *I'm trying. I'm doing the best that I can.*

Lana reached for her face. She traced the line of her jaw with a finger. If she could make Cletus like her more, if she could do the right thing, say the right thing…

"Mama?"

Lana dropped her hand and glanced in the mirror behind her. Magdalena stood in the background, watching her.

"You okay, hon?" Lana turned.

Magdalena gathered her own hair, held it behind her head the same way Lana had. Lana bent, stooped to her daughter, and swept her off the floor. Magdalena rose easily, she was slim and light, long like her father. Lana pressed her close, her little daughter's heart beating against Lana's chest. Lana scooted the wash pan aside and set Magdalena on the dry sink's top.

Lana gazed into Magdalena's pale blue eyes, eyes so much like her father's, not only in color but in determination. But behind the blue Lana saw her own eyes, the ones that had gazed back at her in the mirror. "You're beautiful. You know that, don't you?"

Magdalena frowned, tilted her head, then touched her hair again.

"Hop up on your knees and turn around so you can see yourself in the mirror." Lana helped her daughter rise and turn. Magdalena knelt in front of the mirror and studied her reflection, her fair coloring surrounded by hair that was nearly as wan. Magdalena twisted her head from one side to the other just as Lana had, studying her profile, watching her hair. Lana slipped her hands under her daughter's fine hair, gathered the mass of curls and bundled them on top of Magdalena's head. Her daughter's eyes brightened in her reflection. "See, I told you you're beautiful." Lana held onto the knot of hair as Magdalena turned again from one side to the other, studying her new look.

Someone has asked for you. "Someday a boy will say, 'Look at Magdalena. Why, she's the prettiest girl in town.'" *He's too old to care about pretty, he just wants you to make babies.* "Lots of boys will think so, but you will choose the one you want, the one you think the most handsome and the nicest, because you're beautiful, and beautiful girls can do that." *Those tales of Jeanie's are just that, tales that make little girls' hearts flutter with nonsense.*

Magdalena stopped turning and stared at herself. Lana stared with her, willing, infusing her own heart, the one that was determined to survive, into her daughter. They were mother and daughter but looked nothing alike. Yet she and Magdalena were identical, the vacancy in their eyes where something necessary was missing.

"Someday a young man will ask your father and me if he can marry you. He'll come to our house, and you'll be excited because you love him. You'll want to be his bride." Magdalena's reflection in the mirror shifted. "You'll see." Lana squeezed her daughter's shoulders. "It will be that way for you. I promise to make it so."

Chapter 18

Lana 1935

Lana ran the rag across the top of Cletus' chest of drawers, dust and tiny splinters of wood catching in the fabric. His first wife smiled, she never stopped, as Lana lifted her photo and dusted beneath it. Her hair was dark. Darker than Lana's, and straight. Lana had never asked her name. Her hair was swooped back, swinging low at the sides and disappearing behind her head. Lana set the picture down, touched her own hair, and followed the gentle wave from the top of her head to the ends beyond her shoulders. The waves made her think of a sleigh ride—up, then down, up, then down, easy, smooth, a gentle rise and fall. She lifted his mother's photo and dusted beneath it. His first wife's hair didn't flow like Lana's. She set his mother's picture back in place and grabbed the end of one of her own heavy strands and tugged, pulled it straight to see if she could look the same, look like the woman he'd chosen first, the one who gave only a son and no daughters, who did what was right…except she stopped too soon.

Lana had seen Jeanie straighten her hair once, when they were just girls, by pressing it beneath a hot brick. If Lana fired up the stove earlier than usual, before she cooked the evening meal…more heat and early enough…she could warm a brick and possibly straighten her hair. Something had to help. She was losing him, she was failing…

"Mama?"

Lana jumped. She let go of her hair, and it coiled back, rolled into its natural wave around her shoulders. Magdalena leaned into the room, her head poking through the bedroom doorway.

"He's here, Mama! He's here again."

"Who?" She laid the dust rag on the chest of drawers.

"Outside! Come and see." Magdalena turned and ran through the house. She didn't even gallop but ran like a child. Lana told her daughter every day how ladylike she would grow up to be, how someday a handsome prince would ride up on a horse and she'd go with him instead of riding alone. Maybe Magdalena had put her horse up for now, believing a prince would come, and then she'd ride again, ride away together with him.

Lana smoothed her dress and followed her daughter. The back door stood open, and Lana could hear her oldest children's voices outside, excited, telling everything they knew, to him—whoever he was. She stepped through the door, shielding her eyes from the sun.

"Lana!" It wasn't a man, it was a woman's voice, vaguely familiar. Before she could see who it was, Lana was swallowed in an embrace, a swirl of arms and hair and fabric that smothered her, and blinded her to who it was. "Oh, I can't believe it's been so long!" A happy lilt sang in her ear.

"Jeanie?" Lana pulled back from the hug, wiped

loose strands of hair from her face, and looked…looked at a beautiful young woman who resembled her childhood friend. "Jeanie? Is that you?"

Jeanie was no longer plain, a simple curly-headed best friend from childhood. Jeanie had rounded out perfectly, and her hair made handsome circlets around her face, shiny twists and bends that framed her striking features. Jeanie's eyes, her nose, her cheeks, all fine enough on their own, were accented by a hint of powder, a little rouge, a dark line along the eyes that made them look even larger. She was lovely. Lovely like Lana had never been, never would have been, even if she hadn't married so young and borne five children one right after the other.

"You're gorgeous," Lana whispered.

"And look at you!" Jeanie squealed.

"She's a sight for sore eyes, isn't she?"

Lana stepped away from Jeanie's clutch. Him. That's who Magdalena meant. There he was—Jim—strolling toward Jeanie, and grinning. Lana felt her cheeks fire crimson. She was anything but a sight for sore eyes. She was at her worst, she always was when Jim appeared, but now noticeably worse as she stood next to Jeanie. The wind caught Lana's hair and blew it across her face. She shouldn't have left it loose when she followed Magdalena outside. She shouldn't have been measuring herself against Cletus' first wife. She swept her hair aside with one hand and tugged at her baggy dress with the other. She noticed that Jeanie's dress fit. It was faded like Lana's, but it accentuated the sort of shape Lana envied and lacked.

"Jim." She blushed even more. It was all she could think to say. He stood looking at her, his easy grin warming the places she was cold, drawing her back to Grandma's barn, her cow, the happy times Lana had spent there with him. And sometimes Jeanie.

"You look good," he said.

She shook her head, the blush flushing warmer. Jeanie looked good, not her. Magdalena kicked up a gallop around Jim. Around and around she went, Harold and Alex joining in her train. Jim grinned, but his eyes stayed with Lana. She looked back at him, his content grin, the warmth of his eyes. He would make a fine prince when he finally asked someone to ride away with him someday. It must be Jeanie. Sadly, it wouldn't be Magdalena.

"You look good like a wife," Jeanie said with a happy laugh. "Your grandma tells me all about you every time she gets a letter. Why don't you write me?"

Because you were sweet on Jim. I couldn't... I was being a wife, a good wife so my children would fare well, so my husband would take care of us. "I've been busy," Lana said. She watched Magdalena hem Jim in with a circuit. Lana looked up at Jeanie, at the faint shade of blue above her eyes she hadn't noticed before, the soft tinge of pink on her lips. *I've been being a good wife to my husband so he'd be a good father. Maybe even love these girls someday. I've been doing what I'm supposed to.*

"Well, if you have time to write her, you can write me, too." Jeanie latched onto Lana's arm and dragged her to where Jim stood. Magdalena and the boys swung wider and included Jeanie and Lana in their laps, pinning the three of them into one circle.

"Were you going somewhere when you stopped?" Lana asked, stepping back to widen her children's circle.

"Here!" Jeanie laughed. "I've been begging Jim to bring me ever since he came with your grandma. He was always too busy or had some other excuse. Finally I told him I wouldn't take no for an answer anymore, so here we are!"

Lana tried to laugh with Jeanie. She wanted to steal a glance at Jim, see if she could decipher his excuse for refusing their friend, while Jeanie prattled on, words stringing together in an endless gaiety. Lana wondered if she used to laugh like Jeanie, happy and easy. If she had, she'd forgotten how.

Jeanie kept her hold on Lana's arm and grabbed Jim's with her other, then swung them toward the house. "Invite us in. I want to know everything you've been doing as a wife and what it was like to be a bride. Everything."

Lana pressed her lips into a thin line. She didn't look at Jeanie as they marched forward to the house. She couldn't look at Jim. Wasn't it obvious she'd never been a bride and was failing as a wife? With her free hand she gathered her loose hair and laid it over one shoulder. She hated to wish her childhood friends to be gone, but she did. Cletus would be furious that Jim was here, and he'd never be comfortable around someone like Jeanie.

Magdalena galloped ahead. She turned just inside the door and waited, her eyes on Jim as he came through behind her. The thrum of Magdalena's rapid little hoof beats hammered in Lana's mind. She didn't want her daughter to be that way, a girl who felt she needed to wrangle love and attention from whomever she could since she couldn't wrangle it from her father.

Jim was wonderful; he would make a good prince. But not every man who came along in Magdalena's life would be that way. *I must be a good wife. Give my husband more sons, make him happy, for Magdalena's sake, for our other children's sakes.*

****

It was Jim who helped Lana make the supper and fill the dishes for the table, while Jeanie stayed in the next room and rattled on and on to Cletus about her and Lana's childhood. In one hour Jeanie had filled their house with more words than the seven of them had in all the years they'd lived here together. Lana kept one eye on the two of them from the kitchen, watching for that look Cletus got before he exploded. Cletus' silence had no effect on Jeanie's gaiety. Either her zest for life was more powerful than his stoniness, or her sensitivity to rebuff was more blind. Whatever it was, Jeanie was comfortable. There was no fear in her eyes, no thought that Cletus, or Jim, would be anywhere but there, listening to her, letting her ramble on as freely and gaily as she pleased.

"She does go on, doesn't she?" Jim asked. He leaned against the block table in the center of the kitchen. He grinned and watched Lana mound mashed potatoes into a bowl. "Butter on that?" he asked. He stepped near the washpan and grabbed a bowl of fresh butter, as if he'd been doing this with her for years. Lana glanced again toward the dining room table, where Jeanie pinned Cletus with her unending monologue.

"Yes on both counts." Lana smiled. "But I thought you liked that. Jeanie, that is." She watched him spoon a glob of butter out of the dish. It felt good to work

150

alongside Jim again. She liked to smile. It may have been the first time she'd done it while cooking or serving a meal as Cletus' wife. She glanced at the kitchen doorway, worrying Cletus had seen. He would be suspicious of her and Jim's gaiety, but he was focused on Jeanie, not paying attention while Lana and Jim were in the kitchen. It was only at the moments they stepped through the door with something else for the table that his focus switched. He would stare at Jim then, follow him with his eyes while Jeanie plowed on, oblivious to the shift in attention.

"I don't know if I can live with that," Jim said. He lowered his voice, and kept his back to the kitchen door. "That constant talking."

Lana frowned as she watched him spoon the butter onto the potatoes. "But I thought…"

He looked up the same moment she did, the boy that had been her friend way back then, now a man who still fit so naturally beside her. They worked well together, he for pay, she because she had to. Just like always.

Jeanie droned on in the other room, her words like droplets in a river, meshing into one solid, powerful force that couldn't be stopped. Lana listened to the background hum of her childhood best friend, then glanced toward the doorway the monologue streamed through. She looked back at Jim, the friend who'd spent so many of his evenings helping her…or not helping her, as Grandma used to insist…just like he was doing now.

"I'm quiet," he said. "I like quiet people." His eyes held such intensity they touched her, and she felt them, like a warm attentive clasp that held onto a friend. It looked familiar. It felt familiar. He'd done this before, when they were growing up.

Jim was waiting for her to respond, to say something that would help him. It was her turn to do something for him, to be that friend back. When she said nothing, he went on. "I always saw myself with…you know, with…someone like…"

She lifted the bowl of potatoes and extended it to him, the pool of melted butter sloshing against the rim of the small pond he'd made in the top. He wrapped his fingers around half the bowl, but he didn't take it. His fingertips touched hers, a contact that said he wanted an answer, needed something so he could go on.

"I always saw myself with you, Lana. I never said it. I wish I had, but I had no idea you'd be taken away so young, and without you telling me first. Now I'm trying to see myself with someone else, with someone different, and it's hard. It's easier to at least imagine them like you, exactly like you, since it can't be you."

Lana's heart raced. It ran like Magdalena's pretend pony, but it was galloping away, not alongside Jim like he'd always thought would happen. "I…I had no idea."

"Lana, we were kids then, and in some ways you still are."

"I'm not. I'm far from a child. Just look at my life, my family, all I do…" It sounded like she was arguing, but she felt like crying. They came from somewhere deep inside, tears that simmered like a molten ache.

"I'm talking about the inside you, not the outside. The part that never had the chance to learn about being loved…no matter what."

The scream bubbled up. She didn't want it, not now, not ever. She shook her head, shook it hard until she saw what she'd been unable to see before. "You knew," she said. "You knew about my father…that I really didn't have…"

"Your grandma told me. Way back when, when I first started coming around to help you. She didn't want you to be hurt by some careless remark, or taken advantage of, so she told me. I was careful with you after that, I was slow. Whoever your father was, I grew to despise him. He's the only man I've ever imagined punching in the mouth." The bowl left her hands then. Jim took it, slipped to the other room, and carried it to the table where Cletus sat. Lana's hands hung in midair, a half moon of warmth that was slow to radiate away.

Jeanie's flow of verbiage changed. It took on an extra trill when Jim entered the room. Magdalena's little gallop revived, and Cletus hollered for her to settle down. Lana listened to the life in there that she was a part of, a part more detached than she realized. "I didn't know how…" The interactions in the next room made familiar noises while she breathed, thought who she was, who she was supposed to be.

She lifted a platter of meat and followed Jim. She was alone, an alone she'd always been but had been unaware of. She walked to the opposite side of the table from where he stood, and set the platter far away from the potatoes.

"Oh, how good this all looks and smells." Jeanie made over the meal. Jim stayed where he was, Magdalena near his side. Lana looked at Cletus. His glare left his oldest daughter and transferred to Lana, then to Jim. Jeanie's enthusiasm became background noise again, with Cletus' stare much more distinctive and loud, but not as loud as Lana's heart.

"Let's eat." Lana forced her way into Jeanie's flow of conversation. She gathered her children, brought the oldest to stand behind their chairs, then showed Jeanie and Jim theirs, putting them side by side before she came to stand behind her own.

Cletus never rose. His eyes were on Jim, then Lana. He grunted. Lana and the children sat. Jim and Jeanie followed suit.

"How formal," Jeanie cooed. "I love it!"

Cletus stared at Lana's friend as if he were seeing her for the first time. Lana prayed Cletus would just fill his plate and let Jeanie's comment pass.

"You really are the man of the house. I like that!" Jeanie smiled at Cletus. Lana stared from a cloud that wouldn't go away. She was watching her husband, this man she was wed to but had never smiled at the way her friend did. How did Jeanie do it? How did Jeanie know?

Jeanie's glow cast a radiant reflection on Cletus' face. His usual stoic demeanor was lost in its sheen, his guard softened in its warmth. Jeanie's flattery became infectious, her warmth thawing his icy hardness. Lana watched Cletus' eyes stay on Jeanie as he groped for the bowl of corn. His fingers found it, and he dragged it to his plate. He started to ladle a spoonful for himself, but he stopped, spoon midair, and then he laid it back in the dish and extended the bowl to Jeanie.

"And a gentleman, too," she cooed again, rewarding him. "Thank you."

It was like watching a play she was supposed to be in but didn't know her part. Lana studied her childhood friend handling her husband. Jeanie knew about men because she had brothers, brothers-in-law, and most of all a father. Cletus said nothing. He didn't smile, he didn't blush, he didn't nod, he merely reached for the next nearest dish and served himself a roll, then passed it on. A new look lit his face, not the kind that turned stony, the kind Lana elicited from him. This one was the kind Lana'd always wanted to see. Just not this way. Not when he was looking at someone else.

"Lana, this meal is wonderful! I didn't realize what a good cook you were." Jeanie smiled, a genuine smile, a genuine compliment. Lana knew she should reply, thank Jeanie, but she was frozen, nothing would come out.

Jeanie turned to Jim, her face all alight, and she placed one hand, long slender fingers, on his arm. "Don't you admire the way Lana's husband takes charge of their house? Yet he's so considerate, too. And isn't Lana the perfect wife? Doesn't it just do something to you?"

Jim nodded. He took a bite of corn.

"Now, you eat well, dear Jim," Jeanie continued. "It's a long drive home tonight. But I know you can do it. You're strong too." She squeezed his arm.

The room shifted away, everyone tumbling Jeanie's direction. Cletus stopped chewing and stared at Jeanie's hand. Even Jim. He continued to work the corn in his mouth, but he stared at Jeanie's fingers where they wrapped around his arm. Magdalena scooted her chair nearer Jim's, her face contorting into a scowl as she glared at Jeanie's hand. Lana's other children were entranced by the strange jauntiness and conversation at their table. They watched her old friend, their food barely touched.

Lana set her fork beside her plate. A cold surge

spread inside as she glanced at Cletus. There was no wolfish hunger on her husband's face as he stared at Jeanie's hand, no demand she make sons for him. There was something else there, a different sort of desire, a gentler longing Lana had never imagined him capable of, one she'd never known how to create.

"You could stay here." Cletus shocked Lana with his sudden invitation.

"Oh, could we? Why, thank you," Jeanie gushed. "You're ever so kind. But we mustn't. We will go home. It's more proper that way…since we're not married."

An unsaid "yet" hung in the air. It dangled like an empty noose. It was meant for Jim, but Lana took it. Her husband. Her husband invited them…invited her friend, Jeanie…to stay. Her husband. Her man, one she'd not understood. Her heart beat wildly in her empty breast. She'd never felt so alone.

****

She touched him during the night. The feeling was light and soft, her fingertips gliding up his arm to his shoulder, upward until they traced the line of his neck and cheek and found his lips. Her fingers tingled at the sensation. Fire burned farther down. Lana's whole being leapt into flames. She parted his lips, hungry yet gentle. *I love you.* The words vibrated through her being, anxious to be spoken into life, but her lips stayed still, letting her fingers do her talking.

This was what it was supposed to be like, this was how she should feel with a man, and how she should make him feel.

His body turned, came alongside hers, not on top, his warmth pressing against her gown. She wanted him

156

in a way she'd never wanted him before, a way she'd never imagined possible. There was no hurry. For once he was taking his time. It made her hunger unbearable. She was starving. She wanted him. She ached for him.

The blankets were in the way, and her gown was holding her back. She scratched at them, yanked them aside. "This is how I'm supposed to love you. This is how it's supposed to feel. I didn't understand, you see."

He moved. Away instead of closer. He rolled to his side, farther from her, to the edge of the bed.

"What are you doing? Come back," she whispered.

He fumbled with the light.

"No light." She touched his shoulder. "No light. Just us, in the darkness."

He paused. She squeezed against him and wrapped her arms around him.

"Why not?" he asked. "I want to see you. You're a sight for sore eyes."

"Jim?" Her hands turned to ice. She drew back, scurried to her own side of the bed. Why was Jim here? Where was her husband?

"Jim?" His voice was gruff. He fumbled with the lamp until it lit. He was sitting now, Cletus' long silhouette staring down at her. "Why'd you call for Jim?"

The ice spread throughout her body, dowsing the flames as it went. "I...I didn't." She shrank back into the blanket. "I wanted you, but then you said... Oh...I must have been dreaming... Please, I didn't know..."

Cletus stared down at her. She couldn't see his face with the light behind his back. He yanked the blanket from her clasp, stood, and took it with him. Their bedroom door slammed behind him.

"I thought it was you," she said in the lamplight. "And I wanted you the way I'm supposed to, really I did."

Chapter 19

James 1954

"You look rough, little brother."

James straightened and glanced up into the mirror over the washstand. Beyond his image, fuzzy hair, like a wiry silhouette, stood between him and the light coming from the doorway to the rest of the house. He squinted. He hadn't bothered to turn on the light above the washstand when he came in from doing chores. He was too tired, too worn out to bother. He grabbed the old towel and rubbed the water off his face, then his arms and hands. He scoured hard, so hard his skin stung and turned red beneath the cloth.

"You'll never get that burnt stench off." Magdalena moved closer. She smelled of ashes from cigarettes. James wasn't sure which was worse. Burnt metal scorched into the skin, or smoke, manly cigarette smoke, coming off the skin and clothing of a woman. He felt Magdalena's smile in the shadows. Burnt metal. That's what was worse. No matter how manly the cigarette smoke was, it suited his sister, and she wore it well.

"I won't smell this way forever." He tried to sound glib, like it really didn't matter, but he meant it. He believed it, he just didn't want to discuss it. He didn't want anyone to laugh and say he was stuck as a welder the rest of his life, even though Pop never allowed him to weld. Pop was giving him menial jobs around the shop until he could hire a real man to replace Alex. Alex had escaped, he had gone to the army, and Harold had plans of his own. Just because James was younger didn't mean he wouldn't escape too. He wouldn't sort rods or pile up pieces of scrap forever.

"I told you you're different from Pop. I'm surprised you agreed to work for him."

James stared at Magdalena in the mirror. Funny to hear that again from a sister Pop said always lived at dead ends. She'd said herself she was stuck, and even though James would never say it out loud, he was afraid she was. She was trying, though. Trying hard to get free, and the scars were there, evidence of her internal battle etched onto her face.

"Have to work for him," he said. "For now, anyway." He said that last part a little louder, an emphasis for both of them. He set the towel down, turned, and leaned back against the washstand. "Gotta earn my keep. Pop said boys do that, that's all." He wondered if she understood, if she would snort or argue, but she didn't. When she said nothing, he watched her, then added, "Until I can play ball somewhere. For money."

He'd never said it out loud before. Not even when he was alone, to himself. But there it was, his dream—spoken, exposed to scrutiny, and now, even though he was still so young, something he had to live up to. The words bolted like lightning from the air and through his heart. They lit up his thoughts and feelings. He saw a different future than anyone would ever have predicted for him. A vision coming to life in a blaze of fire.

Magdalena touched his arm, a call back to home and what still was, but he wasn't ready to go there, not now that his heart was out. Her expression was hidden in the dull light, and he wondered if she could feel his excitement through her fingers. He latched onto her hand and held it.

"You're different. You're better. Don't let go of that." She came closer.

What she said sounded like a warning instead of a celebration. He looked up toward her face. She towered above him, just like she always had, tall and lanky, a reminder he was shorter and stouter. His vision vanished for a moment, the excitement of his dream dwindled. *Baseball's not in your blood.* He straightened. He fumbled for the towel behind him. If only he'd been built like her, taken after Pop more...

"You're different. You're better. Remember that," she said again, louder.

She'd read his thoughts. Magdalena knew him too well, and she'd unearthed the doubt that lived in his mind. She'd caused it to flare up so she could wash it away. Magdalena slipped her fingers from between his and lifted her hand to his head and tousled his hair. It didn't flop like it used to. It was gummy with heat and dirt, thick and wiry. "And you're handsome," she added. He could feel her smile.

He smiled back, a ginger smile, but he wanted to hug her. "You staying for supper?" James asked instead.

Magdalena rarely came by in the evenings. She said it had something to do with being married now, but everyone knew it had more to do with Pop. Tonight was council meeting night, so Pop was eating in town. He went to all of the meetings, his war against the city council never ending.

"Yeah, thought I might. Don't bother dragging my chair back to the table. I'll sit in Pop's." She laughed. She really wouldn't sit in Pop's chair, but it wasn't because she respected him or was afraid. Magdalena had her own space at the table and she defended it, making a show of carrying her chair to the table and leaving it there every time she visited. It was hers and she owned it, no matter what Pop said.

"Earl with you?"

She started to glance away, then caught herself and turned back to James, looking him square on. "He's busy."

Earl was always busy. He never came with Magdalena. Earl had come to the house after their wedding, only because Mama insisted. She'd forced him by holding a reception that Pop didn't want either, the two men so much the same, two stoic figures present only in body. The neighbors came, some of Magdalena's friends came, Earl's mother came, but no one else. Mama had done it up big in heart to make up for what she couldn't in decorations and gifts. She'd made Magdalena a princess for the day, a bride, the focal point of the celebration. Mama's excitement had sparkled briefly in Magdalena's eyes, a tiny glitter that flickered, then waned, then went away altogether. Maybe Mama's enthusiasm wasn't enough to infect Magdalena with the idea of being a princess because Earl wasn't much of a prince, or because Pop didn't see his daughter as anything remarkable, much less descended royalty. Mama had tried hard. Her insistence that Magdalena be deigned as special on her wedding day was powerful, but not compelling enough to convince Earl, or even her daughter, that Magdalena was exceptional, even on the one day that was hers.

Magdalena ran a hand over her wiry curls. They bent under her touch, then rebounded back to their normal disarray as her hand passed. She stood differently than she used to, she looked a little harder, more powerful than she had before she married Earl. She smelled stronger of smoke, and chose brighter colors for her makeup. Harold said wearing more makeup wasn't a good sign, especially for a married woman.

"You're different. You're better. Remember that," James said. He said it quietly so only Magdalena would hear. She looked away this time. The profile of her face against the backlight was worthy of a painting, and James wished he could capture it and show her what he saw. "You may not be as different from Pop as you want to be yet, but you're sure different from any woman I know. You're better than all of them, except maybe Mama. You two are equal. You're Mama's daughter, and that makes you beautiful. Remember? Mr. Morgan said so."

Magdalena glanced at him, then turned toward the doorway to the rest of the house. "Come on, let's go help get supper."

He straightened and touched her arm. "One more thing. Don't say anything about me playing ball. Playing for money, that is."

She glanced back at him, an easy smile on her face. "Of course not, little brother. I'll let you tell everyone when you're ready. Tell everyone except Pop. Him, you can show."

Chapter 20

James 1954

"So tell me about tonight's council meeting," Magdalena said as she led James from the washroom. "What are they arguing about this time?"

They stepped into the dining room. It was lit up in more ways than one, vastly different from the nights Pop was home. It was freer, and everyone came to eat on these nights. Sometimes Harold brought Sandra and Gail brought Jackson. Betsy, beautiful as she was, never invited a beau; she refused all their offers, content to stay here with her family, no matter how difficult Pop made it. James felt the freedom and excitement as they scattered dishes of food all over the table instead of just at Pop's end. Silverware and plates were in stacks, waiting for each person to grab their own. No wonder Magdalena came on these nights. These were good nights, when they talked and breathed much more easily.

"Some new fire rule someone proposed," James said as they approached the table. He'd heard that much from Pop's tirades in his and Mama's bedroom at night. Grumbles and rants about a ridiculous law, Mr. Morgan, and *that boy* all jumbled into his complaint, as if James had anything to do with council meetings or town rulings.

Mama spotted the two of them and smiled as she greeted Magdalena, setting a bowl of green beans on the table before she hugged her daughter.

"Hello, Mag," Carla called. She grinned, and their other sisters joined her. Gail scurried to the table with glasses, while Betsy toted hot dishes. They weren't hurrying, they were scurrying, a happy scuttle they actually enjoyed.

James knew someone had proposed all fires be banned within the town, especially downtown. He also knew Pop blamed Mr. Morgan more than he blamed the business owner who wanted his hot and smelly business relocated. Pop had been in the same location for years, fighting to hold on to it the way Magdalena defended her spot at the table. There'd never been an accidental fire in Pop's shop, never been much of an odor escape, either, not any worse than what they carried home on their bodies at night.

Harold tromped into the room, his usual grin on his face. "Cow's fed and watered. We're done for the night." Ever since Alex had gone and James had been working for Pop, Harold helped with the chores, no matter what. "Let's eat! I'm starved!"

Harold grabbed a plate and sat down. Everyone else followed, happy chatter bubbling up everywhere. James grinned. He was exhausted, almost too tired to eat, but he wouldn't miss supper on council meeting nights for anything.

"So what's the deal with the meeting tonight?" Magdalena asked Mama as she passed a plate of rolls to her right. "What's the latest fire rule?"

"Whatever it is, Pop's planning to use it to get Morgan's restaurant shut down," Harold said as he tore a bite out of a roll.

Magdalena glanced at Mama. Mama spooned a healthy portion of beans onto her plate.

"Your father says a fire's a fire," Mama explained without looking up. "They want to make a rule banning fires anywhere near the downtown, so since Glen…I mean, Mr. Morgan, cooks downtown, Pop's going to claim that's as much a danger as his welding." Mama passed the green beans to Betsy.

"I tell you what," Magdalena said, pointing her knife at James. "If Pop can't get Mr. Morgan's restaurant shut down but they're still after Pop, you should start skewering hunks of meat on metal rods and cook them over the welding torch. Say it's soldered sandwich meat. You'll make a bunch of money."

"I wouldn't make that much." James laughed. "I've no talent for cooking in my bones. Nothing I make would be as good as what Mr. Morgan does."

Gail sneered, with a smile. "It would probably taste like you guys smell when you come home, anyway. Who would want to eat that?"

Mama glanced up. "You've eaten there, James?"

"No, not really. I'm just saying anything's got to be better than my cooking."

"Mr. Morgan has good food," Magdalena said, taking a bite of mashed potatoes. She didn't sound brash like she would have if Pop had been there, she being the only one in the family who ignored his war against Mr. Morgan.

"I did have his ice cream once," James confessed.

Mama's brows perked up.

"He made me a sundae. Me and Andy. For playing ball well."

Mama looked at him, but then her gaze drifted away. James wondered if it was longing he saw in Mama's eyes, the imagination of something delectable and sweet. It certainly wasn't ravenous lust, the look Andy had on his face when he'd devoured his ice cream.

"I know Pop doesn't want us there, but that sundae was wonderful. Mr. Morgan covered three mountains of ice cream with melted chocolate. He put candy on each of them, too, and little pieces of bananas and cherries." James rubbed his stomach and smiled. He watched Mama's face as he created the sundae for her, built it in her eyes as if she'd actually been there. "Sundaes are the keys that unlock the soul," James added. "That's what Mr. Morgan said after I ate mine. He was right."

Mama straightened in her seat, her fork making a tiny ping as she set it beside her plate. She raised her napkin and pressed it to her mouth, holding it there, the worn cloth covering half her face.

James stared at his mother's eyes, eyes that led to a soul that needed unlocking with a sundae, a sundae she'd never had, never would have as long as Pop was at war with downtown.

The table noise softened. James looked at his brothers and sisters. They looked back at him. Their usual care was there, just piqued with a sheen of surprise. He set his fork aside and wiped his mouth with his napkin. "Once Magdalena and Carla told me I'm different, different from Pop. You've all said it in one way or another, just not straight out loud." He looked at Mama. "I understand that now. Mr. Morgan explained it to me."

"James..." Mama's eyes grew wide above the

napkin. Harold's chair scooted back and Magdalena stood. He saw "little brother" in her eyes as she came around the table and stopped at his side.

"Mr. Morgan said some people get talent from their parents." James felt Magdalena near, but it was Mama he watched. "And he said some people get heart. He was talking about you, Mama, and me. I know he was. I love playing ball, but I didn't get anything from Pop that makes me play well. Mr. Morgan said when you get talent you don't try hard, but when you get heart, you do. I got heart from you."

Mama's eyes turned red and watery, and tears began to trickle down her face, half moons of darkening fabric growing where they soaked into the napkin.

"Even if Pop doesn't want us in Mr. Morgan's restaurant, I'm not sorry I went that day. It wasn't just his sundae that unlocked my soul, it was him and what he said. He also said people with heart love in lots of special ways. Different ways. That's you too, Mama. And I thank you."

"Oh, James," Mama said again. She scooted her chair back and stood, laying the dampened napkin beside her plate. She walked toward James, tears streaming down her cheeks. "James, if I had some ice cream to give you, I would. Every day. You're a wonderful boy, and you deserve it." Mama's voice trailed off. She came close, and her arms wrapped around him as she bent to him, her tears warming his shoulder. "That special kind of love…you're right. It's in you, it's in your blood."

"I know, Mama. You put it there," he said against her hair. He pulled back, tipped his head to the side, and looked at her, her red eyes, her damp cheeks. "Mr.

Morgan said he'd make a sundae for you someday. When the time's right. I want to be there, Mama. I want to share it with you."

Mama held him tight. "You're my sundae, James."

"That's what Mr. Morgan told me to be. But he promised to make sure you get a real one someday when the time is right."

Chapter 21

Lana 1935

Lana swept around the table with her best imitation of a flounce. She fixed a smile on her face as she glided toward her husband, a bowl of steaming potatoes in her hands. Harold clapped. He liked the show, he liked the extra lift in her step. Alex tapped his hands together twice then laid them in his lap, watching his brother, a puzzled frown on his face.

"Potatoes for you," she sang as she set them in front of Cletus. "For all the work you do for us." It sounded unnatural. It was. She'd never raved about a man, not this man, not any man. It wasn't normal for her, and she wasn't sure how to do it. She was a quiet person, not rambunctious like Jeanie. Jeanie was merry. Jeanie had a boisterous spirit and inner confidence. Lana didn't. Lana was like…like what Jim wanted, like he'd tried to say in her kitchen. Jim didn't want a Jeanie.

Lana watched Cletus over the rising steam of the potatoes, waiting for him to say something. He eyed her, his brows drawing close together as he thought. Jeanie's lack of shyness and her flattery had drawn Cletus out and mesmerized him. Jim may not want a Jeanie, but it was clear to Lana that Cletus did.

"How was your day?" she asked, trying to sound

even brighter. She looked Cletus in the eye. The watery blue irises that stared back at her made her uncomfortable, and she longed to look away. Couples were supposed to look each other in the eye, it was what they did. It just wasn't what she and Cletus did.

"My day was the same as any other." Cletus reached for the potatoes. He looked confused.

She backed up a step, glanced around the table, wondering what to do next. There was nothing else to say. She went to the far end and grabbed her chair and dragged it near his. She returned for her plate, her silverware, and brought all of them to his end of the table. He stopped filling his plate, a spoonful of potatoes midair. He watched as she sat.

"You extra hungry?" he asked.

Her cheeks burned. "I just wanted to talk better, hear about your day, tell you about ours." She nodded toward the children, their faces like their father's, agog, confused. Except for Magdalena's. Hers was fixed in a frown. Lana gave a light laugh. It was supposed to lighten the mood, draw them all out, bring their suppertime to life, but it came out flat. She tried again and it sounded stronger.

Jeanie had written several times since her visit. Over and over, the same way she talked. Her voice, her words, her style were imbedded in Lana's head. Lana closed her eyes and rehearsed the words on the pages. She could see them, she could hear them, but so far, none of them were coming out of her mouth. How was it Jeanie was capable of a never-ending flow of verbiage, while Lana spurted only a halted comment or two, uncomfortable pauses strung together with an occasional thought?

"I fixed the fence the way you told me to. I'm not as strong as you, but I tried to get it right." She glanced his way as she took the potatoes he'd set near his plate. She studied his reaction while she carried them to the other side of the table and began dishing them up for their older children.

Magdalena slumped low in her seat, staring at her plate, her face like stone, her usual antics absent. Lana nudged Magdalena's chair, hoping her daughter would sit up. Magdalena slouched lower as Lana leaned close, stretching between her daughter and her husband as she dished food into Magdalena's plate. Lana glanced Magdalena's way.

"Don't like Jeanie." It was soft. Her daughter's lips barely moved. Lana nearly dropped the spoon she'd ladled potatoes with.

It will be all right. Lana tried to say it to her daughter without speaking, but the stoniness remained, her assurance unable to penetrate her daughter's dislike of Lana's rambunctious friend. Jeanie wasn't safe to invite into their home, and Magdalena recognized her in the room.

Lana brushed one arm against her daughter's shoulder, a touch to comfort, before she glanced up at Cletus. "Maybe you could help me in the morning. Show me how you'd do it, so I can get it right."

Cletus piled meat on his plate and ladled gravy over the top. He nodded. "I could do that."

Lana filled each child's plate, pausing longest over her eldest daughter, then sat and began dishing up food for herself. She moved quickly, her hands frantic like her mind, her thoughts racing, searching for something clever to say. Something to catch Cletus' attention without frightening Magdalena, fill the emptiness with innocent but attractive chatter. The room was like an empty cave without Jeanie's flow of words, just the quiet sounds of eating, the same as every other night. Lana had practiced conjuring an imitation of Jeanie up, but Jeanie just wouldn't come. Lana couldn't create Jeanie from her own personality. They just weren't the same. Exactly as Jim had said.

Everyone ate, spoons and forks clinking against plates. Everyone except Magdalena. She sat, pressed low against the back of her seat, and stared across the top of the table at her mother. Lana took a bite, then another, as she searched for something to say, but nothing about her day or Cletus' was worth discussing. She glanced at her daughter. She wished Magdalena was old enough to understand Lana was doing this for her as much as for any of them. Magdalena's childlike features looked stony, a hardening that showed from the inside as well as on the out.

"Jeanie's learning to drive," Lana blurted. It was about Jeanie instead of a manifestation of her, but she was desperate. Magdalena was brooding, fighting back the only way she knew as a child, envious and despising the one female who'd stolen the spotlight she felt was hers and where she belonged. "Jeanie's mother is horrified, but Jeanie's still determined to learn. She said she can help her father this way. Or her husband someday." Lana couldn't look at Magdalena. Her daughter would take this as a blow. She looked at Cletus instead, hoping and praying.

Cletus stopped chewing and glanced up. He stared at Lana. She braced herself for a correction, a one-word remark, a grunt followed by absorption with his food.

But he was thinking. She could see Jeanie in his thoughts, or her antics in his mind.

"Jeanie said she sits at the edge of the seat because her legs and arms are too short to reach the steering wheel and pedals." Lana took a deep breath and calmed herself, forced herself to speak carefully, draw each word out to give Cletus the picture of Jeanie at the wheel one piece at a time. "She uses pillows or jackets, and piles them behind her." Lana waited, expecting Cletus to just snort and return to his food. He didn't. The idea of Jeanie driving was more powerful than meat and potatoes.

The look on Cletus' face made her stop, afraid to say more. He was too intrigued, more interested than she wanted him to be. She prayed he'd just return to his food. She fidgeted with her fork. She'd said too much. Jeanie was too close. Lana could see it in her husband's gaze. So did Magdalena. One corner of Cletus' mouth twitched upward. He rarely smiled, but this time he almost did.

"I wanna drive," Magdalena shouted. She pitched forward on her seat and looked from Lana to Cletus. She watched him especially, waiting for his reaction. "I wanna drive a big truck," she said even louder.

"Jeanie does, huh?" Cletus said to Lana, never looking his daughter's way. He dipped his spoon into a pile of corn and brought it to his mouth. "I can see her driving a truck." He engulfed the corn, chewed, and looked engrossed by the thought.

"I can drive one, too!" Magdalena shouted.

Cletus glanced at Magdalena, then looked back to Lana. "Jeanie can probably do it," he said. "At least she'll try. Hate to be her father if he's the one teaching her, though."

It was the most Cletus had ever said at the table, the closest he'd come to a conversation. It was about Jeanie, but at least he'd said something. To Lana. She bit her lip, holding back that Jeanie had promised to drive her and Jim to see them as soon as she learned. Lana only wanted Jeanie's fire to ignite her husband and her marriage. She didn't want Jeanie herself to do it, no more than Magdalena did.

"I'm not hungry." Magdalena slid off her chair. She stood near her place and looked at her father. "'Scuse me," she said a little louder.

Cletus looked at his daughter, then at her plate of food. "You ailing?"

Magdalena shook her head.

"If you ain't gonna eat, then get on to bed. Your mama'll be up in a little bit." He turned back to Lana. Lana heard their daughter walk away, her gallop gone, solid footsteps carrying her up the stairs. She listened to Magdalena's retreat, each step a nail driven into her heart. She watched Cletus. He was looking at her, his eyes alight in a way she'd never seen before. The wolfish hunger wasn't there, but something akin to it was, the same something she'd seen when he eyed Jeanie's fingers on Jim's arm. "That's some friend you've got."

"You like her? I mean, she's kind of…well, boisterous." Lana's voice was small, but the enormity of the question nearly choked her. She tried to look casual, as if his answer didn't matter.

Cletus thought. He shrugged. Then he returned to his corn.

A long breath eased from Lana's chest as she stole

a glance toward the empty stairs. She didn't want Cletus to see she might cry. He'd never understand these were tears of relief. She batted her eyes and drew in a deep breath. It had worked. She'd found a way to animate her husband, engage him in a real conversation, draw him out and hopefully back to her. It wasn't Jeanie he wanted. It was nothing more than amusement with her antics. She could hear Magdalena upstairs, stoniness in her steps, pounding out her defiance.

"I'll clear the table after I check on Magdalena." Lana ventured a smile at Cletus. He nodded. It wasn't indifferent, it wasn't cold. "You kids finish up. I'll be back down in a minute."

She rushed up the stairs. Magdalena was too small to understand the sort of hope Lana felt. She'd have to convey it in a way her daughter could grasp. *Your father works hard, he is tired, there is a lot of pressure on him as a man that you're too young to understand. You're also too young to drive, but when you're older he'll help you.*

Lana scurried the rest of the way up the steps. *Thank you, Jeanie.*

****

She came. Not less than two months after she'd written that she was learning to drive, and not more than ten minutes before Cletus was to arrive home from work. Jeanie was in a truck, her father's truck, pillows and blankets stuffed behind her so she wouldn't bounce so far or hard that her feet and hands would fly off the pedals and steering wheel.

"I did it! I told you I would," Jeanie squealed. She dropped down from the truck and held the door open long enough for Lana and her older children to see inside, see the menagerie of rolled up linens and the remains of a sandwich strewn across the seat. "Are you surprised?"

Cletus' truck rumbled in the far-off distance. Jeanie didn't hear it or recognize it, her ears too full of her own boisterous excitement.

"Jim didn't come with you?" Lana was surprised Jeanie would make such a long trip alone so late in the day.

Jeanie swiped her hand through the air. "I told him to come, but he said he was busy. He always says he's busy. So I came without him." There was hurt, or maybe just annoyance, beneath Jeanie's easy dismissal of Jim's refusal to ride along with her. Cletus' truck rumbled nearer, Harold looked off toward the road.

Magdalena inched to Lana's side, watching Jeanie the way a mouse gauges a cat.

"You'll eat with us, won't you?" Lana asked. Of course Jeanie would. She'd end up staying all night. No one would expect her to drive back so far after dark.

"Oh, I meant to get here sooner, but I stopped at my cousin Lilly's house. She's not far from here, and I hadn't seen her in ever so long. I guess we chatted too much, and it got late. Do you mind if I eat here? I had a sandwich with me, but I ate it already."

Jeanie ran on, barely acknowledging Lana's nod. Cletus reached the end of the lane. Harold ran to the edge of the house and peered around its corner to watch his father come up the drive. Magdalena wrapped herself in Lana's skirt, peering out at Jeanie from a gap above its folds.

"Magdalena, what are you doing?" Lana shook her skirt, but Magdalena held on. Jeanie wouldn't know, she wouldn't understand or even realize, what a threat she was. Cletus' truck came around the corner. He let off the gas when he saw them, and as he paused, the truck ambled forward, its engine rumbling submissively, like a tiger subdued. He pulled it next to Jeanie's father's truck and shut off the engine. Lana felt her skirt tug downward as Magdalena wound her fists tighter into the fabric.

"My truck's as big as yours!" Jeanie shouted as Cletus stepped out. She laughed, she sparkled, she meant no harm, but she caused it. Lana saw it, and so did her oldest daughter.

"She's a bad driver," Magdalena spouted from within Lana's skirts. "I could do better. Watch!" Magdalena broke free of the gathers and darted to Jeanie's truck. She was on the running board and hanging from the handle before Lana could grab her. Cletus was quicker. He was out of his truck and, with what seemed like one long, sweeping movement, rounded Jeanie's vehicle and scooped his daughter into his arms, pulling her free of the door's handle. It was graceful, and so natural. Lana had never seen such a movement before. She saw her own awe in her daughter's face, admiration overpowering the surprise at being snatched away from her mission.

Cletus set Magdalena down. He didn't notice how prince-like he'd been in his daughter's eyes, how warm his arms made her feel when they were wrapped around her. Lana felt them along with Magdalena, felt the place a father's arms were to be. They felt good, they felt safe, they made the girl in her feel alive and whole. Cletus told Magdalena to leave the truck alone and stop telling lies about Mama's friends. The warmth vanished. Magdalena's awe subsided. She stared at Jeanie from the spot her father had left her, her face returned to stone. Then she marched to the house.

Cletus didn't apologize to Jeanie. He didn't look embarrassed or angry. But he stood at attention as Jeanie sputtered to a start and gained momentum, explaining how it felt to drive all the way from her house to theirs. Lana studied the two of them, uninterested in Jeanie's narration but wary now, just like her daughter had been, as she watched her husband's reaction. Lana slid her fingers to her stomach, then to below her navel. She rested them there over the new life that was just beginning. *Please be a boy,* she prayed silently. *My husband wants another son, and I need to keep us together, all of us.* She watched. She prayed. She wished Jeanie would go home.

Chapter 22

Lana 1936

It was the first time she'd ever really seen Mr. Morgan up close. She knew of him, knew Cletus' opinion of him, and had vague recollections of how he looked when she'd been to town once or twice before. He was a reputation more than a memory, an emblem of right versus wrong. She wondered if Mr. Morgan knew how the two of them had been inextricably tied in Cletus' mind, her and him together, a pair against her husband. They had been tied, but not quite as much now, now that she was pregnant again, hopefully carrying a son that would put her back on Cletus's side.

Cletus nudged her forward. Walking was difficult, as she slogged from right to left. She tilted back a little to counter the bulk she carried in front, throwing her even more off balance. She prayed her doctor wouldn't be at this dinner, a town council dinner she thought was to make peace amongst its members. She'd never told him she was pregnant. She hadn't told Grandma, either. Lana had worked too hard to get this far, and Ella's glares at Cletus were damaging enough. He didn't need any more reasons to avoid her as a wife.

"Over here." Cletus' fingers were at her back, his attention more frequent, and often gentler, as he waited for the birth of his son. He propelled her toward a cluster of people she didn't know. She rarely came to town, and she felt awkward being here now, the size of a cow with calf.

Faces turned their way, some with smiles, some with half smiles, and others with nothing at all. For Cletus there were nods from the men, most of them without smiles.

"Ow!" She clamped a hand over her mouth and bent forward. The low jabbing pain surprised her, and she stopped.

"Come on." Cletus' fingers pressed at her back. He was nervous about this dinner, the peace dinner. He wanted it to go right. Right, his way.

"I'm sorry." She straightened, slowly, until the pain subsided.

She saw him as he broke from the cluster. His hair was dark, so was his complexion, and she knew it was Mr. Morgan. Lana was taken by his eyes. They were even kinder than she remembered, eyes that smiled, while those of the woman with him were observant.

"Cletus," Mr. Morgan said. They shook hands. Then Mr. Morgan looked Lana's way as he nodded toward the woman beside him. "This is Ida, my sister. And you are Mrs. Paine."

"Lana," she said, at the same moment Cletus said, "Yep." Her protruding belly gave them an excuse to stand apart, away from each other like sparrers might do while they sized each other up. She blushed and tried to shrink back a half step behind Cletus, her stomach still jutting into the midst of their foursome.

"When is the baby due?" Ida asked.

"Any time now," Lana answered. "It's our sixth."

"Sixth! Glory be! You don't look old enough for

six children!" Ida sized her up. "Six! So what do you think this one is? Boy or girl?"

"Boy," Lana answered quickly. "I mean, a son." She looked up at Cletus. He nodded, and she smiled.

Ida began to talk about having babies, something she hadn't experienced yet, still being unmarried, but she was hopeful. Ida paused, then went on. Listening to her was like listening to Jeanie, a running monologue of voice and sound. Lana watched Ida, enjoyed the easy way she spoke, comfortable and rambling on, indifferent to whether her brother agreed or not.

Lana stole peeks at couples around the room, men with their wives, and how they behaved. She'd had no model to go by other than Ella and Carl, and the imaginations Jeanie had put into her head when they were girls. Lana eyed the crowd of men, tall, short, rough, chuckling. Did any of them make love instead of just babies? Did other wives feel frightened, confused?

Cletus jabbed her in the back with a finger. She yanked her head his direction. He nodded to Mr. Morgan.

"I was saying that with so many children you might enjoy a meal free from cooking," Mr. Morgan said— again. She could tell by the frown Cletus gave her. "Bring everyone to the restaurant. My treat."

Ida looked startled, her brows pinched together as she glanced back at Lana.

"Oh, Mr. Morgan…" Lana began.

"Glen. Please call me Glen. And don't argue. Just come and enjoy."

Ida frowned at her brother as Lana smiled.

"I doubt you can afford to feed all of us." Lana looked up at Cletus as she spoke. He threaded his fingers around her arm. It was pleasant. She knew he didn't mean it that way, but it was, and she smiled even more.

"Gather round," a man called. "Time to eat."

Couples paired off, searching for seats at the square of tables. Lana followed Cletus; he led them away from Mr. Morgan.

"We won't be eating at his restaurant," Cletus said as they found their seats. "It's just a ploy, and I'm not falling for it."

The tables were filled with platters of fried chicken, bowls of mashed potatoes, baskets of rolls, ears of corn, and more. It was a meal no different from what she made at home, but it smelled so much better, just because it wasn't her own. When they were settled, she waited for Cletus to fill his plate before she filled hers, but he surprised her by dishing food for her first, then taking care of himself. She eyed the food hungrily. She was starving, she always was, especially now that this boy was so large inside her. Cletus never knew how hungry she felt. He never asked, and she never told him. She wondered now if he had somehow guessed, for he filled her plate to heaping and nodded that she should dig in.

Another pain tore through her abdomen, sharper than the first. It obliterated the pleasure of sitting next to her husband, of having him touch her, wait on her. She wouldn't allow this pain to destroy the occasion. She clenched her teeth and gripped the edge of her seat until it passed.

"Think Ella's doing okay with the kids?" she asked Cletus through her tightened mouth. It didn't sound as casual as she wanted. A tiny sweat had broken out with her pain, leaving her skin cool. Cletus nodded.

She picked up her fork. The hum around them was soothing, and she listened, stowing away the pain and its memory, relaxing into the voices and conversations. She began to eat.

"Why didn't you go big time?" A man across the way asked. He was looking at Cletus. Her husband stared back, a faint tinge of pink coloring his face. "You were the best. You should've gone on."

Cletus shook his head, he looked down at his plate. Not the way he did when she spoke to him. He was still in this conversation, he was just dodging it, not bored.

Stories of baseball erupted around the room, her husband the star of them all. Lana stared at Cletus, a man she suddenly felt she didn't even know.

"You played baseball?" she asked. He nodded. He was taller than any man in the room, longer and leaner, and probably meaner. He must have been quick when he was young. "You were good?" She leaned forward into his gaze. He shrugged. She remembered how he'd moved around Jeanie's father's truck when he snatched Magdalena from its running board. It had been graceful, smooth, and certain. Why hadn't she guessed? He had a gift. He had talent. He hadn't even told her.

"He was the best," Mr. Morgan said from another table. "From what I hear, there was no one like him."

Lana looked at Mr. Morgan, and he winked. It was a fun wink, one meant to tease Cletus rather than her. Mr. Morgan leaned back in his chair and draped one arm across the back of Ida's.

Lana smiled, then she glanced around the room, eavesdropping on tales of baseball, watching men and women enjoy their food. In spite of the enthusiastic bluster baseball brought to the crowd, it was still a strained gaiety, an almost false bravado. She hadn't detected it earlier; she'd been too in awe, too curious about other couples. But now she saw it, the forced effort to make peace she had suspected would be there, the almost challenging tone as the men fired questions, almost accusations, at her husband about why he hadn't played baseball.

Cletus had built bridges, he'd been a war hero, he'd been a husband, and a father. All before her—before her and their nearly six children. When had he played ball? Or hadn't played ball…

"That was a long time ago," Cletus finally said to someone at another table. It wasn't angry, but it closed the discussion like a hammer going down. He stared around the room, men and women stared back at him. He wasn't himself. That's why he'd filled her plate. He was nervous, and she was his anchor.

He looked lastly at her, his pale blue eyes begging her not to ask. She didn't have to. Baseball fit somewhere around the death of his son. She could see it now. He had buried that dream with his family. She wanted to lay a hand on his arm the way Jeanie had on Jim's. She wanted to say with her touch what she couldn't in this crowd or even at home, but the pleading in his eyes warned her not to.

She gave him an invisible nod and turned to gaze around the room again. She no longer wondered what sort of husbands these men were. They were businessmen now, men with stores near her husband's, who wanted him moved. She glanced along the tables, searching through their frivolous conversations that she knew had calculated motives, until her eyes lit upon a man who was watching her. He was very well dressed and immaculately groomed. He was older than she but younger than Cletus, slender, with thinning hair, and staring straight at her.

Cletus' arm pressed against her. She felt his tautness, saw white on his knuckles as he gripped his butter knife. "Don't look at him," Cletus whispered. "That's Kline. He makes trouble."

Kline. She'd heard his name in Cletus' grumblings. She tried to pry her look away from Mr. Kline's, but it was powerful, magnetic. Cletus' leg pressed against hers, and she managed finally, to pull her head away and turn another direction. Mr. Morgan was there in the path of her gaze. She stopped as he nodded, the glitter gone from his look. He was watching, paying attention, but saying nothing. At least not with his mouth. In his eyes she saw a whole conversation.

"We need to go," Cletus said near her ear. "Kline's up to no good." Cletus stood, towering above her, a baseball player, welder, soldier, widower, a man who'd lost his son and was prepared to defend his business.

She scooted forward on the seat and braced her palms on the top of the table. She leaned into them, to pull herself up. Pain fired through her abdomen, and she stopped. She groaned, and tipped her head forward as a familiar darkness stole over her. *No,* she prayed. *Not again, not here, not now.*

Cletus grasped her arm and pulled upward. She cried out, louder this time. She didn't mean to, but it came, that same cry she'd heard when Alex was born. The room darkened, chairs moved, and Mr. Morgan yelled something. Cletus told her to get up, but then it all faded. It was gone. Everything.

Chapter 23

Lana 1936

Grandma was really there this time, not just a shadow, not just the imaginary her. Lana could hear her, talk to her, feel Grandma's hands as she brushed back Lana's hair.

"Thank you, Grandma."

"You're welcome." It came out crisp.

Lana tried to open her eyes and see if Grandma was upset. She raised her hands and rubbed her eyes. It felt good. She dug her fists in and rubbed hard, clearing away the stupor.

"She waking up?"

Lana dropped her hands to the bed. She didn't have to see to know that voice, that her doctor was here. Her fingers crept up to her belly, the mountain that had been there in grandiose proportions the past couple of months... It was gone. She was flat. Her fingers slid back down to her sides.

"Finally." Grandma sounded impatient.

Lana heard footsteps, Grandma moving away? Someone else coming to Lana's side? A hand touched her wrist, then her forehead. It smelled of antiseptic, soap, things she identified with her doctor.

"She's waking up," Grandma said, farther away, talking about Lana to someone else. A man's voice answered. He sounded relieved. Jim? He thanked God, whoever he was. Definitely not Cletus.

Lana listened for the soft whimpering she'd heard when she went through this before, the time Alex was born. The room was still. There was no cry, no warm bundle pressed against her side. She panicked. Horror exploded in her breast. Pools of wet gathered behind her lids. She'd lost the baby, destroyed Cletus' son. Her selfishness, her determination to please and keep her husband had cost some tiny child, a tiny boy, his life. "It wasn't Cletus' fault," she whispered. "It was mine."

The hands left her. She could feel the doctor's thoughts, his judgment, circulating nearby. She opened her eyes, her tears breaking free and racing down the sides of her face. A wobbly image stood near. She closed her eyes, squeezed the tears out, then opened them again. Cloth touched her hand, she clutched it and raised it to her eyes. Tears soaked into the fabric, and she drew it away. She could see now. She could see the doctor.

"You scared the tar out of me!" Grandma appeared at the doctor's side. His arm came up, his forearm raised in front of Grandma. The doctor shook his head. Grandma muffled a snort, but she grew quiet.

Lana looked up at Grandma, at the room behind her, and realized she wasn't home in her and Cletus' bedroom. "Where am I?"

"My office," the doctor replied.

Lana glanced around the sterile room, the whiteness of it, the starkness. It was even barer than her bedroom, this room decorated with steel and glass, cotton, and stringent odors. "How long?" she asked.

"Long enough for me to get the word and come

hightailing it up here!"

The doctor raised his arm again, warding Grandma off once more. Her lips tightened into a thin line, and her brows pinched into a similar shape. It was Grandma's look of love. Lana hadn't understood that, growing up, but she did now.

"Jim bring you?" Lana asked. She prayed not. She hoped it wasn't him thanking God earlier. He couldn't see her like this, know what she'd done.

"Of course. Couldn't stop him. Ella's husband came for me, and when I asked Jim to keep an eye on things while I was gone, he said he was coming too. Got someone else to watch the cow. He's outside the door. Ain't left it since we got here."

"Jeanie?"

This time Grandma snorted and no one stopped her. "It's quiet, ain't it?"

"You got some good friends and family," the doctor said. He looked down at her, kindness couching his frustration at what she'd done.

Lana wondered if that was how her father would have looked at her if... An ache sprang up in her heart. She thought of Magdalena. And Betsy. And the child she'd just stolen everything from—a mother, a father, a life. And what she had taken from Cletus. It hurt too much. A deep agony filled the empty place the baby had been all these months. She closed her eyes.

"Got some good friends here, too," Grandma spouted. Lana opened her eyes. "Lots of food piling up at your house, neighbors cooking for your family. Some flowers, notes, and a few visitors stopping by."

"Visitors? I don't know anyone besides Ella, really." She didn't want to see anyone, either. Not now.

Not even Ella.

"Quite a few people saw you go down at that dinner you were at. They've been checking on you since. A Mr. Morgan's been here more than once."

Lana closed her eyes again. How awful everyone must think she was. Coming to the dinner, eating like a starved animal, then losing her baby. Poor Cletus! He'd never forgive her! Tears sprang up again. She didn't bother to hold them back; hot streams ran freely down her face. Grandma's face and shoulder pillowed against her, and Grandma's earthy smell pressed close as she bent near and held Lana, a cushion of needed comfort. Lana cried into Grandma's shoulder, cried at what she'd done, cried until she could cry no more.

Grandma held her even after she stopped. Her sniffles had nearly ended when she felt someone else nearby. Grandma moved away. Lana tried to hang on to her, hold her there, hide behind Grandma so she wouldn't have to come out and face what she'd done.

Grandma was gone. Lana opened her eyes. Long legs stood near the edge of the bed. She knew them; she knew them as well as her own.

"I'm sorry, Cletus."

The legs shuffled and repositioned. "When you coming home?"

Lana looked up. "You want me to come home?"

"She can't do anything." The doctor stepped alongside Cletus. Cletus flinched and looked away. He was on Magdalena's imaginary horse. Ignore the doctor, pretend he wasn't there. "Bed rest until I say she can get up, and no more children. Both of you need to accept that. No more of this careless stuff."

"I'll be there to help. So will Ella," Grandma

chimed in from behind the two men.

"That's good. She needs it. But even more she needs no more children. None." The doctor turned to the side and stared at Cletus. "You can do what you need to do without having children."

Cletus avoided the look, his eyes focused down toward Lana. He wasn't seeing her. It was what she couldn't give him that was there, what he had to do without having children.

"No," Lana cried. "No, it's okay." She reached for Cletus' hand, but he pulled back and tucked it behind him. "You wanted another boy…"

"And I got another mouth." Cletus saw her this time. His gaze was hard, his eyes cold. He turned, a slow pivot, and then he left the room.

"What? Another mouth? What does he mean?" Lana looked at Grandma, then at the doctor.

"The baby," Grandma replied. "Little girl. Guess that's what he means."

Chapter 24

James 1955

The sound wasn't quite like a truck, but it roared, then slowed. James looked up from the cow's pen, Harold coming to his side.

"What the heck is that?" Harold asked.

They watched the lane. It was council night. Pop wasn't expected home even though the fire decision had been overturned. Pop still kept an eye on things. He didn't want anyone discussing him, even when the meeting topics had more to do with animals, trees, or street upkeep.

"Think Pop bought a new truck?" James asked.

"Naw. He would have said something while we were at work today. Besides, it's not loud enough for a truck. At least not loud enough for one Pop would drive."

A car lurched into view, shot around the corner of the house with a burst of acceleration, then jerked to a stop. The engine faltered, came back to life, and the car yanked forward and stopped again.

"What the heck…" Harold muttered.

The engine roared, the car lurched, its nose swinging in a sharp arch that brought it to face the house, with the driver pitched to the side.

"Is that…"

"God help her…"

The car ground to a stop, flinging a mop of hair over the steering wheel. The engine sputtered, coughed, and finally died.

The driver's door opened, and the head of disarrayed hair appeared over its top. Magdalena grinned and patted the roof of the car. "I drive now."

"That's not driving," Harold said from beside James. "Are you done?"

"I'm parked, aren't I?"

Harold unlatched the gate and stepped through, holding it for James. James latched it behind them, and they walked to the car. Magdalena slammed the door and met them at the rear of the vehicle. She beamed. James hadn't seen such an enormous grin on her for far too long. He stared at his sister while Harold circled the car.

"A Fairlane," Harold said. James heard faint admiration in his brother's voice. "Where'd you get it?" Harold tapped on the metal, peered in its windows. James knew it wasn't Earl's. He was long gone. Magdalena had said she caught him with someone else, and he was no good anyway.

"It's Joe Deeter's. But it'll be mine, too, if I marry him."

Harold stood up from the tire he was bent over. His eyebrows hitched upwards.

"It's a beauty," James interjected. Harold would never insult Magdalena or say something mean to her face. But the look was enough, James knew Harold was frustrated, trying to scrimp enough money from his job with Pop to start his own family. James felt Harold's resentment, or maybe it was envy, at Magdalena's careless ease. Whatever it was, James saw it dampen her smile.

James pounded the car the way he'd seen men do at Pop's shop. "Yes, she really is a beauty." He grinned extra big.

"Joe lets you drive it without knowing how?" Harold's eyebrows pinched together.

"I know how! I'm just new at it!"

"Women don't usually drive, you know," Harold added.

"Some do. One of Mama's friends did." Magdalena's eyes sharpened. "Or at least she claimed she could. Even back then, I could have done better."

"Who was that?" James asked.

"No one important," Magdalena said.

"Someone from a long time ago," Harold answered. "I was pretty little, but I remember. She came with that fellow, then drove here on her own once. She hasn't been back since."

"That fellow was Jim." Magdalena stared at Harold.

Harold dropped back down below the car. "Yeah, Jim. I remember." James heard Harold thump something, then mutter.

James waited for Magdalena to say the name of this woman friend that never came back, the one that wasn't important. She ran her hand over the car, her lips pinched in a tight pucker.

"Will you take me for a ride?" James asked.

"You'll be killed," Harold yelled from somewhere below.

Magdalena guffawed. She sounded like a man. She was good at that. "No one will be killed." She opened the driver's door and pulled out a pack of cigarettes and a lighter.

The back door to the house opened, and Mama stepped out. Betsy and Carla followed in a trail. They approached the car as if Magdalena had parked a flying saucer in the driveway instead of a Fairlane. Magdalena grinned and lit a cigarette.

"You have a car," Carla said in a gush.

"Almost. It's Joe Deeter's. He's my new beau. If we get married, the car will be part mine."

"Married?" Carla asked.

Mama's head was the only one that didn't turn from the car to Magdalena. Mama studied the bright metal, one finger tapping a ping on the fender. Magdalena pulled a long draw on her cigarette and blew out a cloud of smoke.

"I'm happy for you." Betsy wrapped her fingers around Magdalena's arm. "You've always wanted to drive. I remember you saying so, years ago. When we were little."

Magdalena dropped the last of her cigarette into the dirt. She watched her own foot grind it out. When it was thoroughly flattened, she glanced up. At Mama.

Mama stepped to her two oldest daughters and wrapped an arm around each. "That was a long time ago, but it feels like yesterday sometimes. Magdalena, I want you to drive because that's what you want to do. I don't want you driving because of anything or anyone else."

"It's got nothing to do with Joe." Magdalena swiped some dust off the car. "Or anyone else."

"Who's teaching you?" Mama asked.

"No one!" Harold shouted from beneath the car.

"You didn't think Pop would, did you?" Magdalena's face tightened.

"That was a long time ago." Mama leaned her head Magdalena's way. "He probably doesn't even remember."

"Doesn't care, you mean." Magdalena kicked her smashed cigarette butt away.

"Will you stay and eat with us?" Mama asked, a thin gaiety in her tone. "Gail and Jackson are coming. They're working on the house they plan to move into after their wedding. I know Gail would love to see the car."

Magdalena looked up. "Sure, that would be good. Then I'll take you all for a ride."

James watched Mama and his sisters walk to the house. Harold popped up at the front end and rounded the car slowly, his fingers dragging along its metal.

"Who was Jim?" James asked. "And what the heck were Mama and Magdalena talking about?"

Harold drew a small circle with his finger on the hood. "Jim was an old friend of Mama's," he said. "And Jeanie was the other. An old friend who learned to drive." Harold finished his circle and looked up. "Pop didn't care much for Jim. And Magdalena still hates Jeanie."

Harold walked back to the cow's pen, kicking up dirt as he went. James watched small clouds of dust rise and fall around Harold's boots. He should go help Harold, maybe try to say something to ward off the frustration Harold had, watching his sisters marry while he struggled so, but he didn't. James opened the door of Joe's car and slipped inside. He pulled the door closed and gripped the steering wheel in his hands. This was a flying saucer. He was from one world, his family from another. Another world, another time. He truly was different.

Chapter 25

Lana 1938

"I'm hungry." Magdalena craned upward on her toes, stretching over the warm platter of rolls on the kitchen stove. She drew in a deep breath. "Let's eat. I'll put these on the table."

"Your father's not here yet." Lana frowned at her daughter as she stirred the gravy. "You know we don't set the food out until we hear his truck." Lana glanced out the kitchen window. The lane was empty. So was the whole of the outdoors. There was no sound of Cletus' truck. Dusk was fast approaching. He was late. Cletus was never late.

"Can I have just a little bite?" Harold stood in the doorway. At six, he was shooting up like a weed. Cletus trusted Harold with most of the chores, and the boy worked hard. He was wiry. He had good reason to be hungry.

"Hold on just a minute or two longer. In fact, run outside and listen for your father's truck. As soon as you hear him, hurry in and tell me. I'll put the food out right away."

Harold eyed the rolls. "Okay." He lolled his head the direction of the back door and dragged himself that way.

"The table's all set and ready, Mama!" Gail stuck

her head in the kitchen. "I did a perfect job. Just like always."

"Thank you." Lana tried to sound grateful. Gail was so little, but already she was too precise, too helpful, too old for her age. Gail's diligence made Lana more tense, more hurried to make sure everything was just right for her husband. "Please ask Betsy to help Alex wash off, and then go check on Carla."

Carla was their most recent child, the mouth to feed, the last one Cletus apparently ever intended to father. He hadn't touched Lana since Carla's birth, and she was two now, a beautiful child. Carla was graceful, thoughtful, a child with heart. She had Lana's auburn hair and quiet demeanor. Carla was Magdalena's opposite, something Lana thought might have appealed to Cletus, but it didn't. When he closed Lana out, he closed out the mouth to feed, too.

"Magdalena! Get your finger out of the potatoes!" Lana set aside the spoon she'd been stirring the gravy with and gave Magdalena's hand a smack.

"That didn't hurt." Magdalena grinned as she stuck a fingerful of potatoes into her mouth.

"Go help Harold watch for your father."

"I say we eat without him."

Without him. Two words. They struck like a slap. *Without him.* They resounded in Lana's mind, volleying back and forth, creating an echo that reverberated to her heart and through her soul. Without Cletus. Lana dropped the gravy spoon. It clattered to the floor, a splatter of warm gravy stinging her ankles. That's what she was even when he was here. That's what she never wanted to be, not her and not her daughters. But that's what she was, now, this evening. What if he didn't...

What if something had happened… She shook the thoughts away and looked at Magdalena. "Go on. And stop disrespecting your pop that way."

Magdalena tossed her light curls and sashayed out the door. Lana heard the back door slam after a moment. *Without him. Without him.* She didn't like the uneasiness that came with her daughter's careless remark. Lana picked up the spoon and wiped it off. Nothing had happened to Cletus. He wouldn't just go. He had two sons here. He would be home soon, just like he always was.

"Mama, Carla's hungry, too. Can I give her something to eat?" Gail had Carla around the stomach, hugging her like a bag of flour.

"Oh, I guess. Just a little. You know your pop insists we all eat when he does."

Gail lugged Carla to the table. Lana could hear her baby-talking to the youngest, settling her into a chair. Carla wouldn't fight her. She was a compliant girl, thoughtful even at two. Gail came back into the kitchen. She handed Lana a bowl, and Lana filled it with a small portion for Carla. Gail toted the single bowl to the other room. Another slap. A reminder Cletus wasn't there.

He wouldn't… Surely he wouldn't go… Two years he'd stayed away from her, saying nothing, never watching her undress. There'd been no more small talk before bed, either. His silence said what his mouth didn't. It was her fault. He'd been wrong to ask for her. She'd had too many girls. Four girls. Four reasons that kept him away from her, left her without him.

Without him.

Gail cooed and giggled with Carla in the other room, playing as she fed her little sister, barely older herself. Lana moved to the kitchen doorway and watched. Each child was a gift, a unique personality, every single one of them learning to live around their father. The back door opened. She jumped and listened. It slammed closed.

"Mama, he's not coming. Can we please eat?" Harold dragged himself into the room. His legs were bent at the knees, his arms dangling like a scarecrow, his shoulders stooped. At any other time Lana would have smiled, maybe laughed at the way he let his jaw hang slack to prove he was near death. She wanted to laugh, but she couldn't. *He's not coming* was all she could hear.

"He is too coming." She sounded harsh, and she bit her lip. Harold straightened and frowned.

"I don't hear him." Harold nodded in the direction of the road. "And he's never this late."

"I mean eventually. He'll come eventually." Lana glanced around the room, all eyes were on her. "Okay, get Alex and Betsy. Call Magdalena in. We'll go ahead and eat."

"Yippee!" Harold revived. He raced outside.

"Want help getting the food on the table?" Gail asked, a spoonful of food midair in front of Carla's open mouth.

"No, you go ahead and feed your sister. I can get it." If she did it alone, it would take longer. Buy more time for Cletus to come. She listened hard, imagining the sound of a distant engine as she went back and forth, one dish at a time, hoping, praying, listening. Of course he would come. Surely he'd had problems at work. He'd explain when he got here. She'd have his plate filled and ready. And then someday, maybe even tonight, he'd be with her again instead of without her. It would all be fine, surely.

****

The truck finally came. Lana heard it from the dark of their bedroom. The night had been long. Without him. Without her children's Pop. She'd lain through each hour, counting each minute, waiting and listening. The rumble was his, unmistakable although more subdued than usual, like he and the truck were both tired, not in a hurry for a change. It eased around the house and stopped where it always did. The hum of the engine cut, and then there was silence. Interminable silence that made her wonder if she'd imagined the truck. Maybe it hadn't been there at all.

The silence became a living thing, thick and palpable. It filled her ears and blocked all sound. She fought it, tried to hear through it, listened for even the tiniest noise. At last there was something. The back door creaked open, then closed, without a slam. Footsteps shuffled through the house, one at a time, slow, soft, and loose.

The door to their bedroom eased open. Slightly at first, then wider. It was him, home to be with her. She smelled the burnt metal that was so much a part of him. As he stripped in the darkness, the odor grew stronger. More burnt metal.

And then something else. Something sweeter. Another odor that told her he'd been somewhere different. Somewhere without her. Somewhere not alone.

Chapter 26

Lana 1939

"Mrs. Paine." Mr. Morgan bowed, tipping his hat, a black cowboy hat. The sun caught his hair and it shone, a blue sheen off hair as dark as his hat. She'd forgotten that color and the depth of his eyes.

"I think you can call me Lana," she said. She held the back door close to her side, looking out at him. "For all of your kindness, especially when Carla was born. It…it was a difficult time, but the things you brought by now and then—my children still talk about them."

"Happy to help. I was the oldest of five, and I know how hard my own mother worked." His voice was like a gentle song, soothing and calm. She didn't want to hear it, though. It grated across the deadness of her heart, trying to make it bleed again in the places she'd forced it to stop. The kindness of his demeanor, the warm beckoning in his eyes, drew up hidden tears that if allowed to spill over would be tainted with red. She just wanted to be alone. He set the hat back on his head.

Lana stared at him. His countenance was full of life, while she felt solid where she used to hurt. She looked away, beyond him, into the drive behind her house. His car was parked there, with someone sitting inside. She looked back at him. "I'm sorry, you've someone with you." Whoever was there was either small or hunched in the seat. "You should both come in, I'm sorry…my manners…"

Mr. Morgan tipped his hat back and scratched his head. A lock of black hair fell down over his forehead. He glanced at his car, then at Lana. "So, I take it you don't know who that is in my car."

Lana shook her head, stared again at the hump in the passenger's seat.

Mr. Morgan squinted and shielded his eyes as he looked back at the car. Then he dropped his hand and turned back to her. "Guess maybe she doesn't want you to know who she is."

Lana was too tired for puzzles, too broken to care. Talking to Mr. Morgan, trying to guess who that was, took more of her than she had. "I really can't imagine who would be that small, except a child…" She felt the color drain from her face. She looked again at the car, shielding her eyes from the sun. The tiny bump had fuzzy hair. "Well, I'll be!" Lana gathered her skirts and started toward the car.

Mr. Morgan laid his fingers on her arm, his touch was light, but it held her there. She looked down at his hand, his tan fingers, then up into his face. She drew her arm close to her side while she still looked at him, and stepped back.

"She wasn't in school. I assume she should have been," he said, dropping his hand.

Lana knew he was talking about Magdalena. Betsy would never miss school; she would be mortified.

"Where was she?" Lana asked. It felt like his fingers were still on her arm. She ran her hand over the spot, rubbed until she could feel her own heat. "What was she doing?"

Mr. Morgan's brows pinched together beneath the hat. He looked to the side, then glanced at Lana again. "Just talking. That's what she told me."

"Just talking? To who?"

"You know the Olson family?"

Lana shook her head. She knew almost no one. Cletus knew everyone, but he never talked about them, nor did they ever go visiting.

"Well, they don't do any harm, but they're not...well, let's say they're not ambitious. She was talking to Wayne Olson. He's the oldest boy. I'd say he's around sixteen and probably hasn't been in school since fifth grade."

"No..." Lana whispered. "No..." What would a nine-year-old girl have to say to a sixteen-year-old boy? Lana was too hurt to hear her own scream inside, but she heard her daughter's—it rose from each of their hearts and echoed within the other's. "Thank you," she whispered. She glanced at Mr. Morgan. "Thank you for helping my daughter. And me."

Lana looked to the car where Magdalena was hiding. The top half of her face peeked above the dashboard, a rim of curly hair capping it like rays of a rising sun. She understood this daughter so well. She loved Magdalena passionately, fiercely, like a mother bear.

Lana stepped toward the car, one or two steps. Then she quickened her pace until she ran. She ran to Magdalena's door and yanked it open. Her daughter's eyes were enormous, highlighted and lined with an artificial blue as she looked up into Lana's face. Lana nearly fell into the car. She swooped Magdalena into her arms, the thin girl clamped in her grasp. Lana hugged her, drew her out of the seat, and held her tight.

Magdalena's small arms slid upward and wrapped around Lana's neck. Lana buried her face in her daughter's hair. "Magdalena." She held her, Magdalena's feet dangling above the ground. Lana carried her to the house, past Mr. Morgan's dark eyes that said he understood. "Thank you," she mouthed. He closed the back door behind her. Before she and Magdalena reached their front room she heard his car start. She sat on the sofa and nestled her daughter on her lap as his engine purred down the drive and then vanished as he drove away. Her tears trickled into Magdalena's hair, molten tears of melting stone.

Magdalena clung to Lana as Lana cried. How long had these tears been solidified in her? Since she was nine like her daughter? Maybe longer? Holding Magdalena was like holding herself in her arms, two girls trying to escape the terror of being unwanted. Not just unwanted, but also discarded.

Magdalena slipped her arms from around Lana's neck and coiled them at her stomach, pinning them there with knees she drew up also. "I have something, Mama."

Lana leaned her face around her daughter's head and watched one thin arm come out, nine-year-old fingers opening like a bloom.

"It's for you."

Lana looked down at Magdalena's open fist, a small pot of rouge on her palm.

"Magdalena, where… Why…"

"It's for you, Mama. You have to."

Lana looked at the rouge. "Why, Magdalena? Why

do I have to?"

"It makes men notice you more."

Without him. It cut like a knife. The wound was too deep and festered to withstand another blow. And Magdalena, she was only nine… The blue highlighting her eyes. How could she know this or understand?

Lana thought of Jeanie and the colorful accents on her face. She remembered the last time she'd seen Jeanie. The truck, her pride, Cletus' quiet enthrallment with Jeanie's accomplishment. Jeanie'd said she would stay with them that night. She'd entertained them throughout the meal, she'd stayed at the table while Lana cleaned up, her melodic voice singing out her stories, even ones they'd heard before, while Magdalena competed with her, telling taller tales, drowning out Jeanie until Cletus told Magdalena to pipe down and go upstairs. Jeanie continued while Lana put the children to bed, her voice carrying up the steps where Magdalena stood listening. Then it stopped. When Lana came downstairs, Cletus was alone in the living room, settled back in his chair. *She's gone,* he'd said, and that was all. Jeanie'd married soon after that. Not Jim, but another local boy. That's all Grandma had said in her letter.

"This isn't going to help. You know it won't."

Magdalena put the rouge in Lana's hand. "I'll get more for you. I know where."

Chapter 27

James 1957

James shivered in the cool dark. Dawn was approaching. The town was quiet, no one stirring except the milkman, his horse and wagon making deliveries of fresh milk before anyone was ready for breakfast. James tucked farther back into the bushes when the old wagon's creaking drew near. He could hear bottles clink together, and tired bursts of breath from the old horse's nostrils. Mr. Mullen cooed to keep his mare moving, the same horse he'd had forever, stubbornly refusing to retire the ancient beast and deliver milk from a truck. They stopped. The wagon groaned as Mr. Mullen stepped down to deliver a bottle. James waited, wishing Mr. Mullen would hurry and move on. James strained for the sound of Joe's car, praying he wouldn't hear it until Mr. Mullen was gone.

The wagon creaked again, and after a moment Mr. Mullen snapped the reins. "Get along." The horse snorted as if it had fallen asleep, its hooves making a slow start and then padding in the soft dirt, one hoof after the other. They came nearer, two houses away. Mr. Mullen's soft, "Whoa," seemed unnecessary; his horse had already stalled and was probably asleep again.

James wished he and Magdalena had chosen a

different spot to meet. He'd picked this neighborhood so Pop wouldn't discover them, far off the route he drove into town when he opened his shop. Pop would be furious this morning when Harold told him James wasn't coming with them, that he had promised to help clean the churchyard instead. It was a lie, but Pop would never ask Pastor Gordon about it. Pop never spoke to any of the churchmen unless they were customers, and most of them weren't.

The horse snorted awake again. Mr. Mullen turned the mare around, and his wagon moved away, stopping farther down the street.

"Morning," James heard Mr. Mullen say. "You're up and out kind of early, aren't you?"

"Business," someone answered. It sounded like Magdalena. James stretched up from the bushes. "Gotta keep those houses clean." A fuzzy head of hair on a tall slender body walked his way.

"You're a hard worker," Mr. Mullen said as he lugged two jugs of milk to a house. Magdalena slowed, she was coming James' direction, but she was stalling. James shrank back into the bushes. He snapped a twig off a branch and broke it in two. Why was she on foot?

When Mr. Mullen moved on farther down the street, James could hear Magdalena's footsteps. She was hurrying now. Her lanky form appeared above him.

"Where's Joe's car?"

"We broke up."

"What? Why? Couldn't you have broken up tomorrow? What are we going to do now?" James was on his feet. His voice ranged out of control. Magdalena put her hands on his shoulders and forced him back into the bushes.

"Shhhh. You're asking too many questions and someone will hear you."

"Does it matter? We can't go now anyway, without Joe's car!" He dropped to the ground. He snapped off another twig and cracked it in two.

"I'll get you there," Magdalena said above him.

"How? It's almost too late. Dang! Can you go back and make up with Joe? Just for a day?"

Magdalena didn't answer. She stood above him, looking one way and then the other. He snapped the half twigs into quarters. Who knew when another scout for the Lakeland baseball league would be this close again? Even though James was too old to cry, he still felt like it. He might be a little too young to make a major team, but he'd practiced so hard, hoped for so long, and he planned to lie about his age if he had to. He was ready, at least he thought he was. Andy had told him about the baseball scout two towns over, looking for fresh ball players. Ever since James found out, it was all he could think about. All he wanted.

"Hold on. Don't get so excited. I've been thinking about this all the way over."

"Would Joe let you use the car anyway? Just for the day?"

Magdalena snorted. "Forget Joe. I can come up with another idea."

"I can't imagine what it would be. No one's up this early, except maybe Pop. And he's the last person that would give me a ride to try out."

"Get up!" Magdalena snapped. Her hand grabbed the shoulder of his jacket and yanked him to his feet. "Why didn't I think of that? Come on."

"Think of what? Pop? Have you lost your mind?"

James jerked out of her clutch and straightened his jacket. "I'll just walk over to Pop's shop and tell him I'm working today after all. I'll make up something about Pastor Gordon catching a cold or something."

"I haven't lost my mind, and no, not Pop, but close. And I don't want you lying any more, little brother. It's not good for you." Magdalena grabbed his upper arm and hauled him in the direction of downtown, of Pop's shop.

James stumbled along with her. "What do you mean, 'close'?"

"Close to Pop. We'll ask Mr. Morgan to take you. I mean, us."

James stopped. "Mr. Morgan?"

"He's up. I saw lights in his restaurant. Probably got his milk before anyone else. He'll do this for you. I know he will."

"He can't." James refused to budge. Magdalena looked back at him. "He's too busy." And Ida probably wouldn't stand for it. James recalled the way she'd looked at him the day Mr. Morgan served him the sundae.

"Nonsense." Magdalena grabbed his arm again. "Come on." She jerked James her way, and he stumbled after her, his glove tucked under his arm.

When they reached the main section of downtown, James saw that Magdalena was right. The only glow on the street came from Mr. Morgan's restaurant. Not from lights in the front, where people would sit and have coffee and breakfast, but from the back where the work was being done. James cupped his face in his hands and peered through the front window. No one was in sight. Might be better that way. It would be easier and safer to just go on to Pop's and work the day. Magdalena could go clean a house or get on the good side of Joe so she could have use of his car again.

Magdalena marched to the door and rapped on it with her knuckles.

"You can't do that!" James grabbed her wrist.

"How else am I going to get his attention?" Magdalena yanked her arm free and rapped again. A shadow filled the back doorway to the kitchen. When it moved, James recognized the squareish silhouette as Mr. Morgan's. Magdalena waved and called. He laid down a towel and walked to the door and unlocked it.

James felt himself redden. He thanked God it was still dark. He'd never understand how Magdalena could be so bold. Mr. Morgan eyed James' sister as the door came open.

"Morning, Glen. I mean Mr. Morgan. Mind if we come in?"

Mr. Morgan glanced behind Magdalena, then to the side. His gaze lit on James. Even in the dim light James could see Mr. Morgan's bafflement soften. Then he frowned. "You two all right?" He looked back at Magdalena.

"Sort of," she said. "My brother could use a little help."

Mr. Morgan stepped aside. He swung his arm into the restaurant, and Magdalena followed him. She motioned to James. He followed too, lagging behind.

Mr. Morgan closed and locked the door behind them. "What can I help you with?" He glanced from Magdalena to James.

"There's a scout for the Lakewood baseball team over in Marshall today. James was planning to go…"

Magdalena kept talking, explaining James' plans, his and Harold's plot to fool Pop, her inability to get a car to take him, but Mr. Morgan wasn't listening. His eyes were on the glove tucked under James' arm. Magdalena finished. She'd skipped the part about breaking up with Joe, her husband of barely more than a year.

"Would you be able to take him?" Magdalena finished.

Mr. Morgan looked at James' sister.

"I'll stay and help here at the restaurant," she offered. James was surprised. What did Magdalena know about cooking or restaurants? To his further surprise, Mr. Morgan nodded.

"I'll take him," Mr. Morgan said. He turned, walked to the back of the restaurant, and disappeared through the lighted doorway. There were voices back there, two men and a woman. James prayed the woman wasn't Ida.

"You know what to do in a restaurant?" James whispered to his sister. He expected Ida would nix the whole plan, still baffled why Mr. Morgan would trust Magdalena to work for him to begin with.

Magdalena shrugged. "I know things."

The voices were low, and terse. Mr. Morgan appeared in the doorway again. He came to where James and Magdalena stood.

"Ida's in the back. She can show you what needs done." Then he looked at James. "Let's go. My car's at the house. We can walk there and get it."

"Do good, little brother." Magdalena squeezed his shoulder. Then she nodded at Mr. Morgan and headed to the back. Her voice sounded jovial and confident as she disappeared into the kitchen. James couldn't hear Ida, only Magdalena. She was bright and cheery. At least she pretended to be. Ida, no matter how stern, didn't have a chance.

Mr. Morgan unlocked the front door and they stepped onto the sidewalk. James watched him relock it from the outside. As they turned and headed down the walk, something caught his eye in the restaurant. The kitchen doorway dimmed. A silhouette much shorter and fuller than Magdalena filled it, blocking the kitchen light. Ida, he thought. He prayed Magdalena would behave herself and not upset her more than she apparently already was.

"I'm honored you asked me to do this," Mr. Morgan said as they moved quickly beyond his restaurant's front window, Ida left behind. He didn't know if Mr. Morgan saw her or not. Surely he at least felt her. James sure could.

Chapter 28

James 1957

Mr. Morgan stood near the fence. He'd been there all day, never moving to the scanty bleachers to join the other spectators the whole time James played. James glanced beyond him, at the seating arranged around the infield. Mama should be there watching him, but she wasn't. He hadn't even told her about the tryouts. If Pop found out, he'd be furious, and Pop would include her in his attacks on James, yell at her and blame her for *that boy*. Just like he always did.

James tried not to look at Mr. Morgan, but he did, he couldn't stop himself. Mr. Morgan was looking back, his eyes on James, saying the things Mama would have said if she'd been there, maybe even more. James looked away. There were other things in Mr. Morgan's eyes, things a father should say, things Pop never had. He stretched his hands around two bats together and took a practice swing. He could feel the weight, just like Mr. Morgan had shown him years ago. He swung again, waiting for his turn at bat.

Choke up when you use a big bat. James heard the old advice in his mind. It came back, and he almost shouted it at the batter as he watched him swing and miss a fast pitch. James was much stronger now. What he lacked in height, he made up for in strength. He swung the two bats again, even harder, trying to look as old as real ball players were. He rarely choked up on a bat anymore, but that advice had saved him. It gave him strength on the inside where he needed it the most. James glanced at the bleachers, where only strangers sat. He missed Mama's smile and her encouragement. He missed hearing her say his name the right way.

The boy at bat swung and missed again. He whacked the dirt with the end of the bat and stalked to the dugout.

"Batter up!"

James tossed the smaller of the two bats back into the dugout and stepped to the plate. He held the bat high in the air with one hand while he dug his toes into the dirt, positioning himself for the hit that mattered. Lots of fantastic players were here; the competition was stiff. James wasn't the best player trying out, but he was good, good enough to stand a fair chance of being selected if this time at bat went well.

Before he settled, before he lowered the bat and gripped it with both hands, he glanced at Mr. Morgan. He was still there, his fingers laced through the fencing just like they'd been years ago. Mr. Morgan nodded when their eyes connected. *It should have been Pop standing there.* Mr. Morgan's kindness didn't make up for Pop's hurt. It made it worse, if anything, made it more poignant, and made James angry he'd been born to a father that didn't care.

James stared at the pitcher. He twisted the bat in his hands and planted his feet. This pitcher was new. There was a different one each time James came to bat. That kept him from learning one pitcher's style, becoming familiar with how they stood, how their faces changed right before they wound up and let go. This one was tall and lean, just like Pop. He was freckled and fair-skinned. His face was set like a stone, like this was a private war between him and James.

There was no warning nod, no shift in position to let James know the pitch was coming. Suddenly it was there, the pitcher's motion so instantaneous James hadn't even seen him move.

"Strike one!" The umpire roared behind him as the ball smacked the catcher's glove. James stared at the umpire. It wasn't the umpire's fault, but James had to stare at something while the strike registered. The ball whisked past him as the catcher returned it to the pitcher. The catcher pounded his mitt with a fist and walked in a circle before squatting to the ground behind the plate again.

James stepped backwards out of the batter's box. He watched the pitcher rub the ball into his glove and pace off a few steps around the mound. James took a practice swing. He wouldn't let that happen again.

He stepped back to the plate. The pitcher was in place, ball and glove together at shoulder height. He stared as James steadied himself, keeping the bat high in one hand. James dug his toes deeper into the dirt. He'd hit the ball this time. He'd be ready.

James glanced at the pitcher before he settled into the batter's box. His feet were in place, but he kept the bat high. He needed a moment, and he used his power as the batter to hold the pitcher at bay. He lowered the bat and gripped it with both hands, his eye on the pitcher, watching for the clues he'd missed before. Somewhere there would be a wince, a blink, a shift of weight from one foot to the other.

"Strike two!"

A small cloud of dust burst from the catcher's mitt as the ball slapped like a gunshot. James stared down at the mitt and the dust. So quick, so fast. He hadn't even swung, there'd been no opportunity. He wheeled away from the batter's box, walked a few feet back, cracking the sides of his shoes with the bat with each step. He shook his head. This couldn't happen. He couldn't let it. His fielding and pitching had been perfect all day. If he batted poorly, they wouldn't choose him. He could bat. He would.

He pivoted back toward the plate. He needed Mama's voice right now, her pleasant soprano to shout something encouraging. Even if she just said his name, that would be enough. The stands were quiet. No one was there for him, or a particular team. It was every man for himself today. He was alone.

"Move off the plate a little."

James looked up. Mr. Morgan had moved. He was no longer near the dugout, he was behind the umpire now, just off to the side.

"Step back. Get your bearings."

James felt like a little boy again. Like he did the day he wanted to tell Mr. Morgan to leave him alone. He was the little boy who was hurt and disappointed his pop wasn't there.

He stepped to the plate and dug his toes in the same place he had before. He wasn't crowding the plate. Mr. Morgan was wrong. Where he stood wasn't the problem, the pitcher was the problem. The guy was sneaky and quick. He was just like Pop, probably exactly like Pop played. James squared himself at the plate, the same place, the place that suited him. He gripped the bat, squeezing it over and over, letting it quiver above him. He was ready, he was poised, all his strength gathered in his arms and legs.

The pitcher flinched. He nodded. James saw it. He hadn't seen it before. He swung. The ball hit the catcher's mitt, and the umpire called him out as the bat cycled around. No one cheered. No one booed. It didn't matter to anyone except him. James drew in a deep breath and glanced at the scout. There were two of them. They sat at a small table behind the fence where they could see home plate and the infield well. One was writing something while the other looked over the man's shoulder. He was talking low, behind his hand, as the other one wrote.

James wanted to throw the bat. But he hoisted it to his shoulder instead, and walked to the dugout. He nodded as he passed the young man coming up to bat. There was fear in the next batter's eyes. He was right to be afraid. This was an impossible pitcher to hit off of.

Mr. Morgan talked about the day as they drove back home. He analyzed what he'd seen, reiterated plays James already knew about since he'd played them, for Pete's sake, but Mr. Morgan added a different perspective. James let him ramble, glad at least that Mr. Morgan wasn't being critical. But still James wished he'd be quiet. James had missed a day's work for nothing, lied to his pop, jeopardized Mama, compromised his siblings, and for what? For nothing. The scouts had thanked him for coming, but they'd thanked all the players. They said they'd get back with each one who'd tried out, but James knew he had failed.

"You see where the pitcher came from?" Mr. Morgan asked.

James shook his head. Mr. Morgan's monologue was beginning to annoy him even more. He hated himself for feeling that way.

"Came with the scouts."

James perked up. He looked Mr. Morgan's direction.

"He wasn't trying out, he was probably a pro, or semi pro. He was there to bring out the best."

"Or worst." James looked back at the road. If he couldn't hit off a real pitcher he'd never be picked up for a team.

"Part of your best showed," Mr. Morgan continued. They were nearly home. James was glad. He wanted to be alone. He was glad only Harold and Magdalena knew where he'd been all day. He didn't want to talk about baseball, explain how badly it had turned out. "You carried yourself well. You've got your mama's dignity."

James glanced at Mr. Morgan. Dignity didn't make a professional player. Neither did heart. He was glad he had those parts of Mama, but they weren't the same as long, lanky legs, and arms as quick as snakes. Like that pitcher. Like Pop. Pop was right, baseball wasn't in his blood.

Mr. Morgan glanced back at him. They stared at each other for a moment before Mr. Morgan returned his gaze to the road, a small frown furrowing his brow. "You're not like your pop."

"Guess that's pretty obvious," James said. He tossed his glove up and down in his lap. It was still dusty with Marshall dirt.

Mr. Morgan glanced over at the glove, looked up at James, and then back to the road. Mr. Morgan wasn't like Pop either. He was Pop's opposite, from his height, to his dark hair and skin, to his being there. Being at the game and giving James advice.

"Why'd you tell me to step back off the plate?" James asked. "It's not like I have long arms and can reach very far. I have to be right on it. I do better that way."

Mr. Morgan pulled the car in front of the church James was supposed to have worked at all day. He shut off the engine and twisted in his seat.

"Perspective," he said. "Sometimes you're too close to something to see what it really is." Mr. Morgan's gaze dissected James' face, his features, everything there was that made him James. James felt naked. Mr. Morgan glanced past James, then looked out the window behind him. "Let's get this churchyard cleaned so your pop doesn't think you lied. You walked off that diamond with dignity today after you missed that last pitch. That's what real men and players are made of. That's what your mama has, too. And she would clean this churchyard."

Mr. Morgan looked at him again, indecipherable thoughts playing behind his eyes, and then he climbed out of the car. James followed. He didn't ask what Mr. Morgan meant. He trailed him to the shed where the church kept some of its yard tools. He'd wait. He'd let time and distance give him perspective. Then maybe he'd have a better view, and next time he'd whack that ball.

Chapter 29

Lana 1940

Claire. The name spoke of simplicity, of calm, of unassuming beauty. It was what Jim wanted.

Lana stopped reading and laid Grandma's letter in her lap. She gazed around the room at her life, at the room her family gathered together in most often. The one where they ate. Its floors were scrubbed clean, the chairs tight against the table, the fabric of her wedding dress still hanging in the windows as curtains. Mementoes of Cletus, his war medals, pictures, items that made him significant, hung along the walls, just as she'd placed them ages ago.

She looked back at the letter. Claire. With a name like that, what else could she be? What else, except what Jim wanted?

"Remember Jim?" Lana realized Magdalena was standing not far away. Magdalena tilted her head to one side, the young princess who'd once galloped around Jim hoping he'd snatch her up and ride away with her. She was four years older now. Lana couldn't imagine this tall girl slapping her hip and trotting around anymore.

Magdalena nodded. Her eyes flickered as she looked at the letter in Lana's lap. "Is he coming?" Magdalena's voice was bright.

"He's getting married." Lana made the news sound happy. Magdalena was nearing the age of looking for a real prince, someday a real husband. "Isn't that wonderful?"

Magdalena looked thoughtful, her previous six-year-old infatuation flitting behind the gaze of a girl on the verge of blossoming into a young woman.

"Not Jeanie, is it?" Magdalena frowned.

Lana shook her head. "Jeanie married someone else. Guess I never told you." That much she and Magdalena...and apparently even Jim...agreed on. Thank God it wasn't Jeanie.

"Poor fellow, whoever she married." Magdalena turned, then stopped and looked back. "He liked you, Mama. Jim did. And that was good." Then she left, went outdoors, probably on one of the long walks she'd begun to take the past year.

Lana stepped to the window to watch her tall, thin daughter's back. Magdalena let herself through the cow's gate, then struck out across the pasture. Magdalena was quiet most days now, more pensive than she used to be. Quiet until her father came home in the evening. Then she changed, she saved all her energy for him. Spunk, Ella called it. Sass, Cletus called it. Starvation—Lana knew what it really was.

Magdalena disappeared over a small rise. Lana loved the pasture. Maybe Magdalena was learning to love it too. It was soothing, the wind whispering through the flowers as they bowed and nodded along the way. *What way?* She followed her daughter with her thoughts, wanting to guide her, if only she knew the way herself.

Little containers of cosmetics kept appearing

amongst Lana's clothing, a nearly empty bottle of perfume, a ribbon or two. She knew Magdalena was leaving them for her, most of them used or at least opened. Lana dared not think how Magdalena was coming by them. She had enough stashed away now to change her appearance. She had powder for her face, rouge for her cheeks, lipstick for her mouth, liners and colors for her eyes. With those and the ribbons and perfumes that also appeared, she could be pretty. Pretty enough for Cletus? Would pretty really matter?

"One more son," Lana said aloud. "If Cletus would be with me again and I could have a boy, just one more, then maybe…"

Lana looked down again at Grandma's letter. Claire.

Don't know if she's pretty. Lana continued to read Grandma's scrawl from the letter. *Don't matter no how, but I suppose you're wondering. No prettier than you. I know I never said that before and I probably shouldn't now. But you always were pretty. Just not pretty enough for you to believe it until you found out how beautiful you were on the inside.*

The rest of what Grandma said blurred. How could there be beauty in ashes? Lana leaned against the wall and let the tears stream down her face.

Chapter 30

Lana 1940

Lana gazed in the mirror. The rouge was barely visible, the powder almost too faint. She tilted her head one way and then the other to be sure it looked natural. After all, it was Cletus she was going to see. If the colors merely accented what was already there without being too obvious, he might be intrigued. But if they were too much, he'd be furious, most likely shame her in front of his workers. She wanted to look natural, but pretty, just enough to surprise him, make him glad she brought him a lunch.

She'd never gone to town this way before, never taken her husband a lunch. This one was full of his favorites, the house still smelling like lemon from the cake she'd baked. She relaxed her face and stepped from the washroom to the dining area. Betsy and Magdalena were putting out plates, getting ready to serve their younger brothers and sisters.

"You girls know what to do." Lana glanced at the table. "I won't be long. And Ella's right down…"

"Yes, Mama," Betsy said. "We know what to do. You go on and have a good time."

Lana turned to Magdalena. Her daughter tipped her head and studied Lana's cheeks and eyes. "You look good." A smile crept across her daughter's face.

"I won't be long." Lana picked up the pail she'd put Cletus' lunch in and hurried out the door. "Lord, please make this go well, for that girl in there's sake, the rest of their sakes, and also for mine."

At the beginning of the main street of businesses, Lana turned left and traveled a block until she came to the street Cletus' shop was on. It was halfway down on the right, a large, tall building that gaped open at the front like an inferno, the gateway to the netherworld, a black hole with furnaces inside. She'd seen it only twice, but she'd never told Cletus what it reminded her of. Jeanie would have, Jeanie would have and laughed, but Lana never could.

She slowed as she drew nearer. The sound of metal clanging against metal rang from inside, and burnt fumes hung around the entryway like a cloud. She held her breath, her heart beating louder than the bang of the metal. She crept to the edge of the door and peered into the inferno.

Broken pieces of iron lay strewn just inside the entryway, misshapen and grotesque as if they'd been assaulted. Others were welded together, sharp angles that looked more painful than useful. A curse came from within. She bit her lip and clutched the pail to her stomach.

She stared at the dark, avoiding the tiny dots of fire Cletus had warned about when he rubbed his eyes at night. A few shadows moved about the fiery glows, others standing off to the sides. She cupped one hand above her eyes and searched for the tallest form, the one that towered above the rest, the boss, the one they all obeyed, even her.

"Can I help you?" a burly voice called from inside.

She looked the direction of the voice. It coughed. "You need something?"

It wasn't Cletus. The sounds inside the shop waned. Surely Cletus would recognize her and come out. She heard footsteps, metal clattering to the ground, someone shuffling her way. She smiled and grasped the pail with two hands.

"You need something, lady?" The burly voice stepped into the sunlight. The man was filthy, sweaty, and smelled like Cletus.

"I...I was looking for my husband." She stepped back when the man frowned. "Cletus. Can you tell him I'm here?"

The man ducked his head and coughed, burying the rasping hack in his elbow. He straightened, rubbed his stubbled face with a hand, and looked around.

"He ain't here. Ought to be back later. I'll tell him you came." He turned and headed back into the blackness.

"Where is he?" She raised the pail. "I brought his lunch."

The man's eyes grew wide, and his watery irises, much like Cletus', looked from the pail to Lana's face. "Guess he wasn't expectin' that."

"That's right." Another man stepped into the light, just as filthy as the first. "He done took off. For lunch. You're too late. Guess you should take it back home. I imagine he'll be sorry he missed you."

"We'll tell him you was here," the burly man said. He nodded, the other nodded, and they backed into the gaping black hole. "Gotta get back to work."

The pail felt obvious, and her face flushed hot. She backed away and hurried on down the street beyond the shop's gaping front. The sounds of Cletus' workers resumed as she passed. They must think her foolish, trying to surprise him. She stopped a building away and leaned against the wall. She had been foolish, foolish to come and foolish to go this direction instead of back the way she'd come from. She couldn't go past the shop door again. She'd go on and turn down the main street and head back home from there.

Lana's humiliation stayed with her as she brushed past stores and businesses along the main street. Clutching the pail with Cletus' lunch, she crossed to the side of the street farthest from those his shop backed against, her face down, her embarrassment carrying her in a blind rush. She moved quickly, past the movie theatre, a barber shop, an empty store, and then a tavern. She hurried faster, swinging wide of the tavern's doors as they flung open. Two people spilled out, colliding with her, their chatter stopping as she stumbled aside.

"Pardon me." Lana didn't look up. She regained her footing and started forward—until the odor caught her. Sweat mixed with fire, burnt metal on skin, perfume making it sickening—sickening and familiar. She stopped and looked back. The woman, the one she'd smelled that night on her husband, the night Lana had truly become *without him,* was brushing herself off, Cletus at her side.

The pail clattered to the boards at Lana's feet.

"What are you doing here?" Cletus' voice was pinched, and he frowned.

"Who's that?" The woman beside him made disgruntled noises, tightened her posture, and looked Lana's way.

Lana bent, praying this was nothing more than a horrible dream, and retrieved the pail. "I brought you lunch." The pail dangled from her fingers, the smell of lemon overpowered by burnt metal and cheap perfume.

"It's past lunch."

"I guess I'll go." The woman touched Cletus's arm while her eyes stayed on Lana. Lana listened to her boots clatter down the boardwalk, the scent of perfume going with her.

"I gotta get back to work. You shouldn't have come."

The pail dangled from Lana's fingers, the lemon scent stronger now, wafting upward.

"Cletus…"

"A man has needs." Cletus took the pail from her fingers, held it up between them, then stepped onto the street, heading for his shop.

"Cletus!" It came out a scream. Lana couldn't stop herself; she screamed at the back she could no longer decipher through her tears. She stumbled off the boarded walkway and caught him by the arm. Pain erupted inside her, flames exploded from deep within. She yanked the pail from him with one hand while her other rounded through the air, blindly, tears making her target vague as it shot upward until it collided with his face. The slap resounded throughout the street as his head rocked to the side.

He righted himself, a hand over his cheek. He stared in disbelief. For the first time his eyes spoke to her. So did his face. He hated her. He turned and stalked away.

Her palm stung with the feel of her husband's flesh. Her hand trembled as she watched his back. She faltered backward, up onto the walkway, and fumbled the direction she'd been heading. Lana moved fast, past one building, then another, one hand groping along the buildings' rough surfaces. She hit the edge of the third and clung to its wall as she stumbled around its corner, doubled forward, and spilled vomit onto the ground.

That smell in her memory overpowered the putrid smell at her feet, the perfume mingled with fire that had invaded her bed. Lana bent farther over and retched again. Breakfast, hope, the strength to keep doing what she was supposed to do—it all lay at her feet. She rubbed her face and cleared away the rouge, the makeup. Pretty didn't matter. He hadn't even noticed.

Chapter 31

James 1957

"Go okay at your tryout?" Magdalena was propped against the fender of a car, the biggest car James had ever seen.

"Yeah. I suppose. Whose car is this?"

Magdalena patted the car's hood fondly. She smiled. "Wish I'd had this one the other day. We could have gone to the tryouts in style."

James shrugged. Magdalena probably had a good reason for leaving Joe Deeter, but it was still bad timing. Having Joe's car or not didn't matter anyway, in the end. James had botched up the tryout himself. He glanced down at the monstrous car and tried to look at it the way Harold had looked at Joe's. He slumped against it and nodded, as if it met his approval.

"I am sorry about that," Magdalena continued. "I know you were counting on me, but Joe's a...well, never mind."

James crossed one ankle over the other. "Don't worry about it. How'd you do working at Mr. Morgan's restaurant? I didn't know you knew anything about being in a place like that."

"Like I said, I know things. Picked up a little here and a little there."

Alex used to say things about Magdalena's varied

skills, but the way he described them made James blush. Magdalena looked proud.

"Ida okay? You being there instead of Mr. Morgan, I mean?"

Magdalena shrugged and leaned one hip against the fender, crossing her arms. She stared down at the hood, pursing and unpursing her lips. Like a fish.

"I don't think she likes me," James said. He'd decided that the day Mr. Morgan served him a sundae, but she'd looked further irritated when Mr. Morgan took a day to drive him to the tryout. If Magdalena smoked and swore at the customers, even in jest, Ida was probably livid. She might even say something to their parents. So far, Pop still thought he'd cleaned the churchyard, and he wanted to keep it that way.

Magdalena glanced up. There was a feel about the look on her face that reminded him of how she acted the night she'd come to James' bedroom and listened to Pop shout *that boy* downstairs. Magdalena chewed the inside of her cheek while she stared at him. He could see her tug at it from within. She was thinking hard, something she rarely did before she spoke.

"Don't concern yourself whether Ida likes you or not. You're none of her business." Then Magdalena grinned, one of those satisfied, sneering grins she was good at. "She maybe wasn't too keen on having me there at first, but I did such a good job there wasn't much she could say by the time Mr. Morgan got back." Magdalena straightened, went to the driver's window, and reached into the car. She came back to the fender and leaned against it again, a pack of cigarettes and a lighter in her hand.

"Where'd you get a lighter like that?" James stared

at the shiny metal. Magdalena always had plain ones. He leaned closer.

"Comes with the car," she said. A flame shot up from the lighter, blue and gold. The end of her cigarette caught and glowed as she inhaled. She snapped the lid shut and laid the lighter and pack on the hood of the car. She took a long draw on the cigarette, red fire burning at the end. James watched, mesmerized. She withdrew the cigarette from her lips and exhaled a long tornado of smoke. "Don't worry about Ida," Magdalena said again. She coughed a little and tapped ashes from the burning end. "Her opinions don't matter."

"Mr. Morgan took me to the church when we got back. I thought he'd hurry back to the restaurant to keep Ida happy, but he didn't want Pop to catch me in a lie. We worked on the churchyard together until it was done. The pastor sure was surprised when he saw us. Mr. Morgan buffaloed him. Said I'd promised him I'd do it and he was holding me to it. The pastor looked confused, but he thanked us when we were done."

Magdalena grinned. She grinned up into the air as she exhaled another lungful of smoke. "Good story. Glad you told me, but you should probably keep it to yourself."

"I will. I sure don't want Pop finding out I lied and went to a baseball tryout. He'd be even madder to find out Mr. Morgan pulled a fast one on him."

Magdalena coughed. Smoke spewed into the air as she bent forward, hacking and pounding her chest. James couldn't tell if she was laughing or crying, but she made a racket. He slapped her back until the coughing slowed. She straightened and leaned against the fender, holding onto her chest. Tears ran down her cheeks. She looked at him and laughed. "No, little brother," she said, then coughed some more. "We surely don't want Pop ever thinking that."

"What's going on here? You all right?"

James jumped and looked toward the front of the car. A man stood there, a man he'd never seen before. He was thin, too thin, and old. He looked worried as he stepped to Magdalena and put a hand on her back. "You okay?"

Magdalena nodded. She wiped the tears from her face and smiled. "Just having a good laugh," she said.

The man looked at James and then back at James' sister.

"That's my little brother, James. He's a baseball player." Magdalena looked proud. James' mouth fell open at the introduction. "And this is Max," Magdalena continued. She nodded toward the man.

Max extended a hand, long, bony fingers, and veins that looked enormous beneath his thin skin. "Glad to meet you."

"Magdalena clean house for you?" James asked, releasing his hand from Max's grip.

Max frowned. "What? No. Why do you ask that?"

Magdalena snorted and chuckled. "I'm dating him, James. This is his car. And his lighter."

James opened his mouth, a thousand *buts* running through his mind. He looked from Max to Magdalena. She could be his daughter. What would Pop say?

Max put a hand on Magdalena's arm. "You ready to go?"

She nodded and swiped her cigarettes and the lighter off the hood. "I'll drive."

Max patted her arm and looked at James. "Nice to

meet you. I'll probably see a lot more of you."

James closed his mouth and watched them climb into the car.

"Bye, little brother." She winked as the car roared to life. He was supposed to keep this a secret, he could tell by her wink. He nodded. Magdalena smiled and drove away.

Chapter 32

James 1957

James glanced up at the wide open front of Pop's shop. Even with every door pulled up or standing open, the temperature inside felt the same as the white flame at the end of the torches. Customers moved in and out. James wiped the sweat from his forehead with his arm. Only the hardiest stood inside while Pop and his workers fixed their axles, their wagon frames, whatever they brought in to salvage because they couldn't afford to replace them with new. He wished he could go outside and cool off, but Pop wouldn't stand for it. James shoved a few rods aside with his toe. He sorted rods. It was simple inside work, sissy work Pop called it, but with no reason or excuse to step outside.

Pop liked organization. At home it was the way they stood and sat and ate. At Pop's shop it was type of metal, length of metal, age of metal. No mixing. Everything aligned.

Sweat dripped off the tip of James' nose. It splashed onto one of the rods, turning the thin layer of rust darker for a moment, a moment that didn't last long in the intense, dry heat.

"It's too short?" Harold held a long metal bar in his hands. A man stood near him, pointing a weathered finger where the weld had been formed. Harold dipped his head to the side and swiped at his forehead with his upper arm. "You got its mate? We can compare and see what needs fixed."

The man jerked his head toward the door. Harold followed him out, the welded bar in his hand. Harold was nothing like Pop or Alex. They could swear and shout at and with the customers. Harold never did, but he still fit in well. James watched his brother walk out, chatting with the man as if they were friends instead of opposites.

Metal clanked all around, curses sandwiched in between, sounds that stuck with him like the stench of burnt metal. Harold was determined not to stay a welder. He wasn't going to join the service like Alex, either, and he wasn't interested in baseball like James. Harold wanted to run a store. He had his eye on an empty one along the main street, across the way from Mr. Morgan's restaurant, near the theater and the tavern. In his impatience to get married, he and Sandra had already tied the knot and were subsisting happily on little while they scrimped and saved. He talked privately with James when Pop and the customers were far away, how he wanted to raise a family and be a good father, the kind Pop had not taught him how to be and the kind Mama had always been.

Harold appeared in the doorway again, two bars of metal in his hands, the man close at his heels, complaining how much time he'd lost having to come back into town to straighten this out. James smiled. Harold was taking it well. No one would have guessed what a misfit he was here, or where his heart really lay.

"What's the problem?" Pop's voice shattered James' thoughts. He could hear Pop stalk across the shop. James bent and retrieved three more bars of metal to sort and store. Pop reached Harold, had the metal in his hands, looking from the bars to the man.

"Wrong length. One of you welded that bar wrong." The man's weathered finger was pointing again. Pop followed its path. Then he looked up, back over his shoulder at James. Pop never allowed James to weld. James turned back to the rods and grabbed three more, sorting by length, age, and type.

"Time you learned to weld." Pop dropped the two pieces of metal to the dirt behind James, his voice louder than the ringing in James' ears.

"Me?" James turned.

"You need a trade. You can learn this." Pop walked away.

James started to argue. He didn't need a trade. He expected a letter any day from the baseball league, telling him if he'd made the team or not. He probably wouldn't, but if he did, he'd tell Pop he wasn't going to be a welder. Then he'd tell Mama, Harold, and his sisters. He'd send a letter to Alex. Alex was in France right now. If James didn't make the team, he was going to try again. Go to every tryout he could find until he made the cut and could walk away from welding, from Pop, from a trade he didn't want.

"Get a move on." Pop looked back at James. James glanced at Harold. Harold knew James' plans, just as he knew Harold's. Harold shook his head back and forth, almost invisibly, and James knew to do as Pop said. He set the last rod in the pile, picked up the two pieces Pop had dropped, and followed his father. When the letter came, if he made the cut, he'd be gone. If not, he'd try again. He recited his plan in his mind to the cadence of his steps behind Pop's. Someday, somewhere, he'd go. He couldn't stay here and work for Pop. Pop didn't want him. *That boy* was in Pop's eyes, in his gestures, in the distance he kept his youngest son.

Pop took the two bars from James when they reached the corner where light welding was done. He nodded toward a face shield, and James lifted it from the bench and set it over his head. It tipped to the side. He straightened it and tried to see Pop through the glazed glass.

Pop was talking. He was lifting the bars and pointing at the welder. James had watched from a distance for months, but no one had told him the details, the gas names, the pressure, the metal types he'd need. Pop ran on, fast, authoritative. Then he laid the bars down, stared at James, and walked away.

"That boy know what he's doing?" the man called after Pop. Pop stopped, looked his way, and shrugged. *That boy.* Did *that boy* know what he was doing?

"James can do anything," Harold said. "You should see him play ball."

James aligned the bars on the floor with his foot. One was barely shorter than the other. He measured the difference and lifted the smaller one to the bench. He turned, glad for the weeks and months he'd spent sorting, learning about metal, understanding the types.

"Come on outside," Harold said to the man. "It's cooler out there. James'll let us know when he's finished."

The man muttered, then shuffled behind Harold, James' brother leading the man away so James could have enough air and space to breathe.

"Got the right one?" Pop stood over him again.

"I think so." James held up the pieces he'd chosen. There was no indication in Pop's face if he approved or not. He stood like a silent sentinel. James carried the metal to the welder and began to work.

Pop stayed nearby, his eyes measuring each step, every move James made. Welding had looked simpler from far away where the flame wasn't as hot, the metal not so heavy. He appreciated how tired Pop was at the end of the day, how disappointed he must be with where his life had ended up.

James strained under the work and under Pop's stare. He was careful and slow, but he was accurate. When he finished, he laid the repaired bar on the floor next to the other. They were identical. He'd done it right.

"That's not as easy as it looks," James said, glancing up at Pop. "But I did it. I got it right." James felt a smile inside. He'd done something good, as good as Pop. Maybe not as fast as Pop, but the result was the same.

"It's the same way you play ball," Pop said.

The smile froze inside. Ice formed in James' gut. It hurt. Something inside burned cold, and hurt.

"You can do it, but it's not in your blood." Pop walked away. He walked outdoors. James had relished the thought of hearing Pop tell the man his bar was ready, but now all James could hear was, "It's not in your blood."

The ice began to thaw. The pool turned to tears, a hot puddle of anger brewing inside. The tears simmered, they gurgled, they roiled to the top in a geyser James couldn't stop. He was gone before Pop returned. Out the side door before Harold could congratulate him about how well he had done.

He could hear the face shield spinning on the dirt floor behind him. The door slammed. Fresh air blew the scent of burning metal from his nose, the wind scattered small splinters of iron and steel in his trail.

James ran. He ran the opposite direction of home. He ran past the ball field, past the neighborhood Andy lived in. He kept running until town was behind him. He ran until his heart beat like a locomotive, the heart Mama had given him, the heart that made him weld and play ball, the heart that pumped blood that had nothing in it.

He ran. Ran, and ran, and ran.

Chapter 33

James 1957

It was Mama's heart that turned James around. Her heart and Magdalena's headlights. Max's headlights.

It was dark, too dark to know where he was, but the moment he decided to turn and go back the way he'd come, lights shone. They came from behind, wide apart and rumbling, wide and loud like a large car.

He walked toward the beams, but off to the side and face down so they'd pass. He didn't want to talk. He didn't want anyone offering him a ride. His lack of worthwhile blood had taken him this far, but his heart could carry him all the way back.

The car stopped before it reached him, its engine a loud purr. He looked down, lengthened his stride, and moved farther off the road. Just as he moved past, the side door opened, and a cloud of smoke rolled out.

"Want a ride, little brother?"

James stopped. The interior of the car had a faint glow, enough to highlight the mass of curls.

"Mama's at the house. Max's house. She's worried sick. And she's mad."

James walked over to the car and stood at the edge of Magdalena's door. The door to the back seat opened and Harold stepped out. James could see Sandra in the middle of the long seat, she'd evidently been pressed at his brother's side, the way a couple should be.

"Get in, son," Max said from within. James glanced at the back seat, the other side of Sandra.

"No, up here with us. I'll scoot over." Magdalena disappeared inside, squeezing over next to Max.

"I…I don't know…"

"It's okay," Magdalena said. "Pop's not at the house. Just Mama."

James felt Harold's hand on his shoulder, tightening into a reassuring grip. James laid his hand over his brother's and squeezed. Then he slid in beside Magdalena.

The interior was quiet as Max rumbled forward, looking for a place to turn his monstrosity of a car around. Magdalena lit up a cigarette, giving Max suggestions, smoke filling the car every time she offered advice. James drew in a deep breath. Magdalena's smoke tasted good; it smelled reassuring. He liked her for it. He liked the way it was a part of her.

"Your letter came," Harold broke the silence from the back seat.

James stopped, holding onto a lungful of Magdalena's smoke. No one said anything. Magdalena put a hand on his leg.

James blew the air and smoke out. "It came after I ran out?" James wheeled toward the back seat when Harold didn't answer. "I said, it came after I ran out?"

"It came a couple of days ago." Harold spoke softly from the dark.

James turned farther around, squeezing Magdalena against Max. "A couple of days ago? Why didn't anyone tell me? Why didn't you tell me?"

"I didn't know. Honest, I didn't. If I did, I would

have told you."

James stared into the dark where his brother sat. Sitting next to his bride, mapping out their lives the way they wanted them. James was glad for Harold and Sandra, but that didn't stop his anger. Why hadn't Mama told him a letter came? Anyone?

"Pop had it," Magdalena said. "No one knew until tonight."

"Pop?" James turned toward his sister. "When? How?"

"I don't know. Mama found out when you didn't come home. She went after Pop. Wish I'd seen it. Harold did. He took Sandra to the house when he realized you'd taken off. He said no one had ever silenced the house like Mama did tonight, not even Pop."

James could feel Magdalena's grin in the dark. She was proud of Mama. No wonder she wished she'd been there. He looked into the dark back seat again. He waited. He wanted Harold to tell him what happened.

"Mama said 'that boy' was her son. She jabbed Pop's chest with her finger. I was afraid he'd hit her, but he didn't. He kept backing up while she advanced. She kept at him until he spit out what had happened at the shop. His side of it. Mostly."

"The letter," James said. Mama's heart beat inside of him. He was her son, and he was glad. Pop's contribution to his life was minimal. It meant nothing. James didn't care what wasn't in his blood, because Mama's heart was there. "Did Mama get the letter?"

Harold was quiet again.

"I said, did Mama get the letter?"

"No. Pop burnt it."

"He had no right!" James yelled. He seized the back edge of the seat and glared into the dark. "Did he read it, at least?"

"Said he did. Said he thought it might be for him. But when he saw what it said and realized what you'd done, trying out and all, he burned it."

James looked to the side. At Magdalena. He could see the orange glow where she drew on her cigarette in the dark.

"He said you didn't make the team." She said it as she exhaled, her words framed in a cloud of smoke. "You're going to try again, though, right?"

Max's car rolled onward, but the world stopped. The vibration James felt was steady, a hum beneath him that took him nowhere. He turned forward, leaned back against the seat.

"Son, I know it's not my place." Max broke the silence. He was right, it wasn't his place, and James wished he'd keep quiet. "But from the bits and pieces I heard about your Pop and your day, he did what a father's supposed to do."

There was that scream again. The one that lived inside and never came out. James felt it come to life.

"Stop the car." James' hand was on the door's handle.

"That thing he said about needing a trade. That's probably why he said it." Max leaned forward, steering, looking around Magdalena at James.

"I said, let me out!" James opened the door. Max stopped with a jerk, and everyone rocked forward.

"Son..."

James slammed the door behind him. He banged his fist on the car's roof to tell them to go. They did.

Max crept forward, probably at Magdalena's insistence. As the car disappeared, the scream emerged. It was like a howl in the night, empty, long, and painful. It came from James' depths. It sounded like "that boy." It was too painful for any other words.

Chapter 34

James 1957

"You'll need a trade" stuck in James' mind with the same mulish insult "that boy" did. Magdalena better not marry that man. How dare he address James as "son." Max was just like Pop. They were probably the same age, so no wonder.

James kicked the dirt. Daylight was just beginning to creep into the sky, encroaching upon the darkness, trying to devour the worst night of his life and mute it to something hopeful. James preferred the dark. He didn't want to come back into town when people could see him. He probably looked as horrid as he felt. He'd walked all night; he had nowhere to go. He couldn't go backward to being a welder. And the letter—he couldn't go forward either... He kicked the dirt harder.

He could hear Mr. Mullen's milk wagon, a cruel reminder of the foolish hope he'd had the morning he'd hidden from him, the morning he'd gone for the tryouts. Mr. Mullen was coming his way. James turned to the right, took another street toward downtown.

You'll need a trade.

Andy's house was ahead on the right. It was still dark. Andy would probably take over his father's hardware business someday. He didn't seem particularly interested in it, but Andy wasn't particularly interested in anything. His life was fairly simple. All he had to do was live it. He didn't have to carve it from stone, like James did.

James thrust his fists into his pockets. He watched the toes of his boots move forward. His feet hurt. These boots were for welding, not walking. His feet hurt, his legs ached, his heart was broken.

"You lost?"

James jumped and wheeled around. A man approached from behind, a dark squareish figure advancing his way.

"Looks like you could use a walking partner."

The man came alongside James where he could see him. Mr. Morgan smiled in the wan daylight.

"Mind if I join you?"

James thought of the number of times he'd wanted to shoo Mr. Morgan away. He always appeared at the worst possible moments, always James' lowest, and offered advice. He was too tired to shoo him away this time, so he shrugged, and continued down the street.

The dull clop of Mr. Mullen's old mare could be heard a street over. It was like a drum in harmony with James' slow shuffle and Mr. Morgan's refreshed clip. James tried to step it up a bit, not sound so sluggish. Anyone who wanted to play baseball should walk briskly, at least. Wanted to. Past tense. He slowed to a shuffle.

"You drink coffee?" Mr. Morgan asked.

James shook his head.

"Time to try some. It'll give you a little clarity. Help you get started."

They reached the restaurant well before Mr. Mullen. Mr. Morgan let them inside and locked the door behind them.

"Come to the back with me. You can sit and rest while I start some coffee." He turned and studied James. "Maybe some eggs and ham, too. Juice. Even toast. Looks like you could use it."

"Mr. Morgan," James said, "I think one of your sundaes is what I need."

Mr. Morgan grinned. "Maybe that too."

James followed him to the back and took a seat near the wall. He turned sideways in his chair and leaned back against the wainscoting, his right arm resting on the table and his left arm on the chair's back. It was surreal watching Mr. Morgan work in the dim light. He said he kept it that way until he was ready for customers. Too often they saw his lights and pounded on the front door, wanting in to eat or drink something. Mr. Morgan moved smoothly and quietly, back and forth. James' eyelids drooped. Mr. Morgan became a shadowy blur, his dark hair, his tan complexion, his stout stature, all flowing together in a haze. James drifted along with him.

Mr. Morgan set a cup of coffee on the table. James straightened in his chair and wrapped his hands around the cup the way he'd seen Mama and Magdalena do when they sat and talked. Mr. Morgan disappeared, and James let the black steam clear his mind. It smelled wonderful. He didn't know why he'd never tried drinking coffee before.

"Here's your food." Mr. Morgan set two plates in front of James, one of eggs, toast, and ham, the other of potatoes and gravy. "Eat up." He pulled out a chair across from James and sat down.

"Thank you, Mr. Morgan." James lifted his fork

and began to eat. As soon as the sensation of ham hit his mouth he was ravenous. He dug in; he ate everything. And then he remembered the coffee. It had cooled, but it was wonderful, too. Mr. Morgan was right. He needed starting, and this helped.

The back door opened and closed. James heard a key turn in its lock. He wondered if it was Ida. He cringed. No matter how dazzling Magdalena was in the restaurant that day, he still thought Ida wouldn't care to see him sitting there. He started to stand, just as she appeared behind Mr. Morgan. She spotted James and stopped.

"Good morning," James said.

She looked from him to Mr. Morgan, then hung her jacket on a nearby hook. "I'll get biscuits started," she said and disappeared.

"What's the main thought running through your head?" Mr. Morgan asked when Ida was gone. She could be heard dragging out canisters and lard buckets, spoons and tins.

James thought of everything that had run through his mind as he'd walked all night long. Several were important, some just hurt. "Baseball," he said. It was one of the hurts.

"Tryout didn't pan out the way you wanted?"

James shook his head.

"There'll be others. Don't give up. You're too good. And the lessons you learned from the last one will make you ready for the next." Mr. Morgan tapped the table with a finger. "What next?"

James drew in a long breath. What was next? Something important or more pain? *That boy*? Mama? He shook his head. "I need a trade."

250

"You need a job. Baseball's your trade."

James snorted. He sounded like Magdalena. He didn't mean it, though. He didn't mean to be cynical when what Mr. Morgan said felt right inside.

"You can work here. I'll hire you to help in the back. Maybe even teach you to cook. You can bus tables at first. Fair enough?"

"It's probably not in my blood."

"What?" Mr. Morgan stopped tapping his finger.

"Nothing." James looked up. "Are you sure you want to do this?"

"I'm as sure about this as I am that baseball's your trade. You can begin tomorrow. In the meantime, go find your mama. No doubt she's worried about you, and she's not a woman to keep worrying. She's too fine for that."

There was a noise behind Mr. Morgan. James looked up. Ida was standing there. The lights were still dim, but he could feel the look on her face, one even shadows couldn't hide. "I need you to light the oven," she said.

"Sis, I want you to meet your new employee." Mr. Morgan turned and looked at her, raising a hand and gesturing toward James. "He starts tomorrow."

Ida looked at him, murmured a small welcome, then disappeared to the back.

"Well, I have work to do." Mr. Morgan stood, and James followed.

"How did you know, sir?" James asked. "How did you know my mama might be worried about me?"

"It's a restaurant. I hear everything eventually. You will too, when you work here. But let me tell you something, and always keep it in mind."

James nodded, and Mr. Morgan continued.

"Don't believe everything you hear. Or you'll end up like…" Mr. Morgan nodded toward the back where pans were banging even louder.

"Ida?" James whispered. "What did she hear?"

"Doesn't matter what she heard. Or thinks she saw. Her problem is believing. See you tomorrow."

Mr. Morgan disappeared into the back. James didn't know where Max lived, but surely Mama had gone home by now. He didn't want to see Max anyway. Pop would be going to work soon, so James would go home first. He'd find Mama and let her know he was fine. Just like Mr. Morgan said to do.

Chapter 35

James 1957

James liked the new smell on his skin. He drew in a deep breath—pine soap mixed with a little bit of grease, cooking grease. He smelled like a fried potato. The burnt metal odor from Pop's shop had almost faded, thanks to the number of hours his hands and arms were submerged in water, washing dishes, scrubbing floors, shining counters and tables. Pop said it was a sissy job. He'd always said that about Mr. Morgan and the restaurant. Now he said it every night, now that only Pop smelled like iron that had been burned.

Mama's face was tight as she brought supper to the table. It had been that way ever since he'd taken the job with Mr. Morgan. Her eyes had grown huge when James first told her Mr. Morgan had hired him. She shook her head back and forth, tears pooling in the rims. "Please don't," she'd whispered. But now she never said anything about it. She offered faint smiles, and once she even said maybe he could cook for her someday.

James stood near his chair watching her. Mama put the last dishes on the table, Betsy at her side, aligning the silverware and plates. Gail was married, tormenting poor Jackson with her preciseness, Carla was with her fiancé, planning their wedding, and Magdalena was with Max. Mama paused, ran her eyes over the table. James could see her mentally counting out each setting, each dish on the table, and the seconds until Pop came into the room.

Mama realigned the meat platter near Pop's plate just as he strode in from the back room, rubbing his hands together. James had heard Pop's entrance so many times he didn't have to turn to know what Pop was doing. Mama brushed her hands down the sides of her apron. She nodded at James and Betsy, and they moved behind their chairs.

Pop paused at his, one hand on its back as he surveyed the steaming bowls and platters. He dragged his chair out, sat, then jerked it forward. They all did the same, no sound other than wooden chair legs raking across the wooden floor, followed by the clink of ladles against pottery as Pop began to fill his plate.

"That girl of yours got herself married again." Pop finished and slid the last dish down the table. It stopped in front of James. Pop took a mouthful of potatoes.

"What?" Mama's eyes were wide as she stared at Pop.

Pop finished chewing and slid his spoon beneath the mound of potatoes on his plate. "I said she got married again. Magdalena." He shoveled in another bite. "She married some old guy this time." Pop looked at Mama now, as if what Magdalena had done was Mama's fault. He shook his head and switched to his fork and knife and dug into his meat.

"Max?" Mama looked at James.

James couldn't tell by her expression if she approved or not. Mama had said nothing when

Magdalena married Joe Deeter, and she'd said nothing when Magdalena divorced him. Joe had slapped Magdalena for scratching his car, and she left him, scratching it again as she walked away. She'd told James what really happened one afternoon at Mr. Morgan's restaurant when she'd come in alone. James didn't care for Max. He couldn't forget his comment that he'd need a trade. But when Magdalena told him about Joe and said Max would never do something like that, mostly because he was afraid what Magdalena would do back, James thought he might forgive Max. At least Max was safe for his sister.

James gave Mama a nod. It would be Max. Magdalena was quick to change men, but it was unlikely she'd have two old ones this close together.

"We should do something for them." Betsy spoke. James looked up. She was leaning toward Mama.

"Shouldn't," Pop said around a bite of biscuit. "She won't need a thing, marrying an old man like that. She'll have everything. He's got a car, a house, probably got some money stashed away."

Betsy looked down at her food.

"The girl married for money this time. Not sure why she married before." Pop reached for the platter of biscuits and snatched another.

"She married for love. Or at least looking for it."

James turned toward Mama. He couldn't believe what she'd said. She was staring at Pop.

"Earl didn't love her, but that's what she wanted. She was done looking for it here, so she went elsewhere."

Pop laid down his biscuit. He gazed across the table at Mama. James couldn't tell if he was baffled by what she'd said or angry that she'd said anything at all.

"Here?" Pop finally snorted. "You go *out* and find a man to love you. It's not going to be at home."

"Exactly." Mama stood. "She had to go out because no man here loved her. Women do that."

"You women all addled in the brain? Of course there was no man here to love her."

Mama stepped to the side of the table. She eased around Betsy, her eyes on Pop. She came to his side and stopped. He looked up into her face, something James had never seen him do before. Everyone always looked up to Pop. He never looked up to anyone.

"The first love of every little girl's life is her father. That's where she first feels loved and knows she's special."

Pop frowned, his eyes narrowed.

"Why do you think your daughter chose a man your age?" Mama leaned close to Pop. "That little girl who rode pretend ponies to get away, who was determined to drive, who wore makeup when you told her not to, who sassed you just to get your attention…did all of that to no avail. When she couldn't get love here, she went out to find it."

Mama had painted the clearest picture of Magdalena James had ever imagined. She'd drawn her precisely from the inside out, so precisely it was as if Mama saw inside Magdalena, reading the lines of the life her daughter had lived.

"That your excuse too, then?" Pop spat, a sneer on his face. "No father? No grandfather? And your husband wasn't enough, so you had to…"

The sound of Mama's hand on Pop's face was like a gunshot. Pop's head rocked to the side, a red imprint the shape of a flame blazed on his cheek. Before Pop could regain his balance and get to his feet, her hand shot out again, hit the same red mark like it was a target.

"That first one was from me. The second was from Magdalena. I'm done slapping you. Forever." Mama stepped past him, her feet moving quickly, nearly at a run. And then she was gone, the outside door slamming behind her.

Chapter 36

Lana 1940

Cletus' welding shop emitted sounds even more brash than before. Harsh metal clanged as pieces fell against each other, while fiery hot flames hissed and sizzled in the background. These were man noises, Cletus noises, sounds without feeling.

Lana stood, her children with her, in front of the wide open doorway lit only by tiny bursts of fiery flames inside.

"Wait here." She looked at Magdalena and then at the others. "I'll get the money, and then we'll go."

She bundled the smaller ones close together before she stepped into the darkness. Clusters of men looked up as she wove between them. She didn't glance their way. She was searching, only interested in the tallest one, and this time she'd find him.

When she reached the back of his shop, she turned. She hadn't found him, Cletus wasn't there. Her eyes, adjusted to the faint light, looked around again, across men who refused to look up or offer a hand. To her left, in the far back corner, she spotted a doorway, closed and likely his office, built like a notch cut out of the shop's floor space. Her heart began to pound like a fist knocking against his door as she walked that way.

She glanced toward the large lighted square where

her children stood outside waiting for her. The youngest were distracted, engrossed by the fire and noise, but Magdalena was staring at her, as if even in the dark she knew just where Lana stood.

Lana nodded, even though Magdalena couldn't see her. Then she rapped with her knuckles, loud and sharp. No one answered, so she knocked again. Her knuckles burned; the wood scratched the skin where her bones hit the door. Men were watching now. She could feel their eyes, the sounds of their work diminished.

Lana felt someone at her side. They weren't tall enough to be him. She didn't look. She rapped harder, refusing to be dissuaded. Cletus' workers couldn't make excuses for him this time. The person pressed close and she knocked harder, her face down, her knuckles numb. A hand touched her arm. A small hand with long fingers. It wrapped around her forearm, and she paused. The shop was silent.

"It's okay, Mama." Magdalena pulled Lana's arm from the door. "I got the money."

"You? You got the money?"

Magdalena nodded. Her fingers squeezed Lana's arm, and she drew Lana toward the large front opening. In Magdalena's other hand, the off-green color of dollars peeked from her fist.

Magdalena towed her through a sea of faces. The men were silent, but they knew, at least one of them knew. Lana stopped, wrenched the money from Magdalena's fist, and threw it on the shop's floor. "We won't have this!" She kicked the money across the packed dirt. "I won't, and she won't either!" Lana grabbed Magdalena by the elbow and rushed to the street. She gathered her children and hurried them away, down the walkway and around the corner to the main street. They stumbled forward when they reached it, the little ones at her feet and the stores a blur at her side.

"It's okay, Mama, really it is." Magdalena tried to slow her.

"It's not okay." Lana spoke in a hiss. It wasn't okay Cletus was missing, it wasn't okay his workers protected him, and it wasn't okay she had to beg and look foolish.

"Mama…" Magdalena stopped. They were beside Mr. Morgan's restaurant. Lana watched Magdalena's hand on the door as she pushed it open.

"Come on, Mama." Magdalena eased inside. "We can sit and relax."

"No. Let's go home." Lana saw past Magdalena into the restaurant. It looked warm inside, and she felt it touch the iciness in her heart. "We shouldn't…" She just wanted to go home, be away from town, away from Cletus' shop and him, wherever he was.

"Please, Mama." Magdalena stepped inside, holding the door open. Her brothers and sisters looked up at Lana expectantly. She'd promised them an outing. She'd promised when she really had nothing to offer at all.

The ice inside Lana's heart fought everything behind Magdalena and on the faces of her children. Small crystals bound together fought the eagerness of their eyes and the warmth of Mr. Morgan's restaurant. She was so cold, so tired, so empty. "Okay," she conceded. They'd sit, she'd relax, and then they'd go.

"This way, Mama." Magdalena led them to a booth, shiny chrome surrounding bright red seats and a matching tabletop. "Sit here. We can all squeeze in."

Lana stared at the table as her children crowded in. They looked foreign for a moment, happy and excited, clambering to have fun instead of to hurry or hide. A cry rose inside her. The scream. She stared at the nearly full seats, just enough room for her at the end of one side or the other. The scream stirred. It wanted out, but not here, not now.

"Would you like a chair? I can sit you at the end of the table."

Then she saw them, as if she were seeing them for the very first time. Eyes that said so much without ever a word, dark eyes against dark skin, crowned with black hair. Mr. Morgan, posed like a prince, waited for her answer. The cry simmered. It stirred. Something about the way he looked at her set it on fire. Tears dowsed the fire on their way up, leaving only a sob to escape from her throat.

It was like Jim's kindness and Grandma's hug all at once. Mr. Morgan moved close and held her, he let her cry while he said soothing things to her children. She could hear them stirring and felt Magdalena at her other side.

"I'm going to make food for all of you," he said near her head. "I promised your family a free meal a long time ago. Now's the time." She felt him look down. "Magdalena, would you take your mother to the back? I have a small room back there that's comfortable. Sometimes I stay the night there, even."

Magdalena touched her. Lana let her lead her away, to the back, to the room Mr. Morgan said was comfortable, and he was right, it was. Comforting.

Chapter 37

James 1957

James' gut felt steely and cold, his insides heavy, as he bussed tables, carried food to Mr. Morgan's customers, and did dishes in between. His world had shrunk to a tiny orb, drawn so tight no one could get in.

"That your excuse?" Pop's voice rang in his mind. *"No father? No grandfather? And your husband wasn't enough, so you had to…"* Then the slap. The red stain of Mama's hand on his father's face.

Ida dumped more dishes into the sink. James' back ached from bending over the deep basin all day. Water splashed upward. Suds clung to the hair of his forearms. James didn't look at her. Ida wouldn't say anything even if he did. He just shoved her stack aside and kept scouring the silverware and plates they needed for the unusual lunch crowd they had today.

It was only supposed to happen at death, your life flashing before your eyes, but James' sixteen years played over and over in his head, visions of things that had been said and done suddenly taking root, showing themselves for what they were, looking different in the daylight of being older. *Step back, gain perspective.*

The tepid gray water swirled, the rag became soggy, and James wrenched his arms from the sink and walked, then ran for the back door of the restaurant. He pushed through, doubled over, and heaved. Heaved in the dirt behind the building, years of scream coming out in putrid bile. He leaned over the foul puddle and braced himself with his hands on his knees. *Baseball's not in your blood.* The scream came up again, more yellow fluid, soaking into the dirt.

He spit. White foam floated on the mess he'd made. Looking at it made him retch again, but nothing came up. He was empty. No more scream, no more illusions about who he was, no more heart. Mama's heart. He didn't even know if that was in there.

He straightened. Every muscle ached. He leaned back against the restaurant, happy voices coming from the other side of the wall. People whose lives were intact. Who knew what to expect, knew what they were made of, had no surprises springing up like little warnings their whole lives.

The hum of the restaurant made him angry. He envied those people. He'd never been a part of them, and now he knew why. Even Ida's coldness made sense. He looked down the narrow alley between the backs of the buildings that faced the main street and the backs of the buildings that faced the other way, the ones side by side with Pop's business. It was as if he'd been in this spot his whole life, between Pop and the others, thinking he belonged with one when maybe he never did.

He brushed his hands on the apron. It was wet from doing dishes, cool in the shaded air. He undid the back tie and slid the apron over his head. Restaurants didn't suit him either. It wasn't in his blood. He wasn't sure what was, but he needed to find out. Finally, and for sure.

James turned to go back inside. He'd at least let Mr. Morgan know. The door swung open before he touched the handle. Mr. Morgan stood there, their eyes meeting. The noise behind Mr. Morgan was loud now that the door was open. He stepped outside, pulling it closed behind him.

James wished he'd kicked dirt over his vomit. The sour stench was strong, and he was ashamed it was there. Mr. Morgan surely was aware of it, but he said nothing as the door latched and the two of them were alone in the alleyway.

Mr. Morgan was never silent. Even when his mouth said nothing, his eyes always did, those dark eyes that said so much, called in such a familiar tone. James wanted to fall into them and run from them at the same time. They were too familiar, too painful when they drilled so deep.

"You're thinking about going." Mr. Morgan dropped his gaze to the apron dangling in James' hand. James looked down and nodded. He lifted the apron and extended it to Mr. Morgan. To his surprise, Mr. Morgan took it. "Don't expect you'll need that apron where you're going," he said.

Mr. Morgan couldn't possibly know where he was going. James didn't even know. James frowned as he wondered what Mr. Morgan saw that he couldn't.

"Everything else I gave you, you can keep, though."

James frowned more. Mr. Morgan had only given him an ice cream sundae and some tokens. James shook his head.

"Well, like the advice I gave you when I told you to choke up on a bat. If what you're handling is too big, choke up. Place your grip where you can manage it even if the hit isn't as strong as you want."

James' gut began to swirl. This time it wasn't bile, it wasn't a scream, it was something childlike, the yearning of a boy who'd always wanted something but never got it.

"Or like when I told you to step back off the plate so you can gain perspective. Step away, look things over. Find out what you didn't see because you were too close."

Tears pooled somewhere deep in James' chest. He thought Mr. Morgan had been teaching him to play baseball all those years, but he wasn't. He was teaching James about life. James looked down, stared at the toes of his shoes.

Mr. Morgan moved close, his head near James'. "And I said don't believe everything you hear. I know I said it about in this restaurant, but it's true everywhere. Don't."

James swallowed. *No father? No grandfather? And your husband wasn't enough, so you had to...* A too-large wad of saliva lodged in his throat. He gulped. The tears came up against it, creating a lump that was huge and painful.

Mr. Morgan put a hand on the door's handle. He turned sideways, ready to go back inside. "One more thing."

James looked up. He knew his eyes were red, but he wasn't ashamed. Not in front of Mr. Morgan. His place was safe. It always had been. That's what he'd seen in this man's eyes his whole life.

"What's that?" James tried to clear the lump from his throat.

Mr. Morgan put a hand on James' shoulder. "I told you once your mama's got heart, and that heart's in you." He looked hard into James' eyes. "And she's the most beautiful woman I've ever known. She is. I meant it. And that you can believe, wherever you hear it. She gives you value. Hold onto that."

James stared at the man as his chest heaved outward, then in, with breaths as hard as if he'd just run up and down the street. "Thank you for the work, sir." James nodded as he said it, then looked away. The alley stretched before him, Pop on one side, Mr. Morgan on the other. James passed between them. Left them behind. He had to find what was in the blood pumping through Mama's heart.

Chapter 38

James 1957

James felt odd stepping onto a porch, knowing it was Magdalena's. Max's, but now hers, too. He'd never thought of her really having a house, a nice house like this one. She and Earl had lived with Earl's brother. And Joe Deeter, that hardly lasted. This little house was neat and simple, nice. It just didn't remind James of his sister. She would have to change to fit this house, or she would be changing it to suit her.

He brushed his hands on his pants, then raised his fist and knocked. Not loud, but sharp, his knuckles stinging against the door. Max's car was parked alongside the house. That alone said Magdalena was home. She loved cars, she loved to drive, and when he'd been working at Mr. Morgan's restaurant he saw her going up and down the street all the time, her window down and an elbow hanging out, sometimes her whole arm with a lit cigarette being fanned to ashes in the wind.

The door opened. Magdalena stood there. James was glad it wasn't Max. He still hadn't warmed up to him. Max had no business saying James would need a trade, even though he was right. Magdalena's face lit up. James thought she looked relieved. "Hold on," she said, and whisked away. She was back in a moment, pulling the door closed behind her.

"Let's go," she said, heading off the porch.

James frowned. "Go? Go where?"

"I don't know. Go talk. Isn't that why you're here?" Magdalena was off the porch and at the driver's side of the car. "Get in. Let's go."

James shrugged and followed her. He was barely in his seat when the car roared to life and Magdalena was backing toward the street.

"Slow down a little," he said, fighting the door closed.

Magdalena managed to light a cigarette while she edged into the street. She shifted to a forward gear, the cigarette dangling from her lips. She grabbed the steering wheel with her right hand while she lowered her window with the left. The car cruised forward, and she took the cigarette in her left fingers, blew out smoke in a big sigh, and settled back, a smile on her face.

James frowned at his sister. "You happy I came by, or what?"

Magdalena took another draw on her cigarette and turned toward downtown. She smiled more. "I'm so happy you came by!"

"Why? You that glad to see me?"

"Of course, little brother," she said, grinning his way. "But more glad to see life! I was going insane in there. Max is asleep *again*! I swear, that man takes naps to recover from naps. It's like living in a coma with him."

James settled into his seat and looked straight ahead. He didn't know what to say. He was right, that house didn't suit his sister. He wondered if Max slept to escape Magdalena's energy.

"He doesn't like it when I smoke in his house, but I can't help it. He doesn't like it when I pace, either, but there's nothing to do, so I smoke and pace. Back and forth, back and forth. Thank God for cars!" She leaned out the window and waved her cigarette in the air, she smiled, she inhaled the fresh air. Her freedom.

She headed down the main street. James slid low in his seat. He'd just come from here, from Mr. Morgan's restaurant, and he wasn't ready to see it or anyone just yet. Magdalena yelled from the window, shouting and waving cheery hellos at almost everyone she saw. James sank lower. He hadn't come to find her for this. He'd come to get some things straight before he reappeared in town. If he ever did.

"What if Max wakes up and finds you're gone?" he asked, hoping she'd feel guilty enough to turn around, even though Magdalena never felt guilty about anything.

She snorted. "Won't matter. He'll probably be happy I'm not there smoking on his furniture or wearing a path on his rugs."

They reached the end of businesses along the main street and headed into the residential area. James hoped she'd keep going, drive out of town into the country where no one would see them.

"So what's going on, little brother?" she asked.

James repositioned in his seat. He looked out the side window at house after house flowing by. "I need to know something," he said without looking at her.

The car slowed, Magdalena quieted, and James could feel her attentiveness. "I figured," she said.

He glanced her way, and she turned to him, her

face serious, the joviality set aside. She looked straight ahead then, both hands on the steering wheel, the cigarette gone. James looked ahead with her. The houses were thinning, country taking over the scenery, the privacy he needed to ask what he had to know. "What Pop said about Mama the other night when she slapped him... The thing I told you about..."

Magdalena didn't say anything. James had never seen an expression like the one she had on her face. It was years older than she ever behaved; it was full of everything he didn't know about her, things she probably didn't want to know herself. "You talk to anyone else about this?"

He shook his head. "No."

In Magdalena's silence he thought he heard the answers to what he wanted to know. Voices that sounded like Pop and her shouted in his head—*that boy*…you're different from Pop…you're not stuck like I am…baseball isn't in your blood. He thought he was going to be sick again. He reached for the door's handle.

"I told you Pop made his own mess," Magdalena said.

"Who was Jim?" He gripped the door's handle. It was slippery from the sweat on his palm.

Magdalena tucked her head forward, her brows knit into a frown. She pulled the car to the side of the road and stopped, killed the engine. She twisted in her seat so she looked James square on. She frowned for a long time, and he let her. He wanted to know. Harold had said there was a Jim, but he'd said little more. Finally Magdalena drew in a long breath, then let it out. "Jim was Mama's friend," she said. "He used to visit when I was little. Pop never trusted him. I told you, Pop made his own trouble."

James shook his head. "That doesn't tell me anything."

Magdalena settled deeper into the seat. She gazed out the front window, stared up toward the sky, then looked back at James. "Mama grew up with Jim. They were always friends, good friends. Probably would have been better if…if Pop hadn't asked for her." She paused and shrugged. "You never knew Mama's grandma. She came around now and then when I was growing up. She finally died, but not before she tried to make up for sending Mama off to marry the way she did. I heard Mama's grandma say once, 'There's lots of girls with no man in their lives, too many girls with a bad man in their life, and one girl with a good one.' She wished Mama had been that girl, that one girl, but she wasn't. Grandma thought sending Mama with Pop would be good for her. Jim would have been better."

"But Jim never was?" James asked, not sure he wanted to know any more. "He never was good for her? Not even once?" He felt his insides grow cold. He ran his fingers along the door's handle, just in case.

Magdalena shook her head. "He married some woman named Claire. Jim never came after they got married, except to bring Mama back home when she went there once. It was an especially bad time. She said she had to go see her grandma. She was gone a little bit, then she came back, pretty sick. Jim brought her, but he didn't stay."

James didn't ask when Mama went there, he didn't ask why he bore Jim's name.

"It ain't what you're thinking," Magdalena said.

271

Choke up so you have more control, step back for better perspective, don't believe everything you hear, and your Mama's the most beautiful woman I've ever known. "I'm ready to go back," James said, and he looked forward. Even with Magdalena staring at him he refused to look her way. Maybe he should walk back to town, spend some time thinking. No, he wanted to ride. He wanted to do like his sister did, ride and think. Maybe he'd ask for a cigarette and smoke while she drove.

Magdalena finally straightened in her seat and started the car. James listened to her light up a cigarette and inhale. The car filled with smoke as she let her breath out. She hung the cigarette out the window and let the car creep forward. He leaned back on the seat. If it wasn't what he was thinking, then what was it? He was either *that boy* or he was James Paine. He couldn't be both.

Chapter 39

Lana 1940

A small bell jangled as Lana entered the store. A few faces turned, men and women both, then all went back to their own business. Lana closed the door gently, holding onto the bell so it wouldn't jingle again, and slipped to the nearest aisle.

She had money in her pocket. Cletus had never done that before, but he'd laid money on the table after his breakfast and said, "Go to town. The boys are growing out of their pants." He hadn't set much there, but he'd said it would be enough. "Get what we need and try to look decent when you go." She wondered if this was a penance, an effort to erase the shame of never being there, leaving her without him at his shop. Being caught with more than the stench of burnt metal on his skin.

She'd done her best to look decent, for her own sake as much as his. Her dresses were all worn and plain, faded and cinched around her waist with a tired belt. Magdalena'd stood over her while she fixed her hair, insisting Lana wear some of the makeup Magdalena had given her. Magdalena had said it made her more beautiful, but Lana knew it only masked the emptiness behind her face, nothing more.

She ran a hand over her tired dress as the store

opened up in front of her, exploding with odors plentiful and pleasant. She inhaled deeply, drawing in scents different from dirt, cow, grass, and roast pork. It had been so long since she'd been in a store, long enough she'd forgotten how fragrances intertwined with confections, burlap softened pungent spices, and leather competed with soaps. She inhaled again as she drifted down an aisle, turned into another, touching, inhaling, and forgetting her own world.

"Would you like some help?"

Lana glanced up. A man stood above her, the same man she'd seen here before, ages ago when she'd come in with Cletus. He was slender, clean shaven, and balding. A white apron covered the front of him, a crisp collar above and neat shoes below. He smiled.

"No. Thank you, though." Her face felt hot. She felt like a naughty child, touching things that weren't hers. "I'm just deciding what I want."

"Let me or the missus know if you need help." The man nodded at a counter at the far end of the aisle. A plump woman stood behind it, her curly gray hair bobbing up and down pleasantly as she helped a customer. Lana noticed how much wider the woman's apron was across her top half than her husband's. She smiled. They suited each other.

"Thank you." Lana nodded at the man. He strolled away, and she watched his back. He was peaceful. His wife seemed the same. The whole of the store felt serene. No one yelled, no one was sour. She envied this sort of calm and wished she could buy it instead of dry goods. He disappeared around the end of the aisle, and she continued to stare where he'd been.

"I know how you must feel."

Lana glanced up.

Mr. Kline stood above her, his face expressionless, the same as it had been at the peace dinner ages ago. She moved away, to the opposite side of the aisle. He followed, and stepped in front of her.

"He's careless with his home life. It's in your eyes. I see it there. Will he be as careless in his business, as well?" Mr. Kline was close. Behind his empty expression she saw worry, he was genuinely afraid, but not for her.

Lana backed away, groped her way down the aisle toward the door. "I don't know what you're talking about."

Mr. Kline's eyes stayed on her as she stumbled backwards against the door. The bell clanged again as she pushed it open. It rang as she darted through, letting it close her off from Mr. Kline.

"Mrs. Paine?"

Lana fell against Ida, the woman with dark hair like her brother's, a blur in Lana's tears.

"You're white as a ghost. Are you okay? Are you expecting again?"

Lana nodded, then shook her head. "I was just leaving, going home."

The bell jangled again, and the door to the store swung open. Mr. Kline stood there, the question, the accusation still on his face.

Lana stumbled backwards, away from Ida. Ida stared from Lana to Mr. Kline, a frown creasing her brow.

"I need to go." Lana turned away.

Ida's fingers were around Lana's arm before she could escape. They were strong, jerking Lana to a stop.

"I need to go," Lana insisted. Ida's grip intensified, and the woman steered her forward, stepping at a quick gait. "You can let go of me." Lana wrenched her arm loose and stopped. Ida stopped with her and glanced back. Lana tried not to, but she followed Ida's gaze. Mr. Kline was gone. Ida looked back at Lana, the handsome face so like her brother's but pinpointed and sharp, her dark eyes shouting instead of speaking. "I don't know you, but my brother seems to have taken an extraordinary interest in you. And your family. Now it seems that Mr. Kline has also…"

Lana shook her head. She didn't understand. "Your brother's been kind, but…" She glanced back to the store where Mr. Kline had been.

"A woman has to know her place and understand men at the same time. Don't confuse your needs with their behavior. It's too easy to flatter yourself, especially when…"

Lana backed away. "I need to go."

Ida's eyes stayed on her, drilling staves into the cold barren emptiness she felt inside. Lana pivoted. She tried not to run, but she hurried toward home. The money, money that felt strange in her small cloth bag, was suddenly heavy. The clanking of the coins jangled out what she didn't want to hear. *It's too easy to flatter yourself, especially when… Will he be as careless in his business as he is with his home life?*

The cavern where the scream lived swelled, the emptiness so immense the scream seemed diminished, a tiny sound that ricocheted, searching for a way out. She ran when she was out of town and out of sight, but still the accusations and questions stayed with her.

Chapter 40

James 1958

Pop's shop was hot, the warmest place in town in the winter. James stacked iron rods on top of iron rods, same length, same type.

"See how I did that?" James asked Toby, a boy of twelve Pop had hired to take James' old job. Toby nodded. "Do it right, or my pop will make you sorry." James knew Pop had hired more than one boy since James had quit ages ago. None of them had lasted. No one could stand working for Pop. Toby nodded again.

James walked to the welding station, the one Harold used to work at. Harold had finally opened a store across the street from Mr. Morgan's restaurant, one that had been empty since James could remember. Pop hadn't asked James to come back and work for him again. James had just shown up after Harold quit. Neither Pop nor James said a thing. James just went to work. He was going to find out if he was a Paine. He'd do his best, and he'd find out what was or wasn't in his blood.

The fires were hot, forming a formidable wall against the encroaching cold. Pop left the front doors open all year long. It was the only light during the day, except for the flames inside. It was the only air worth breathing. It kept them from the cough one man said welders always got. James didn't want the cough. He looked up at the snowflakes melting against the wall of heat, a clash of cool beauty and fierce hotness.

Three heavy brackets hit the dirt at James' feet. Clangs such as that no longer startled him. Surprises and loud noises were Pop's way of telling him there was something to do. Bars banged and clattered to the ground. James looked up. Pop nodded toward the man beside him, then walked away.

James looked at the man. He tried to be like Harold had been, softer than Pop, good to the customers. "What can I do for you?" he asked.

The man sized up James' arms. He was muscular beneath his shirt. The sweat made it cling to his skin. He was stronger than he'd ever been. If he hit a baseball now, no one would ever find it; it would go too far. But that didn't matter. He didn't hit baseballs anymore.

"Got plenty more of those." The man jabbed the rails with his boot toe. "They're out on my truck bed."

James waited for the man to say more. The man was like Pop, he said nothing, so James looked toward the open door. "Show me where they are."

What the man wanted was impossible, too large for the shop. James nodded as he stood in the snow, listening to what the man wanted him to construct. *He's lazy*, James thought. *Too lazy to build a proper building, so he's cheating and wanting me to do something out of metal instead of him doing it with wood.* James nodded. "Sure," he said. He sounded like Harold, but his thoughts were like Pop's. "I can do that." *But then you've got to figure out how to haul it away.*

"He'll do it in sections," Pop said from behind

James. "Then he'll bring them out to your farm and weld them all together for you."

James clenched his hands into fists, then straightened his fingers.

"That'd be mighty fine," the man said. He looked at James. Pop walked away, back into the shop, his boots making crunching noises in the snow.

"I'll unload this for you," James said. Already the mountain of metal was blanketed with snow and icy cold. He'd have to store it inside so no one would steal the iron, do bit welding a piece at a time, then carry them outside as the monstrosity grew. It was impossible.

The man moved inside and talked to Pop while James unloaded the iron. His shirt became soaked with sweat and snow. He wanted to pull it off and put his jacket on instead, but he didn't. Pop was watching. He could feel his eyes like tiny beads of fire. He worked long; he worked hard. Pop shook the man's hand, and the man rode away, his tires noisy in the snow.

James sorted and stacked long, rusty, cold rails of metal while Pop looked on. What James had learned to do with the welding rods he did with this man's unruly mess. James made noise, more noise than he'd ever made before. It was music to his ears, the ring of frustration. He heaved, he dragged, he kicked, and he threw. It took the rest of the day. It took all of his fury.

Pop shut down the shop at the end of the day. He closed the gas bottles. He dowsed the lamps. Pop said goodbye to his workers and shut the huge front doors. After he'd latched them, he walked to the small door he'd leave through, locking it behind him. James followed, his jacket slung over his shoulder, the icy snow a blessed relief on the heat of his muscles. Pop stepped to the truck and climbed inside.

"I'm not riding with you," James said. "I'll be home later."

Pop started the truck and backed away. James watched him, listened to the deep throaty growl of the engine he'd grown up terrified of, the sound that haled his pop coming home, the roar that had said *hurry* all his life. The truck disappeared, tracks mashed in the snow, the rumble of its engine fading away. James waited until Pop was completely gone and he was alone on the walk. It was peaceful, it was still. He shivered. It felt good.

James cut behind Pop's building and into the alley between it and the main street stores. He veered to the right and entered Mr. Morgan's restaurant from the rear. He could hear the familiar clang of pans and dishes, the rush for the evening crowd. Ida shouted orders, and someone said they got it. He was too tired to smile. He nodded at the cook who glanced up as he made his way to the main restaurant. He spotted the first empty table and dropped into a chair. It was the one he'd sat in when Mr. Morgan hired him ages ago. He draped his jacket over the seat next to him and settled back against the wall, watching the din around him.

James drifted away with the hum of the restaurant. He closed his eyes and rested, a blanket of soothing sounds and smells easing his tired muscles, trading places with the stench of rust and burnt metal.

"This is for you," a voice said. James started and opened his eyes. "I thought you looked like you needed a steak and a stout cup of coffee, but Mr. Morgan said to give you this." The waiter disappeared. James looked down at the table. A dish of three mountains of ice cream sat there, each covered with chocolate lava, fruit, and candies sprinkled on their sides like trees in a forest. He looked up. He looked through the bustle of bus boys and waiters, harried waitresses and customers. Mr. Morgan stood behind the fountain, wiping his hands on a white towel. He grinned and nodded. The busy restaurant closed in again, obliterating Mr. Morgan from view. James looked down at the sundae in front of him. He felt it crack open. The door to his soul.

The restaurant was quiet when James finally stood to leave. He'd savored the sundae, letting each drop explode in his mouth. If Andy'd been here for this one, he wouldn't have got a single bite, again. James had smiled through the whole dessert, and he smiled as he walked to pay.

Mr. Morgan was at the cash register, his employees cleaning the tables, Ida somewhere in the back. His dark eyes smiled at James as he approached. "On the house," Mr. Morgan said as James fished in his pocket for what little money he had.

"What?"

"You looked like you needed it," Mr. Morgan said.

James glanced at the bill he'd extracted from his pocket. Mr. Morgan was right. Again. Something about a sundae did open up the door to the soul. Each spoonful took James back in time, to days of boyhood, baseball, and mysteries that were carefully veiled back then. James nodded and looked into those eyes that felt like home. "I did. It made me forget some of the rough stuff and reminded me of good things. Thank you." He extended the dollar.

Mr. Morgan raised his palm, warding off James' offer.

"You've given me a lot of good things, Mr. Morgan." James stuffed the bill back into his pocket. "I never thanked you, but I'm thanking you now. Like your good advice. Your help. Compliments to me and my family. You drove me to the tryout."

Mr. Morgan looked James in the eye. "I gave you one other thing."

James frowned. He wasn't sure what he'd missed. There'd been a lot, but he thought he'd summed it up well.

"Your glove."

James frowned at Mr. Morgan. Christmas was there in those dark eyes, that Christmas long ago when he'd received the glove. Pop had been upset, Magdalena had been thrilled, Mama had… Mama had been beautiful. That's when James had seen it, seen Mr. Morgan was right, Mama was beautiful. James didn't know what to say. He hadn't touched the glove in maybe a year. He hadn't played ball since he'd failed at the tryout.

"I want you to use it again."

James shook his head. "You gave me the glove?"

"What were you thinking about when you ate the sundae this evening?"

"Baseball." James sighed and looked down. "And Andy." The things that lay in his soul. He looked up at Mr. Morgan.

"It's time to be James again. James the ball player. You're ready."

Something bubbled to life inside. James didn't know if he could drag Andy away from the girls he'd discovered long enough to help him, but these muscles he had were surely good for something. He could pitch again, somehow force Andy to catch. Mr. Morgan was right, he needed to be himself again.

"I'll provide the sundaes." Mr. Morgan grinned.

James wanted to hug him, but he didn't. His life was charging forward, like a burst of acceleration when riding with Magdalena. "Thank you, thank you again, Mr. Morgan! We all thank you!" James couldn't wait. He couldn't wait to slip the glove over his hand. He couldn't wait to tell Andy, Magdalena, his other sisters, and Harold. And Mama. Beautiful Mama. Maybe this would bring beauty back into her eyes.

Chapter 41

Lana 1940

Magdalena opened the door to Mr. Morgan's restaurant and held it, waiting for Lana to enter. Her daughter's ease at what she was doing impressed her. There was no shyness on Magdalena's face, no evidence of feeling ashamed.

"Come on, Mama." Magdalena stretched to her toes. She grinned. She was excited. "They'll be all right. Even Carla. You and I will sit here for awhile until their movie's over. We'll have fun!"

Lana stepped through the door. She wanted to ask about Ida, whether Ida was here and what she'd think of Lana's children seeing their first movie while she spent some leisurely time at a restaurant. "Maybe we should go to the other café. Maybe we should have stayed at the movie."

"Mama, you know Betsy wanted to be in charge. Let her. She'll be proud." Magdalena wasn't fooling her. She had chosen Mr. Morgan's restaurant because she knew how her father despised the man. "Come on. The food's good here."

Harold and Alex had begged Cletus for money before he left for work. They wanted to see a film and had promised to work extra hard if he'd let them. Lana was shocked when Cletus slapped money on the table.

Magdalena swiped it up the moment he walked out the door, counted it, did the math, and said there was enough for her and Lana to have a soda, something Lana'd never had.

The restaurant buzzed with a pleasant early afternoon hum. Booths lined both walls and small Formica-topped dining tables with matching covered chairs were scattered throughout the center. She hadn't noticed the colors before. She'd only seen the darkness of Cletus' shop, the closed office door. In the back of the restaurant and off to one side was a long, shiny counter with silver fountains and glass containers full of brightly colored candies.

"It's sure pretty, ain't it, Mama?"

Lana scoured the faces for Ida. If she was here, she was in the back. "It's wonderful, but…"

"Let's sit down." Magdalena headed to the left, passing a number of booths until she came to the same one the children had sat in before. Magdalena slid in one side and pointed to the seat across from her. "Sit there, Mama."

Lana slid in opposite her daughter, almost missing the seat, her eyes taking in the colors, the lines, and the bustle around her. "This really is nice."

Mr. Morgan fell into her line of perusal. He was behind the fountain, leaning an elbow on a tall silver canister. His face danced with animation, he was engaged in conversation with another man, who was feasting on something colorful in a tall fountain glass. Mr. Morgan's laugh carried above the restaurant din. He sounded happy, he looked content. He threw his head back as he laughed, and then he spotted her and his eyes changed. He finished his conversation and looked her way again. He snatched up a small white towel, wiped his hands, and walked toward their booth.

Her face heated as he drew near. Mr. Morgan certainly knew, knew what Mr. Kline had insinuated and Ida had fairly stated. He had to know what Ida thought of her, also.

"Maybe we should go." Lana leaned forward and whispered to Magdalena.

Magdalena scrunched up her face. "Why?"

"Good afternoon, ladies." Mr. Morgan was beside the table, an aroma sweeping with him, a blend of fried food, sweet fruity flavors, and pine soap.

"Hello, Mr. Morgan." Magdalena looked up and grinned. "I brought Mama back."

Lana looked up as Mr. Morgan looked down. His eyes sparkled, but still she knew. She could see it in his gaze, what everyone thought, what everyone probably was aware of. Her face grew warm.

"Welcome to my restaurant. Since you didn't have anything the first time, my offer still stands. For both of you. Whatever you want is on me."

"Oh, goody!" Magdalena bounced in her seat.

"No, no, we couldn't." Lana reached across the table toward her daughter.

"You could. And I insist. What would you like?"

"One of those big burgers with cheese and onions and catsup. Oh, and dill pickles. And some of those fried potatoes, with pepper on them, and a soda. Make that a root beer float." Magdalena fired her order off. Lana frowned.

"How about double that?" Mr. Morgan grinned.

Lana wanted to ask—ask what she should do. His eyes were so kind, and so was he. *Don't get your needs confused with the way men are.* He turned and walked away. She watched him disappear to the back and through a door.

Her needs. She didn't even know for sure what they were, but they were there. And they hurt.

"See that man over there?" Magdalena leaned across the table and whispered, her eyes alight, almost with sparks. Lana looked at a man she didn't know, while Magdalena whispered on, telling a bit about him, and then another. Sitting in Mr. Morgan's restaurant with her daughter was like watching a movie. A panorama of people strolled in, ate and conversed, then walked out while Magdalena kept a running narration, whispering everything she knew about each person.

Lana eyed her daughter. "How do you know so much?"

Magdalena shrugged.

"Here you go." A waitress appeared with their food. "Anything else?"

"Nope," Magdalena said, stuffing a fried potato into her mouth.

The waitress disappeared, and Lana lifted the sandwich from her plate. It looked delicious. She tasted a fried potato—crisp, salty, peppery, and greasy. This was nothing like what she made at home, nothing like anything she'd ever had before. She devoured every bite.

"This was truly wonderful." Lana closed her eyes and leaned back in her seat. There were fewer people now, fewer customers, and more sounds of cleaning than cooking and talking, the odor of pine overpowering the smell of fried food. Lana relaxed, drifting along with the last few minutes of quiet, of adults interacting with each other, before she was to meet her children outside the theater.

The bell tingled on the door. She heard it open, and she listened, counting the footsteps of whoever'd come in. It was one person, not two. Soft steps, rather brisk, probably a woman. The footsteps approached from behind, passed near their booth, and continued to the back of the restaurant. A chair scooted out, and Lana heard the person sit. She imagined the person looking around, deciding what to order…

Then that smell. A sweet odor caught her, billowing in the wake of whoever had passed. Lana straightened and opened her eyes. She saw the back of her, the woman she'd only seen once but now smelled for the third time.

"Let's go." Lana slid to the end of her seat and stood. Magdalena followed Lana's gaze to the woman's back.

Lana fumbled with her cloth bag, searching for the money Cletus had given her.

"No need for that." He was near. She hadn't heard him or seen him approach. Mr. Morgan was there beside her, between her and that woman.

"Please, I insist," Lana whispered. She glanced around Mr. Morgan, at the woman's back.

The woman turned, out of curiosity, nosiness, or impatience. She stared at Lana for a moment before her face changed and Lana felt the color drain from hers.

Suddenly Magdalena was there between them, her back to the woman and her face toward Lana. Mr. Morgan's arm threaded through hers, but she pulled back. "I can't," Lana said. "Your sister, other people…"

"Pay no attention to Ida," he said close to Lana's

ear. "She means well, but she imagines far more than she knows." He steered her to the door, her arm wedged within his, Magdalena behind them closing off the view between Lana and the woman.

Mr. Morgan opened the door and let loose of Lana's arm. "Do come back," he said. "Any time."

Magdalena thanked him as the door closed between them and the woman. Lana looked back.

"Don't, Mama." Magdalena turned toward the theater. "We'll go back, like he said. And next time we'll have beef stew. But don't look back. I never do."

Chapter 42

James 1959

"Whose car is this?" James looked at the red and white monstrosity Magdalena drove into the lane. She idled to a stop and cut the engine smoothly instead of throwing it into a violent death. Mama stood next to him. They watched the driver's door open and Magdalena's curly head pop out, a cigarette balanced between her lips.

"Kevin's," she said, squinting in her own smoke.

James looked at Mama, *Who's Kevin?* in his glance. Mama was probably wondering the same thing, but she kept it to herself, nothing in her expression letting anyone know if she was surprised.

"Ready to go?" Magdalena took the cigarette from her mouth. She gazed over the top of the car at them.

"Sure." James opened the passenger door for Mama. She slid in, and he closed it for her. He slipped into the rear seat and slid to the middle so he could lean on the back of the front seat to hear and talk. Magdalena jumped in, started the car, and backed up. They were on their way. A baseball game. James patted the glove on the seat next to him.

Playing baseball was harder than it used to be. James didn't play for fun now, and it was no longer because he wanted to be good enough so Pop would come. He played for real again, even more so than he had before, played more than town games. He had to go farther away, try harder to find games and teams that would challenge him, put him in front of the people who mattered. This game, the one Magdalena was driving him to, was that game. A tryout. Scouts were supposed to be there, scouts from the Lakewood team he'd tried out for before. James stared at the road. Magdalena drove plenty fast, but not fast enough. He dug his knees into the back of the seat, pushing the car harder and faster. He wanted to be there now.

"You ready for this?" Magdalena shouted over the engine, the sound of the wheels biting at the dirt and rock in the road.

"You bet," James shouted back. He thought of all the nights he and Andy had stayed late in Pop's shop because it was cold and wet outside, Andy crouched, catching, while James pitched. Over and over, night after night. Pop never knew. James never told him. Pop would have locked James out, taken back the key James carried. He and Andy pitched and caught, pitched and caught, until finally Andy would beg for relief and they would cut through the alley to Mr. Morgan's restaurant, where he waited for them, ready to make two heaping ice cream sundaes so they could talk baseball.

Mama smiled over her shoulder at James, her gaze resting on Magdalena before she returned it to the road. The smile waned. James knew Magdalena would tell them who Kevin was when she was ready. And she'd let them know about Max, whether he was still her husband or not. Pop made sure Magdalena had no safety net. He wasn't there to catch her between beaus or between husbands. She wasn't allowed to stay at home anymore. She had to go from one fellow to the next if she wanted a place to stay. It didn't seem to bother her. She never asked to come home, she never seemed heartbroken, either, for the Maxs, the Earls, or the Joes she left behind.

Dexter was over an hour away. James had left work early, and Mama had left fixing supper to Betsy. Neither he nor Mama said it to the other as they'd stood side by side in the drive, waiting for Magdalena. They both knew this was the way things were now. Pop would manage without them.

"There it is!" Magdalena shouted like a child. James jumped, craned farther forward against the front seat. Dexter loomed ahead, houses and buildings waning to insignificance as James spotted a big crowd of cars on the right. That must be the ball diamond. He grabbed his glove and scooted to the door. Magdalena pulled in behind the cars.

"See you after the game." He slammed the car's door behind him and ran toward the field. Other players, some he'd played with before, milled around, tossing balls back and forth while they waited. He became lost amongst them.

James forgot about time, the rest of his life, the parts of it that pitted failure against success. Mama's voice pierced his concentration when he was near the fence or coming to bat, Magdalena's Indian war whoop embarrassing him. He pitched, he batted, he played infield and out. He watched the other players, he studied the crowd, anyone who looked like a scout, anyone who didn't.

Finally he saw him. Them. One he'd seen before, when he'd tried out last time. The man next to him was new, different, but there they were, notebooks on their laps and pencils in their hands.

"Batter up!"

James tapped the sides of his shoes with the bat, then let it swing loosely at his side as he walked to the plate. This was his third at-bat. The first two had been easy, and the pitcher this time didn't look any tougher than those. He stepped to the plate and squared himself, the bat high in the air until he was settled. Someone said something—it came from the stands. The umpire raised his hands and stepped back. James looked around. One of the scouts was at the fence. He was pointing his pencil, and the umpire hollered, "Time out!"

James backed out of the batter's box, swinging the bat just to keep moving. He scanned the field, wondering why they'd stopped the game. A man called the pitcher off the mound. James watched him go, the young man looking as puzzled as James. James looked back around the bases, infielders slapping their gloves, watching. He gazed along the fence, past the waiting batters, beyond the bleachers, then stopped. He let the bat hang down, the tip resting in the dirt at his feet. Mr. Morgan. His fingers were woven through the fence, his eyes on James.

Mr. Morgan tipped his head to the left. James frowned. Mr. Morgan stood straight and stepped back, his fingers still looped through the fence, his arms outstretched. The baseball hit the catcher's glove. It sounded like a gunshot. James yanked his gaze from Mr. Morgan to the catcher, who flinched, shook his glove hand, and threw the ball back to the pitcher. James followed the ball, followed its lazy path to a pitcher he recognized. Long and lean, the one Mr. Morgan had said was pro at the last tryout. James wheeled back to Mr. Morgan. He nodded, he moved close to the fence then stepped back again. *Step back. Gain perspective.*

In the hot afternoon air James felt a chill. Why had the scout switched pitchers on him? He stared at Mr. Morgan, hoping he had the answer. Mr. Morgan nodded. He let go of the fence and clapped his hands once.

"You can do this, James," Mr. Morgan said, at the same moment his mother's voice called the same thing.

Step back. Gain perspective.

James looked from Mr. Morgan to his mother, her auburn hair, her slender arm raised in a wave. She was beautiful, beautiful like Mr. Morgan had said, beautiful and didn't know it, like Magdalena had said.

"Batter up!"

James didn't know how many practice pitches had sped by. He hadn't heard any after the first one. He'd only heard Mama and Mr. Morgan. He glanced back to where Mr. Morgan stood. He wasn't there. He'd moved. James looked but couldn't see him. He stepped to the plate, bat high.

Step back. Gain perspective.

James held the bat in the air while he stared at the pitcher, but it was Mr. Morgan he saw, in his mind. He kept the bat up; he needed another minute. Mama was there next; he saw her lithe form in faded dresses, always at the games. James stepped back, several inches farther from the plate than he usually stood. He lowered the bat to his shoulder and dug in. He was ready. He had his perspective.

There was no warning, barely a motion. But James didn't need a warning this time. He was ready for the pitch. His bat was as quick as the pitcher's snaky arm. James swung, he connected, and the ball sailed away.

"Go, James!" Mama yelled, her voice rang with excitement, while Magdalena whooped.

"Go, James, run!" Mr. Morgan's voice came from behind, like two hands at his back, pushing him.

James jetted off the plate, his legs carrying him around the bases as fielders ran after the ball that dropped behind them. It wasn't over the fence, but almost. James pounded the dirt, his heart beating in stride. He rounded third. He ran, and ran hard. He knew Mr. Morgan was to his right and Mama somewhere ahead. He dug deeper, he pushed forward, he flattened himself and slid feet first, slid under the smack of the ball in the catcher's glove. People cheered, the catcher helped him up and congratulated him. Mama screamed with excitement, and somewhere nearby Mr. Morgan clapped. James just knew it without even seeing the man.

****

His sweat didn't seem to bother Mama or Magdalena when the game was over. James' two best fans wrapped themselves around him when he finally stepped off the field. Mama held onto his arm, Magdalena grinned, bobbed up and down a little, and ran her hand through his damp hair.

"You did good, little brother. If there was a scout here, he noticed you!" Magdalena tussled his hair, then let go.

"Oh, they were here," James said. Magdalena raised her eyebrows, and James nodded to his right, toward the other bleachers where the two men had been sitting. Magdalena turned, so did Mama, and when James looked along with them, the scouts were gone. It was Mr. Morgan they saw, he was standing there, watching them.

Standing back. Gaining perspective.

James looked at his mother. Lana was staring at Mr. Morgan. She dropped her hand from James' arm. He couldn't tell what she was thinking, but Mr. Morgan seemed to understand. He came their way, a warm smile on his face.

"Mama?" James touched her arm with the tips of his fingers. She was lost in a communication he was afraid to interrupt, but he felt a part of it somehow. He just didn't know what was being said.

"Mama."

Lana looked his way. She was younger suddenly, yet sage in her expression.

"Mama…"

"Son?"

James turned. He looked into the face of the scout, the one from the first tryout, the other man James didn't recognize standing beside him.

"You're James Paine," the scout said.

James Paine. Magdalena had said it, James had said it himself. James glanced at his mother, then turned back to the man. "Yes, sir, I am."

"I remember you from Marshall, where you tried out before. You were good then. You're even better now. Stronger. But even then you were good enough for an offer, though you looked a little young. Why didn't you take it? Why are you trying again?"

James sputtered. Surely he misunderstood. Or the

man was confused. He glanced at his mother, at Magdalena. Neither one seemed to understand either.

"I beg your pardon," James stammered. "What offer?"

"The one we sent you. You never responded. Just wondered why."

"Sent me…?"

"In the mail. A letter. Didn't you get it?"

Mama's eyes grew wide, Magdalena's fierce. James read in their faces all the agony he'd felt every time Pop missed a game, every time Pop ridiculed him, every time Pop called him *that boy*, or every time James' enthusiasm was dashed by Pop saying baseball wasn't in his blood.

"Pop," he whispered.

"I'd be willing to offer you a second chance at a contract if I knew for sure you were interested. You have a reason why you weren't before? And would you be now?"

"He sure would." A hand clapped over James' shoulder. Tan fingers squeezed as Mr. Morgan spoke near James' ear. "Not sure what happened to that last offer. I vouch this young man never saw it, or he would have been playing for you long before this."

Pop. The name lay dead in James' gut. Pop.

"Be happy to send you another offer, then," the scout said.

"Send it to me. I'll make sure he gets it. Name's Glen Morgan. Here's where to send it…"

Pop. James heard Mr. Morgan recite his address. He saw Mr. Morgan move and lean over the paper the man was writing it on, making sure the scout had it right. Why hadn't Pop given James the letter?

Chapter 43

James 1959

Choke up on the bat. You won't hit as far, but you're more accurate. James inched his fingers higher on the bat the way Mr. Morgan had showed him years ago. The bat quivered in his hands, his fingers tightening, then loosening, repositioning as he stared at Pop's desk.

"You thought all these years I didn't know how to handle a bat, didn't you?" The end of the bat circled high in the air, making rings and loops as James held it off his shoulder. "You wanted me to be no good. Baseball was your game, and I wasn't good enough to be your boy. I was *that boy.*"

James inched around to the back of the desk where Pop sat. He kicked Pop's worn desk chair aside, the rusting casters catching on the gouged floor, sending the chair toppling over. James kicked it again, harder. It skidded against a cabinet, knocking a binder to the floor. James sneered at the scattered papers as he eyed the drawers of Pop's desk, all closed, probably none locked, but it didn't matter. He was going to open them with this bat, one by one, until he found what he was looking for.

"Choke up on the bat. Who taught me that?" James yelled, his voice resounding in the shop. It was empty, dark except for the lamp he'd lit in Pop's office, and it echoed back at him. James' voice sounded bigger than Pop's as it bounded against walls and the high ceiling. "Not you, that's for sure!"

The light from the lamp flickered in his eyes, wetness and light distorting his perspective. He rubbed his eyes against his shoulders, drying away the moisture, keeping the bat up, ready to swing. He inched his fingers higher for stronger impact. "I never cried. I wanted to. I wanted to cry and scream my whole life. Seems now screamin' ain't gonna be enough!"

James raised the bat over his head. He squared himself with the row of drawers on the right. If that letter was in there, the first one from the scout, he'd find it, he'd get it out. Even if Pop really did burn it, he'd beat the desk until he knew for sure. Tears rose again, blurring his vision, but it didn't matter. The desk was his target, the envelope, Pop.

"James."

The bat was at its peak, heaved backward over his head. It quivered as he stretched, every muscle taut, ready to throw the wood forward and smash the desk.

"James."

The voice was closer. He couldn't see who it was.

"Look the other way if you don't want to see this," James yelled. "I came to get something out of this desk, and I aim to get it."

"Don't, James."

The bat sailed across the room. It cracked against the wall, a satisfying splintering of wood, an explosion almost as gratifying as if he'd destroyed Pop's desk. James closed his eyes after the impact. He squinted hard, forcing the wetness out. He drew in a deep breath.

He was trembling.

"He deserves it," James spit out.

The smell of cigarettes came near, cigarettes and a whiff of automobile, and gasoline.

"But Mama doesn't." Magdalena moved in front of him. She was facing him now, standing between him and the desk.

James looked up. He felt fierce as he looked into his sister's eyes, but when he saw them, saw Magdalena's heart, he stopped. "What's Mama got to do with this?"

"When I told you you're different from Pop, that means you're like her. Fight your battles like she does, not like him."

You got your mother's heart, not your father's talent.

"Your battle's not much different from hers."

Be patient, be kind, and fight above the hurt.

Mama never fought Pop. She reasoned. She discussed. She never got anywhere except the time she slapped him. Once for herself and once for Magdalena. Pop shut up after that. Kept quiet around the house for several days. "Mama didn't fight."

Magdalena leaned against Pop's desk and sat back on its top, her long legs stretched out in front of her the same way Pop did when he was talking to a customer. "She doesn't fight like Pop, but she lives a battle."

They'd all lived a battle. Alex joined a war to get away from this battle. A war could destroy his outsides, but this family battle was destroying his insides. Harold chased a girl until he caught her and got married. Betsy withdrew, Gail lived on a tightrope, Carla emulated Mama and followed her shadow, and Magdalena…

Magdalena fought. She fought every day by living in rebellion and hardening her whole being so she didn't care. "What'd Mama do?"

Magdalena frowned, her eyebrows pinching together. "What do you mean, 'What did Mama do?' "

"I guess I don't know anything. I'm five years younger than Carla. It's like I'm a separate family, one Pop made pretty clear he didn't want. Who are we? How did Mama and Pop end up like this with me?"

Magdalena looked up toward the dark ceiling. James liked it when she thought before she fired off a comment. Beneath her bristly exterior was some depth, a wisdom born out of desperation. "Pop didn't end up like this. He was always this way, but the path he chose made him worse. I told you before, he caused his own problems. Mama didn't end up either. She had a tiny spark hidden inside. The battle was so constant no one ever saw it, not even her. Until it got fanned."

"Fanned? How?"

Magdalena shrugged.

"Did I help fan it?"

Magdalena grinned. "Let's just say you keep it alive. You're that boy Mama always hoped for, James. You were the love child that was supposed to make Pop change. She pinned everything on you."

"That boy. I really was *that boy,* then. That boy that Pop didn't want as much as Mama thought."

"It was too late by then. Pop kind of ruined things."

"Five years too late. So why did they do it? Why did they have me? Love seems like the farthest thing from Pop's mind. He doesn't love anyone. How could I be a love child?"

"You're Mama's love child, James."

"Mama's love child?" There was no love in Mama's life except what she brought into their family and what he and his brothers and sisters returned to her. Mama's was a loveless existence. Her marriage was mechanical, a union formed merely to get two humans through adulthood, and nothing more. "Pop never loved Mama." James looked at Magdalena. "Pop was never good to her. He wasn't even kind."

Magdalena stared, a thought teetering on the tip of her tongue. She straightened, lifted herself off Pop's desk. "It isn't kindness that makes a baby, James. Kindness is what turns a boy to a man." She turned and left Pop's office. James heard the outer door close behind her.

Kindness is what turns a boy to a man. He looked through the back wall of Pop's shop, through the wall and across the alley, to the only kindness he'd ever known.

Chapter 44

Lana 1941

He seemed to know what they wanted. Mr. Morgan didn't even bother to ask anymore. When he saw Lana and Magdalena come into the restaurant, he nodded at the booth they had sat in from the first, and they took their seats.

"You look beautiful, Mama," Magdalena said.

They came to town more often. Cletus left money for movies or whatever they needed, and he left it fairly often, left it and left her, never suggesting what she should buy or asking where it had been spent. When they came, Lana wore some of the cosmetics Magdalena had given her, a touch of color that felt obvious but nice, just never nice enough to cover over the hurt that sometimes bled through the artificial tones on her face.

"Thank you." She smiled at her daughter. It felt good to smile. She did feel richer inside, and more alive. Her timidity had begun to dissolve under Mr. Morgan's welcomes. And her courage had strengthened each time she came in, with her hope that other woman wouldn't come in also, the one whose sweet smell blended with Cletus' burnt odor. But if she did...Lana looked across the table at her fair-haired daughter... Lana would be bolstered by two friends, Magdalena and Mr. Morgan. Maybe that small budding of mettle was the real beauty Magdalena saw, or maybe it came from the sundaes Mr. Morgan served, the doorways to her soul.

He'd laughed the first time he said that to her. She'd never seen a sundae before, except from a distance. And she'd never imagined what one would taste like until he brought two to their table that first time, sliding one in front of Magdalena and the other in front of her. She'd gasped. Magdalena had clapped and squealed. It was then that he first said it, that sundaes unlocked the soul.

When that first sweet savor of ice cream covered in chocolate touched the inside of her mouth, an explosion of sugar, a blast of sensation, coursed through her. There was nothing quite so delectable anywhere. Her troubles disappeared and, for a moment, nothing else mattered. The sundae had trickled deep inside, awakening her as it created a world she'd given up fantasizing about, one where all was right, all was perfect, all was pleasant and enjoyable.

Mr. Morgan appeared alongside their table, one sundae in each hand, two spoons sticking up from the pocket of his white apron. His dark skin contrasted with the pools of white below the lava of chocolate dripping down from the mounds of ice cream. He smelled of chocolate, fried food, and pine soap. He smelled clean and safe. He was good, delivering another key to free her soul.

Lana glanced across the table. Magdalena was watching Mr. Morgan's hands as he set the dishes of ice cream in front of them. Then she looked up, her eyes on his face as he retrieved the spoons from his pocket and placed them beside each dish.

"Eat well," he said, "and enjoy."

Magdalena grinned, and Lana saw it, the longing in a girl for a prince. Magdalena...her invisible pony long gone, her first prince, Jim, now married. Grandma had written a little about Jim's wedding and that he still came by to help her even though she'd tried to shoo him away. Jim came because he was kind and he cared. He was a good prince, just like Mr. Morgan.

Oh, Lord, when my little girl chooses a real prince someday, let him be like Jim or Mr. Morgan.

"You should join us." Magdalena's eyes flashed. She latched her fingers around the table's edge to scoot aside and let Mr. Morgan sit next to her.

He glanced at Lana, then turned and surveyed the restaurant. There was only one other customer, the kitchen was quiet, it was a lazy afternoon.

"Certainly," she heard herself say. "Of course you should join us. You're always so generous. You can share my sundae." Lana scooted her dish toward Magdalena's side of the table as her daughter slid toward the wall.

"I really never do things like this," he said. Mr. Morgan wiped his hands on his apron, watching Lana, then looking at the empty spot next to her daughter. "Maybe for a minute."

It was strange yet right to see someone like him across the table. She was so used to harsh looks and a head bent in silence. Now she looked into a smile, into dark eyes that flickered, at dark hair that shone. She put her fingers on the edge of the cold ice cream dish and pushed it farther. "I would be honored to share with you."

One side of Mr. Morgan's mouth kicked up. It somehow reminded her of Magdalena's pretend pony, the way it kicked up in glee. "That one's for you." He slid the dish and spoon her way.

Magdalena suddenly disappeared. She disappeared under the table and reappeared at its edge, where he'd been standing before. She raced to the fountain counter and ducked behind it. Lana watched as her daughter emerged and ran back to the table, a dish in one hand and a spoon in the other. They clattered on the tabletop as she ducked under again and popped up next to Mr. Morgan. Before Lana could say anything, Magdalena dipped ice cream from both of their dishes onto the clean one, splitting the sundaes into three equal amounts.

"There," she said, sliding the new dish and spoon in front of Mr. Morgan. "Now we'll all share."

Lana stared. "Magdalena, how did you know… How did you…"

"I learn things," she said. She retrieved her spoon and scooped a big bite from her own dish. "Let's eat!"

Two thirds of a sundae was the most satisfying treat Lana'd ever had. As the silky sweetness went down, a gentle flow of conversation rose up. The three of them laughed, shared stories, compared life in the country to life in town. When they finished, Magdalena disappeared once again under the table. She stacked their dishes and spoons on one arm and toted them away, promising to return with glasses of water.

"I don't know how she…" Lana commented as Magdalena walked away, the dishes balanced on her arm.

"But you know why," Mr. Morgan said. He was

watching Lana instead of Magdalena. If she hadn't known why before, she did now. She saw herself in his eyes, in a way she never had before. She was beautiful, she was a woman, she had value. Something she'd never recognized but something she'd always wanted.

He said so much by saying so little, his silence full of meaning as opposed to silence that suffocated. Mr. Morgan's silence elicited conversation from her, even though she didn't feel compelled to say anything in return. He somehow evoked meaning in their quietness, answered thoughts even his sundaes couldn't reach.

"Three waters," Magdalena said, scooting under the table and popping up next to Mr. Morgan again. The water was good, cool and clear. They drank in silence, a beautiful silence that said more, meant more, than all of the sundaes and conversations she'd ever had.

Chapter 45

James 1959

The letter came. The offer from the Lakewood team. James would begin training in the spring after a brief winter practice to introduce the players to each other and touch base as a team.

"You sign the top page down here. Use the carbon paper between them so you have a copy. Send the one you signed back to them." Mr. Morgan stood at James' shoulder, the two of them on the street in front of Pop's shop, looking over the sheet of paper in James' hands. Dirt and rust from the iron rods left spots where his fingers rested. He brushed his hands on his pants, one at a time, then tried to blow the faint grime away.

"I can't believe it," James said. He couldn't. The sounds and echoes of the welders inside the cavernous building disappeared, and all he could hear was the smack of a baseball into a mitt, the crack of a bat as it sent a ball out of the field. "Can you believe it?" He looked into Mr. Morgan's face. His excitement was reflected there. James threw his arms around Mr. Morgan's neck, held the man in a squeeze, and couldn't let go. "I won't be all that far away," James said in Mr. Morgan's ear. "You can come and watch. So can Mama and Magdalena. At least when we have home games." James felt Mr. Morgan nod, felt the man's hands reach around him and hug him back. "Thank you, Mr. Morgan. Thank you."

The sounds from Pop's shop grew louder, as if a window had opened. Then they quieted again, as if the window had shut. James didn't look up. He didn't let go of Mr. Morgan. His mind was full of baseball, his heart sailing through the air like the first homerun he'd ever hit.

"You can have that boy you've got ahold of there. You can have his mama, too." Pop's voice cut hotter and more fiery than a welding torch.

James had never felt such searing hatred. He dropped his arms from around Mr. Morgan and looked behind him. Pop was close, closer than he'd ever been. James looked up into his father's face at the hatred, the intense dislike.

"Go! Get on out of here!" Pop roared. Two men stepped out of the shop behind Pop.

"What do you mean, get out of here?"

"I said get out! Both of you! I've put up with this long enough. Never should have to begin with!"

James looked from Pop to Mr. Morgan.

"Your son got his baseball contract today," Mr. Morgan stated. "His second one."

"My son!" Pop laughed. James had never heard his father laugh before. Men trickled from the shop, began to line up along the front. "My son!" He laughed again.

Mr. Morgan moved next to James. "This is his second one because something happened to the first."

Pop's arms were like snakes, quick and limber, shooting out faster than lightning and striking true. Before James could react, there was an ugly sound, a fleshy sound, and Mr. Morgan was on the ground.

Someone gasped, someone hooted, while James dropped to the ground beside Mr. Morgan.

"I said get out, and I meant it!"

Blood trickled from the side of Mr. Morgan's mouth. He curled upward, and propped himself on one elbow. A mountain of red, like a mound of strawberry ice cream, rose on his face. James' heart exploded. Men moved closer, and his father's legs were right behind him.

"Get out of here, both of you!"

"You okay, Mr. Morgan?" James asked, bent over the man. Mr. Morgan nodded.

James burst backwards then, threw all his weight into the knees behind him. A gasp of surprise sounded above him, and men scurried away as Pop toppled to the ground. James was on him before Pop could move. He'd never wanted to hit his father, never thought it would make him feel any better, but he'd never been this age before, with this many years of frustration pent up and the only man who'd really been a father to him lying on the ground behind him.

Pop was slower than his hands had been a moment before. There was surprise on his face, making his arms and legs lag behind the realization that James was on him, hitting him, had knocked him to the ground. Dirt, rust, blotches of red and blood appeared on Pop's face. He threw his hands up in defense, but then he caught the rhythm and got past his surprise. He went from warding off James' blows to throwing a few of his own.

There were words, but James didn't care what Pop said. There were hands on his back, grabbing at his shirt, but he shrugged them away. Pop was fierce now, hands that had worked hard all his life turning to fists that had hated for years. James felt Pop's hatred, felt the years of silence screaming in Pop's blows. More hands grabbed at him, some at Pop, men's voices shouted above and around them.

James felt himself yanked upward, dragged off his father. As he was pulled away, he was no longer like himself, he was like an animal—no thought, no heart, just furor and fervor. He clawed at air, reaching for Pop. He yelled. Pop wasn't clawing toward him. Pop's arms were down as his friends dragged him back. Pop had stopped. When they released him, he rose to his feet and shoved the men aside. He stepped to James, one finger raised. The finger came to James' face. More threatening than Pop's fist, it stopped, poised.

"Never come back. Not to my shop, not to my house. Same for your mother. Neither of you come back." Pop turned, brushed through the crowd of men, and disappeared into his shop.

Hands dropped James. Men disappeared through the same door Pop had gone through. Only James was left. James, Mr. Morgan, and dirt clumped by drops of blood. James kicked the dirt. He kicked it again, his toe digging into the gullies cut by their brutality. He turned to Mr. Morgan, stared into his face, retrieved the contract from the ground, and marched away.

Chapter 46

Lana 1941

"Do you ever intend to marry?" Lana cupped her hands around the mug of coffee, wondering why she had asked and whether he would answer.

Magdalena had gone with her brothers and sisters to the movie this time, leaving Lana to shop, to spend the extra money as she saw fit. She had—on fabric, flour, sugar, and more. Too much to carry on her own, so it was stacked just inside the door to Mr. Morgan's restaurant while she sat at her usual booth, the remaining few cents she'd had left buying the cup of warm coffee she had her hands wrapped around now.

Mr. Morgan was relaxed across from her, taking a break while business was slow. He ran a fingertip around the rim of his cup, hemming in the steam and the black drink with an imaginary circle. "I don't think marriage is something we should intend to do. We can't plan it, as if the sort of love we want is secondary to making a ceremonial commitment. I see it the other way. To love well is essential. With or without a ceremony. With that sort of love, I'll be married in my heart."

Lana felt it, a tiny ember so layered under years of just being asked for, of so much hurt and ice that she'd forgotten it was there. It jumped from deep within—

longing, forgotten longing that had been there her whole life. What Mr. Morgan said fanned it and brought it to life. Tears followed, roiled upward behind it, and she looked into her cup.

"That probably was more than you wanted to know. I'm sorry. But I couldn't just tell you yes or no. Not you. You needed to hear the truth because it's there in you, the same as it is in me. You haven't really forgotten it's there, you've just tried to."

That scream, it wasn't a scream at all. It was an ache, a deep need to love and be loved. It resented mockeries, it despised superficial imitations, and it wanted to live. Be let out and live.

The flames glowed, lighting up the dark cavern inside. "I can..." She didn't know what else to say or how to say it. There weren't words or fables for what she could. It was just there, the ability in her to love and be loved. "I can."

"Yes, you can. That's what's beautiful in you, the love that knows no bounds. Love like yours is a law to itself, limitless, only confined by the nature of what love is."

She understood deep within. The ember leapt even further to life. His hand touched hers, his warmth helping to thaw her ice. He slid from his seat and drew her up, the ache bubbling up like a fire into her throat. By the time she was beside him, it came out, it came out with tears, deep sobs of joy and agony, all rolling out onto his shoulder.

She'd never known the smell of a man without the scent of burnt metal. Or cheap perfume. She'd never known that beneath the smell of pine soap, sweets, and fried food, Mr. Morgan smelled like heart, like soul, like strength and kindness. She drew him in, inhaled him. He was the same as her. She felt his cheek on top of her head and his arm pulling her close. It tightened around her middle and forced the rest of the ache upward, making it spill out even more, soaking his shoulder.

"Glen…" It was Ida. She was at the back of the restaurant, her fists on her hips.

"Not now," he said. Mr. Morgan took Lana, like a child, like a woman being born, and lifted her from the room. She didn't know where they were going, but the restaurant was behind them, along with Ida's accusing glare. He was close. He drew her into himself, as he took her away. To a place her heart could bleed, and heal, and love.

Chapter 47

James 1959

Mama came through the door, the door to the small bedroom Kevin had let James use after Pop threw him out. James was packing; so was Magdalena. Kevin hadn't panned out like she'd planned. "He's too much like Pop," Magdalena had said. It was all she'd said, and James left it at that. Even though Kevin had allowed James to stay, James had never felt welcome. Maybe that's what Magdalena meant, why it didn't work out. It didn't seem to matter to her, so it didn't matter to James either. He was packing for the brief winter baseball session. After that, he didn't know what he'd do until the team began its spring practice session. James didn't know where Magdalena was going, she hadn't said, but she always found a place.

Mama looked thinner, worn, and tired. James stopped layering his clothing into his bag and stared at her, the paleness of her face, the red rim around her eyes as she stared at what he'd packed. "You could come with me," he said. Mama had stayed with Pop, even when he threw them both out. James had begged her to come to Magdalena's with him, but she had refused. *It can't be any worse than it's ever been.* She hadn't said it, but James had seen the thought in her eyes. There had been plenty of disappointment, plenty of hurt. She didn't think there could be so much more that she couldn't take it.

Mama shook her head. She crossed her arms and looked at his bag.

"I'll only be gone a week. You could be gone for a week. Please come."

Mama looked up, and her gaze drifted to the window behind him. She stared out at nothing. She was just traveling the only way she ever would, by imagination.

There was a thud by the front door, and Magdalena appeared behind Mama. She brushed her hands together as if she'd just built something instead of taking it apart. "That's done," she said. "I'm packed and ready. Need any help?" She eyed James' lone bag.

"I got it," he answered. "I want Mama to go with me."

Magdalena eyed their mother, then looked back at James. She shook her head. "She can't." Something about the way she said it told James she was right. He didn't understand it, but he knew. He slapped his remaining clothing into the suitcase. He trusted his sister, but he was fed up with the way things were, tired of the fact that he never understood.

"I'm ready," he said at last. He latched the suitcase and yanked it off the bed. "Tell Kevin thanks for letting me stay here."

Magdalena snorted. She turned and walked to the front door. James and Mama followed as she carried her two bags out of the house to the front yard, where she set them down. "I've got a ride coming," she said.

James looked at Mama. She didn't return the glance. He knew she wouldn't. Magdalena's life was always a puzzle, one James knew Mama always hoped would finally piece together. They stood at the edge of the yard. Magdalena lit up a cigarette and waited, watching down the street to the left until it came, Max's big lumbering car moving toward them.

"Max?" James didn't mean to say it out loud.

"Just borrowing it," Magdalena said. She blew smoke in the direction Max was coming from and watched the slow advance of his car.

Magdalena drove. She never dowsed her cigarette, but she hung it out the window as she dropped Max off at his house.

"Got some time, little brother," she said as they pulled back into the street. "Your train doesn't leave for over an hour."

James looked at Mama. She'd chosen to ride in the back seat with him, even after Max got out at his home. Her skin was sallow, her gaze a pool of vacant sorrow.

"Take us to Mr. Morgan's," James said. Magdalena stopped drawing on her cigarette. She held the smoke in and stared straight ahead. "Mama needs one of his sundaes." He looked at his mother. Her face flushed, her eyes grew wide. She looked down at her hands in her lap. "I should have taken you for one years ago, Mama. It's just what you need."

The car lurched forward. James saw the curl of a smile on Magdalena's mouth as smoke seeped from between her lips out the window.

Chapter 48

James 1959

The bell Mr. Morgan had on the door of his café tinkled as Magdalena and Mama stepped through. James followed. He eyed the table in the back, the one he'd used most often when Mr. Morgan sat with him or served him, helped him find the right path. It was empty. He reached for Mama's elbow. He wanted to take her there, let her share the same balm he'd found, but she'd moved. James watched as she walked to the restaurant's side wall, to a booth, as if it had her name on it.

James followed. Mama reached the booth, touched her fingers on the table's top, then slid in. Magdalena slid into the seat opposite her. James frowned, then bent to slide in next to Mama.

"Over here, little brother," Magdalena said. She pushed up against the wall and patted the bench seat next to her. "Sit by me before you go."

James frowned again, but he obliged her, sliding in next to his sister. He looked across the table at Mama. There was color in her cheeks, a flush that went with the deeper breaths she seemed to be taking.

"You all right?" he asked.

"So, you got your place to stay all set up?" Magdalena interrupted.

James looked from Mama to Magdalena. His sister's eyes were bright. She was excited. He couldn't imagine why she'd interrupted him.

"Yeah, all set." He started to turn back to Mama, but Magdalena grabbed his hand. "You need any money?"

"What?" Sometimes Magdalena could be annoying. He frowned at her. "No, I don't need any money. Besides, you don't have any."

"I always have money. I work, remember?"

She hadn't talked about cleaning houses in forever, but she was right, she always had money, or a way. "No, thanks, I don't need any."

He pulled his hand from Magdalena and turned back to Mama. She was looking across the restaurant, and he followed her gaze. Mr. Morgan was walking toward their table, his eyes on Mama, the white towel flopping in his hands as he rubbed and wiped them. He stopped at the edge of their table. He stared at James' mother. James looked at Mr. Morgan, then Mama. Something beat in Mama's gaze. It was life. It was beauty. She'd gone from cadaverous to living. And even without one of Mr. Morgan's sundaes.

"I…" James began. "I mean, we…"

"Sundaes?" Mr. Morgan asked.

Tears, a tiny rim of wetness, pooled in Mama's lower lids.

"Work your magic," James said. It was too quiet to hear, or so he thought. But Mr. Morgan smiled at him, turned, and disappeared.

There was nothing to say. The clink of glassware and silver came from behind the fountain where Mr. Morgan worked. Even Magdalena was quiet. The three of them sat there. James wondered if Mama was afraid Pop would find out she was in here, especially now.

Mr. Morgan appeared at the booth's edge, two dishes of sundaes in his hands. He slid one in front of Mama and the other in front of Magdalena. He laid a spoon near each one. James eyed the two dishes, white and chocolate and bright colors glistening in the light. Mr. Morgan disappeared, then reappeared. He put two more dishes on the table, one in front of James and the other near Mama. Mr. Morgan slid in beside Mama and pulled that dish to himself. He gave James a spoon and kept the last.

Something beat in James' chest. Something far away was trying to come to life. Something was familiar, something was right. It was as if he'd always seen this moment, hungered for it, but yet never knew for sure.

"Cheers." Magdalena waved a dripping spoonful of ice cream in the air.

James watched them dig in. His mother. Mr. Morgan. Side by side. Hadn't he seen this somewhere before? Wasn't this buried in his mind? Maybe in a dream? How could it be? A gulp formed deep inside. It simmered. It was a cry. It was what was left of his scream. It hurt, but it was right. Mr. Morgan looked up. Their gazes caught. Their hurts meshed, their silence said the same thing. James saw Mama there in Mr. Morgan's eyes. He saw himself. Just as he had years ago when Mr. Morgan said to choke up on the bat.

Someone screamed, but it was outside instead of in James' heart. People were running. Some ran into the restaurant and all the way through to the back.

"Fire!"

James smelled it then, the unmistakable scent of burnt metal. Wood, heat, ashes, and smoke billowed out of the sky and rumbled down onto the street in front of Mr. Morgan's restaurant.

More people ran in and cut through, words piecing together all James needed to know.

"Pop!"

James sprang to his feet. He ran to the back, Mr. Morgan beside him. The back of Pop's business was still there, but the heat and smoke coming from it forced them back, down the alley, to one end or the other to get away or to get help. James threw up an arm and pushed around the building. It hurt, it burned, but he pressed on, around Pop's building, to the front.

Flames licked up the sides of the shop, the front a furnace. Black smoke lunged for the sky. James scoured the crowd, smoke and heat burning his eyes. He threw his arm over his eyes and tried to move closer. Men he recognized were backing away, men who'd worked for Pop for years.

"Where's Pop?"

James turned. Harold, clad in an apron from his store, stood at James' side. They looked at each other, the heat beating them back.

"Ran back in," a man coughed.

James felt Harold's hand wrap around his arm. "In there?" James yelled. Harold's hand tightened. James threw it off, stripped out of his light jacket, soaked it in a pail of water, then threw it over his face and plunged forward. Pop would only go back if there was something he really wanted. Maybe in his office. He had to be in the back corner.

A hand touched his back as he reached the

building. The heat blazed; the smoke blinded him. He shrugged away from the hand and shoved it off with one arm. "Get back, Harold!" James shouted. "You have Sandra to think of."

The hand came again. It held on.

"Get back!" James screamed. He kicked at the small door to the side, one that would get him to Pop's office the quickest, farther from the main shop floor where the bulk of the fire seemed to be. The door crumbled, sparks exploded, and James stumbled backward into the person behind him. "Harold, get away!"

"Your brother's back there."

James turned. He squinted against the smoke. Mr. Morgan looked at him, his face dark, sweat making rivers of black down his tan face. James turned back to the open doorway and pushed through, Mr. Morgan behind him.

It was impossible to breathe, impossible to see. James heard Mr. Morgan cough. He wheeled around to tell the man to get out when he saw it, a long, lanky body stretched nearby, both arms clutching something to the chest. Pop.

James hurried forward, fumbling, closing his eyes against the heat and smoke. He felt his father's back and latched on. He tugged and pulled, dragging him inches at a time toward the door. James yanked hard and stumbled, lost his hold and fell. Scrambling on all fours, he grappled in a circle like a blind man. "Pop!" He tried to call, but he choked, his chest constricted into a deep cough. He squinted to the right, where the light of outdoors should be. There was nothing but black smoke. He tried to stand, holding back a cough, panic setting in. Where was Pop? Where was the door? Where was Mr. Morgan?

Crouching, James broadened his circle. He stumbled forward and fell again, wind exploding from his lungs. He gasped for air, drew in a deep breath of smoke, and choked, lights bursting in his head. Whatever was beneath him kept him off balance…he fought against it…a body…it had to be Pop. He grasped at the figure. His hand hit something sharp and hard. He shoved at it and tried to stand, pawing over the body, searching for an arm. He tumbled to the side and rolled to the floor and lay there. Something clutched him from behind. He felt himself heaved upward. The body beneath him moved also. He tried to get a foothold, use his legs to help, but his coughing erupted; it was fierce. He couldn't breathe. He couldn't see.

The smoke began to thin. The air lightened. Whatever had him by the back let go and dropped beside him. James landed on a body. He coughed, he gagged, and then everything went black.

Chapter 49

Lana 1941

Lana stared at the baby boy in her arms, his black hair, his almost olive skin. Babies change. Sometimes they started with dark hair, then it lightened. Had blue eyes at first, then later brown. "What will you be?" she whispered. He slept. He was peaceful. He was to have been her miracle child, love's child, the one that made Cletus happy again. Another son, the only thing he wanted for children.

"He came early," she'd told Cletus. "He's small because he wasn't ready to be born." Cletus had stared at the baby, then at her. "He resembles Carla, don't you think?" The boy did resemble Carla, but Lana saw in Cletus' eyes there was no similarity.

"That boy," he'd said, "isn't mine."

"He is, and you know he is." Lana had said it firmly to his back as Cletus left the room. He didn't believe her.

She'd been gone too long, several months ago. She'd left town and stayed with Grandma. Ella had taken over for her for a few days. Jim had brought her back, stayed to eat with them, then left. Cletus' silence had been deafening. He really didn't care, yet he did. Some strange part of him claimed her yet didn't want her. She'd tried to explain how sick she'd been at

Grandma's, how she couldn't suffer a long ride on the train, how Claire was heavy with child and couldn't ride with them but didn't mind if Jim brought Lana home. Jim was kind, a childhood friend, but nothing more.

Lana had vomited then, spilled out the undigested supper she'd eaten, all over their bedroom floor. She stared at her meal at her feet. Cletus had come near, stood over her in nothing but his long johns. She'd touched him, forced herself to reach for him, her fingers tracing the weave of fabric around his waist. She thought she'd vomit again. The room seemed dark, the floor swirled and spun, but she held on, following a trail around his back, her fingers leading her arms around him.

"Please, Cletus. I'm so tired..." Then everything went black. She woke up the next morning in their bed, nothing on, last night's vomit dried on the floor. He was gone, and she wondered. Had he? She'd run her hands down her bare body. He must have.

The baby repositioned in her arms. One tiny fist struggled free from the blanket. He brought it to his face and rubbed the ball of fingers against his nose and cheek. Lana smiled. He was so small, so soft, and so warm. This birth had been easy, maybe because of his size. She thought of his father, and tears came to her eyes. "You're special," she whispered. "You need a special name. One that will dub you with kindness all your life. I think I'll call you James."

Chapter 50

James 1960

They came, they all came, and they stood just as they had stood around the table James' whole life. But there was no table here, and there were no chairs. Just a train platform and a waiting train alongside it.

"All strikeouts," Harold said. "Pitch those no-hitters." One arm was around Sandra. She smiled, her face rosy, and James wondered. By the time he came back from his first season of playing ball, he'd know, but he suspected by then Harold would be the father he always said Mama had been.

"I will," James promised. "Only winning games."

Betsy stepped forward and hugged him. Gail and Jackson handed him a bundle wrapped in burlap.

"From Harold's store," Gail offered. "A good jacket. Want you to look perfect while you're out there in the world."

James smiled. Perfect. It's what Gail did. Poor Jackson.

The whistle blew on the train. James' heart jumped. He wanted to go, yet he wanted to stay. Carla and Miles stepped forward, and Carla wrapped both arms around James. She felt like Mama. She smelled like Mama. James was glad Carla hadn't married a Pop like Mama.

"Alex will be sorry he missed you," Harold added. "Just another week and you could have seen him before you left."

James thought of Alex as he'd last seen him. Muscles that loved enough to break a wooden post for James' sake, muscles that had fought in a war to escape the hurts at home, now coming back to take over Pop's shop. Pop...

"Don't think about it, little brother." Magdalena slipped an envelope into his hands. "It's his own fault," she leaned close and whispered. "I told you that before."

The stench of welded metal scorched into James' skin was nothing compared to the smoke that had seared his lungs. Two days? Four days before he came around? The white of the hospital room's walls couldn't erase the black smoke James saw in his mind, or the burning cloud he tasted with every breath. James had survived the fire. Magdalena and Mama were at his bedside when he first awoke. "Pop?" he'd tried to ask. He sounded like an old man, his throat burned raw. Mama laid her hand on his. James couldn't read what he saw in her eyes. Love? Fortitude? All of the things Mr. Morgan had said were there? Certainly beauty. "Pop made it," Magdalena had said. "Barely. He won't be the same ever again, though." That's when James saw him, just after Magdalena said it, those dark eyes, that dark hair, standing back and watching. Mr. Morgan, also in hospital attire. Magdalena had nodded. She knew James' question, and she knew he had seen the answer. Mr. Morgan had saved them, saved James and Pop. Mr. Morgan was there.

The train huffed impatiently behind him. James

fingered the envelope and looked at his sister. "Save it for later," Magdalena said. He slipped it into his shirt pocket and nodded.

"All aboard!"

James glanced at the conductor, a car away, waving his arm toward the train. He turned back to his family, the ones who had loved him all his life, protected him, told him he was different without ever really saying why.

Choke up on the bat. Passengers filed past, heading to the train. James glanced around them, through them, searching for the one who'd given him that advice years ago. He wasn't there, but everything he'd given James, over the years, was.

"It's time to go." James turned to his family. They pressed close, they touched him; no one said goodbye. "I'll write," James promised, looking at Mama.

Tears formed in Mama's eyes as she drew him to herself and hugged him. He felt her nod, her head close to his, a faraway look in her eyes when she stepped back and released him.

"I know you will, James," she said. "I know you really will. It's what family does, but you really will."

He boarded the train at the conductor's final warning. Pop wouldn't have come to say goodbye even if he could have.

James found a seat near the window. He laid Gail's bundle beside him and put his satchel at his feet. His family stood on the platform. They spotted him, and he planted his palm on the window's glass as if he could touch them. *Stand back and gain perspective.* There he was. Mr. Morgan. Far back, his dark hair, eyes so like James' own, so like Mama's, also. *Your father will be there today.* The train lurched forward, James' family passing by on the other side of his hand.

He couldn't see them.

His eyes were drowning in tears.

Epilogue

Magdalena 1960

Mama had six children after she had me, one right after the other except for James, mostly because Pop couldn't leave her alone. It wasn't that he was in love with her. He just loved hard the same way he worked hard. He worked her hard too, and us kids. Mama never complained, not for a long time, no matter what Pop did, so we mostly didn't either. My brothers and sisters were too afraid of what Pop would do when they were growing up. I learned later in life I was only afraid of what he didn't do.

"Guess what, Pop. Got another letter from Jim!"

Pop flinched. It was all he could do. James had walked out of the hospital after the fire, but Pop never could. He was carried home. The disfigurement the fire left made his flesh match his heart. That was an ugly thing to say, but it was true. While James went on to play baseball, Pop took to his bed.

Sometimes I borrowed Max's car and took Mama to one of James' games if it was fairly close. James traveled a lot, and when he was on the road, he always wrote. He described every inning of every game in great detail. For Mama's sake, so she'd feel as if she was there. He wrote each letter well, because I heard her cheer when she read them. When she was finished, I always took his letters into Pop's bedroom and waved them in the air. I waved one now as I dragged a chair near his bed. Pop hated it when I said "Jim." I did it because it was medicinal. It made me feel good and it kept him alive.

As I read James' letter, Pop never interrupted. I'm not sure he could. He never responded when I finished, either. He never did. I know he reacted on the inside, though. He just never let it show. I stuffed the letter back into the envelope.

"Alex says everything's fine at the shop." I waited. I could see Pop thinking, but there was nothing to say. No thanks for reading, no thanks to Mr. Morgan for saving him, nothing to Mama, me, or Betsy for taking care of him.

I did want to thank Pop for something, though, but it would have been cruel. When Mr. Morgan had pulled Pop and James from that fire, he had taken something from Pop's arms before the three of them were carried away on stretchers. A box, a small metal box that housed some papers, a letter, and a key. Mr. Morgan handed it to me when I went to visit him in the hospital. The papers were a ledger of the money Pop had given Mama years ago when he paid for us kids to see a movie or her to do as she pleased. Guilt money. Probably to counter the key, a key to a house Pop had bought. I claim that house now. Mama and I chased away the woman he had living there, and I made it my own. The letter was James'. I'd handed it to him before he boarded the train, his first acceptance from the scouts, never burned after all. But almost.

"Need anything before I go, Pop?" I still didn't mention the house.

Silence. I left his room.

Mama kept all of James' letters in a small box on her dresser in my old room where she slept. I set this one at the back, all of James' letters in a row in the order they'd come. I walked back downstairs through the living room, through our old dining room, and onto the back porch. I stopped at the washstand and gazed into the old mirror. I lifted my hair the way Mama had done once, then let it drop. I call myself just Magdalena now. I live in a house paid for by Pop, and I help take care of him, but I'll never be Magdalena Paine again. That girl grew up and became so many Magdalena somethings I lost track. Each one was different, yet each one the same. I didn't see it until Mama pointed it out to me. Every last name I took on was attached to a man who was like Pop in some way. Magdalena Paine died then, and a new Magdalena was born. I like this one. This one is beautiful.

Beautiful like Mama. Just like Mr. Morgan had said. I turned from the washstand and stepped outside.

Mama was out there. She really was beautiful. She looked better than she'd ever looked. The wind whipped her faded housedress against her legs. She was still tall and slender, her auburn hair fluttering around her face.

I walked up beside her and stared out over the pasture where she was looking. She was smiling. I reached down and took her hand. I pressed a small token into her palm and closed her fingers around it.

"What? More?" Her eyes twinkled. "I swear…"

"Save 'em up, Mama. Someday you're going to be ready for one of those sundaes again. And you'll have enough tokens to last you the rest of your life."

Mama smiled and turned toward the pasture, but not before I saw James in her eyes. I watched her let herself through the gate and disappear over the rise. Mama loved the pasture. Mama just plain knew how to love.

A word about the author...

Born and raised in the Midwest, Colleen is at home in that rural atmosphere but enjoys experiencing other cultures also. She works as a laboratory technician by day, but devotes her nights and weekends to literature, both reading and writing. Other hobbies include outdoor activities, treasure hunting in antique malls and flea markets, yard work, and theater.

Colleen's multiple awards for her short stories, include:

2nd Place, Mighty Mo Award, 2008;
1st Place, Jim Richardson Memorial Award, 2010;
1st Place Ozarks Writers League Award, 2012;
Honorable Mention,
Ozark Creative Writers Nostalgia Short Story;
Honorable Mention, Mighty Mo Award, 2012.

~*~

Also by Colleen L. Donnelly
and available from The Wild Rose Press, Inc.
Mine to Tell

Thank you for purchasing
this publication of The Wild Rose Press, Inc.

If you enjoyed the story, we would appreciate
your letting others know by leaving a review.

For other wonderful stories,
please visit our on-line bookstore at
www.thewildrosepress.com.

For questions or more information
contact us at
info@thewildrosepress.com.

The Wild Rose Press, Inc.
www.thewildrosepress.com

Stay current with The Wild Rose Press, Inc.

Like us on Facebook
https://www.facebook.com/TheWildRosePress

And Follow us on Twitter

https://twitter.com/WildRosePress

www.ingramcontent.com/pod-product-compliance
Lightning Source LLC
Chambersburg PA
CBHW071522260626
47170CB00002B/467